Let the Children Come
The Life of George Müller

Tom Fay

COAST PUBLISHING

Copyright © 2021 Coast Publishing

All rights reserved

The characters and events portrayed in this book are fictitious, but some are based on real persons and occurrences. The author does not claim to accurately portray any real persons without error.

No part of this book may be reproduced, or stored in a retrieval system, or transmitted in any form or by any means, electronic, mechanical, photocopying, recording, or otherwise, without express written permission of the publisher.

Paperback ISBN-13: 978-0-9746374-4-0
Paperback ISBN-10: 0-9746374-4-0
Ebook: 978-1-7374503-0-6

Printed in the United States of America

For the next George Müller to rise up.

Table of Contents

Introduction	1
Prologue	7
Chapter One	20
Chapter Two	39
Chapter Three	49
Chapter Four	58
Chapter Five	67
Chapter Six	77
Chapter Seven	85
Chapter Eight	92
Chapter Nine	101
Chapter Ten	106
Chapter Eleven	117
Chapter Twelve	124
Chapter Thirteen	133
Chapter Fourteen	143
Chapter Fifteen	151
Chapter Sixteen	159
Chapter Seventeen	168

Chapter Eighteen	173
Chapter Nineteen	179
Chapter Twenty	182
Chapter Twenty-One	188
Chapter Twenty-Two	195
Chapter Twenty-Three	207
Chapter Twenty-Four	211
Chapter Twenty-Five	219
Chapter Twenty-Six	224
Chapter Twenty-Seven	231
Chapter Twenty-Eight	237
Chapter Twenty-Nine	253
Chapter Thirty	263
Chapter Thirty-One	279
Chapter Thirty-Two	293
Chapter Thirty-Three	295
Chapter Thirty-Four	305
Chapter Thirty-Five	317
Epilogue	326
Acknowledgements	331
About the Author	333

Introduction

I first heard of George Müller as a freshman in Bible College over fifty years ago. I was impressed by his genuine and unconditional faith. The story of his life both encouraged me to trust Jesus Christ more than I did at the time and challenged me to live by faith every day.

I started writing this book about George Müller over six years ago. Frankly, I didn't know exactly how it would turn out, but I knew his story had to be told again to this generation.

As I talked to friends about writing this book, many had heard of George Müller's life of faith and had been inspired. And that is the way it should be—testimonies of living by faith inspiring us to do the same. The author of Hebrews in chapter eleven lists person after person in the Old Testament who lived by faith, and they continue to be our exemplars.

Recently, though, as I read about his life once again, it occurred to me that it's hard to understand Müller's world since it begins before automobiles, airplanes, telephones and even electric lights were invented. George Müller was born in 1805 and died in 1898. This is a time that very few of us can relate to: no computers, internet, or smart phones.

Yet in the latter half of George Müller's life, there was an explosion of technological innovation. Guglielmo Marconi, Nikola Tesla, Heinrich Rudolf Hertz and others figured out how to transmit radio signals. Thomas Edison was working on a light bulb, telephone, and a phonograph. Louis Pasteur and others developed methods for isolating and characterizing bacteria. The advanced development of the steam ship and the opening of the Suez Canal in 1869 greatly increased trade with China. An increase in electric and other technology, medicine, international trade, and globalization was unprecedented at that point in human history.

Now that I think about it, George Müller lived in a very exciting time, perhaps in a way, not too different from our time in the 21st century.

Humankind has not changed much. We still grieve at the loss of a loved one. We still have poor health care, poverty, and lack of education among many. We still strive to learn, believe in God, work long hours, have families, get sick, and ultimately die. We still start wars. We are still selfish, though our selfishness is interspersed with great acts of kindness.

I didn't want to write a history book of his life; there are plenty of those. History books about preachers are not generally that interesting. I didn't want to write about someone that wasn't relatable. I wanted to tell the story of a complicated man who decided to put his complete faith and trust in Jesus Christ. This was a man whose faith grew over time. Each time God answered his prayer, George's faith got stronger. But he started out just like us. His story could be your story; in fact, he wanted you to live like him in faith.

George Müller was an amazing man, and his story needs to be retold to those who have read of him and told to a new generation that needs to emulate his faith. I have taken George Müller's life and put it all five years into our future. It is a novel, which is a fictitious prose narrative of considerable length and complexity, portraying characters and usually presenting a sequential organization of action and scenes. I have tried to write a compelling story rather than attempting to strictly write the historical events that took place over a century ago. However, I have taken actual events that happened in George Müller's life and "modernized" them. I gave him email, a cell phone, computers, PayPal, and other things that are strictly 21st century. Had George Müller lived in the 21st century, I feel quite certain that he would have used all this technology. Furthermore, I am quite certain that he also would have spent the same amount of time in prayer and with the scriptures. And God would have led people to give to his ministry as He did in George's lifetime. He would still have been a beloved preacher. In his old age, in the latter part of his life, he would still be loved by young and old. So, while the setting is different, the George Müller of this book is no different from the George Müller of the 19th century.

I wanted the dialog in the book to present the human side of George Müller. Some dialog we have recorded, but most we don't. I created the dialog to be able to present an accurate picture of who George Müller was. The dialog and the stream of consciousness of his thoughts are inspired by what he wrote and the actions of his life. They are generally not verbatim, but they do reflect what he probably did say and think. I have tried to respect his life.

And so it is with this in mind that I felt it was absolutely essential that George Müller's faith be told afresh, more than a century later, so that it might inspire some young man or woman, some person searching for a ministry, some pastor or missionary who is discouraged, some adult frustrated by living according to "do's and don'ts," or even one of the baby boomers who are now approaching the fall and winter of their lives and see the futility of living a life that is not completely by faith.

My prayer is that whatever stage of life you are in, even if you have refused to trust in Jesus your entire life for the salvation of your soul, you will now be inspired to trust in Jesus, the Christ, who arranges the affairs of the world as we trust in Him. It is never too late or too early to begin living a life of faith.

Further, it is my prayer that God will raise up another "George Müller" who will be an example of the power of prayer and faith for a future generation. That person is no doubt alive today and will read this book and will begin to trust God for extraordinary things in their life just as George Müller did. And if you are that person, your life will inspire another young person perhaps 200 years from now to simply live by faith in the Son of God who loved us and gave His life for us. Will you be that person? Will you be the one that God uses to show His disciples how to live by faith? Will you live today by unconditional faith?

If, after reading this book, you have an account of living by faith, I would love to hear about it. Has George Müller's life affected you? Tell me more! Write me at tom@tomfayauthor.com .

Let the Children Come

Prologue

The deafening sound of traffic passing by on the street below and the quiet rustling of the green leaves overhead seemed to be at war with each other. Every sound vying for his attention fell on deaf ears. Tears stung his eyes, but he refused to let them fall. He was fifteen—a man. Men didn't cry.

His gaze remained on the rays of light flickering through the oak leaves above. He couldn't peel his eyes away, no matter how much he wanted to.

How cruel, he thought, glaring at the brilliant light. How dare God make the light so beautiful on a day like this? Somehow, the beauty only made his contempt grow.

He was so consumed by his own feelings of pain and anger that he barely heard it when the window behind him slid open, and even then it didn't register to him to turn around.

"George."

Fred's voice was too concerned, George thought in annoyance, and suddenly his anger shifted toward his older brother. Yet he refused to turn around and acknowledge that Fred was standing there. Just as he'd refused to acknowledge...

George couldn't finish the thought.

Fred sighed. "George. You can't stay out here. You need to come downstairs."

"Why?" George hissed. "So a bunch of hypocrites can use my pain as an excuse to talk about themselves and how much this has affected them?"

"No," Fred answered. "Because she was your mother, too."

George flinched. *She was more my mother than yours*, he thought. It wasn't true, but it made him feel better to think so. At least Fred had Dad, who so adored and praised him. Fred had college and friends and a bright future. George? Well, through his own rebellion, he'd ensured that he had practically none of those things, except for his mother. He'd had her.

His mother, who stood up for him when his father yelled. Who cared for him when he was ill and tended to him when he needed help. George knew that he was the furthest thing from a golden boy, yet his mother had always defended him when his father caught on to his antics. Who would defend him now? Certainly not Fred. Surely, George thought, he was too comfortable in his new life at college (and outside of his father's controlling reach) to risk defending his hellion kid brother.

"George," Fred said again softly. It was hard to resent him when he was being so compassionate. "Come down. You need to at least make an appearance."

He didn't want to. With every fiber in him, George wanted to stay on this rooftop. To forget what had transpired…and his role in all of it. But he knew he had to.

George stood unsteadily and climbed through the window. Fred offered to help him down, but George batted his hand away and headed out of his untidy bedroom to the stairwell beyond. He could already hear the voices of the mourners downstairs, murmuring respectfully.

Mom would have hated this, he thought.

She was so full of life. She would have been horrified if she knew what her wake looked and sounded like.

With Fred following close behind him, George made his way through the small group of guests invading his home. Some people stopped him and told him about how much his mother meant to them, while others just cast him sympathetic glances or placed a hand on his shoulder as he passed. He could hardly feel or hear a thing. Everything felt strangely numb, as if he'd been sitting in a bath of ice too long.

Then he saw his father, and his senses returned to him.

His father wasn't an abusive or mean man, but to say he and George didn't get along was putting it lightly. Being the prestigious lawyer he was, he expected only the best from his two sons.

Fred didn't disappoint. He was the epitome of the perfect child—like father, like son. He was tall with light brown hair, just like their father's. He excelled in school and rarely ever got into trouble with either parent. He kept his head down when he was around their father, though, knowing the expectations laid out for him.

Their father had expected the same of George: excellent grades, meek and kind behavior, perfect scores on the SAT, and a long future as a lawyer after college. George didn't know what he hated most about those expectations. Or maybe he didn't hate the expectations at all—maybe he hated that he could never seem to achieve them. It didn't matter either way. Long ago, he'd decided that if he couldn't meet his father's expectations of him—if all John Müller ever saw him as was a delinquent and a failure—he'd resign himself to being the most rebellious hellion of them all.

And he had been. Only, the person he ended up hurting was the one person who had always defended him. He had hurt his mother.

His father didn't look like his normal self. He wasn't collected or powerful looking. Instead, as he stood amidst a group of people with his shoulders slumped, he looked…shattered. Exactly the way George felt.

Then Mr. Müller looked up, and his eyes locked with George's. George's stomach dropped immediately. His father's gaze went from pained to enraged in the blink of an eye, and George wasn't about to stand around to find out if there would be more of a reaction. He ducked into the crowd of people and made his way into the family kitchen where he thought maybe he could find some peace, but there were more people huddled around the finger foods set out on the island.

"George," Fred called out as he followed him into the kitchen. He set a hand on his little brother's shoulder. "Talk to Dad. You two need each other right now. He's just hurting, and he's taking it out on you. It isn't right—"

"Yeah, it sure as hell isn't right."

"George," Fred chided quickly, looking around to make sure no one else had heard him swear. *If only these people knew…*

George shook off his brother's hand and was just about to break free of the crowd when someone else stopped him.

"Oh, George!" exclaimed Mrs. Baker, George's teacher. She took his hand in hers, tears in her eyes. "I know how painful this must be for you. Cancer is…" She hesitated, as if she suspected George was too fragile to even hear the word. She continued with a shake of her head. "But your mother is in a better place."

A better place? George scoffed internally. Why did people keep saying that? She wasn't supposed to be in any better place; she was supposed to be here, where her family needed her.

Where I need her.

But he forced himself to nod and say, "Yeah. I know."

She wiped a tear from her eye. At least Mrs. Baker had known his mother. The two had been friends for a while. Her tears seemed genuine.

"Well, it was good that you were here with her when she passed."

Here? So his father hadn't told anyone what he had really been doing or where he'd really been.

His heart sank with the weight of his own guilt, and he felt sick to his stomach. He immediately clamped a hand over his mouth and managed to mutter the words, "Excuse me," before racing to the bathroom and doubling over the toilet.

A knock at the bathroom door. "George."

Damn it, Fred. Would he really not leave him alone?

The door opened, and George immediately regretted not locking it behind him in his haste. Fred stepped inside hesitantly, but not because he was afraid of George by any means. He was just that way—thoughtful, kind, and gentle. As closely as he resembled their father in looks and life choices, he even more closely resembled their mother in his character. It was, George thought, why it was so difficult for him to be around Fred now.

Fred knelt beside him. "I know you. You're beating yourself up for not being here for her."

"No, I'm not," George sputtered in indignation. "I just—Well, where were you?" He quickly changed tactics. If Fred was going to play the blame game, then so would he. "You don't think she wanted you here, too? You stayed at college. She was sick for months. Dying for months. You never visited once."

Fred looked away. "I…" He shook his head. "I don't have an excuse. And I'll own that. What's your excuse?"

George opened his mouth, but he couldn't answer.

"Sneaking out. Drinking. Taking drugs. I don't know what's gotten into you. You're blaming me for not being here while you've been out partying and getting high? Dad said she asked for you. He called and called."

"I know," George muttered miserably.

"Where were you? You were right here. Why weren't you with her?"

"I was with friends, okay?"

"Doing what?"

George knew he shouldn't answer, but he did anyway. "Sneaking out. Drinking. Taking drugs." He snidely threw Fred's own words back at him.

Fred seemed unfazed by the declaration. Their father must have let him in on George's shortcomings already, as he always did.

"Yeah. Wanna know why Dad *hates* me right now?" George continued. If he'd already dug himself into a hole, he might as well bury himself alive in it. "I was out with friends getting high, and when Dad called me, I was too stoned off my ass to notice. So Mom died...and I wasn't there."

He did everything he could to hold back the tears, but they just weren't listening to him. They streamed over his cheeks freely, but he wasn't about to acknowledge them. As long as Fred didn't point it out, he thought he could handle a little crying.

Fred sighed. "This isn't you, Georgie." He paused for a second, then said, "I'm coming home for the summer. You and I...we're going to be spending a lot of time together. It'll be fun. We'll go fishing and camping and to the movies—"

"Yeah, as thrilling as fishing sounds, I think I'll stick to drinking and smoking, thanks."

"Oh, no. That ends now. Dad's beyond pissed. He wants to send you to military school."

That snapped George out of his fog. He hadn't been the picture of an obedient child his whole life, and it wasn't like he and his dad had ever gotten along...but military school? It was unfathomable!

He immediately sat up straight. "What? Because of the drinking? He can't do that! I'm not cut out for military school!"

Fred shushed him. "Keep it down," he chided. "I've convinced him to wait until fall. That gives us enough time to turn things around."

George huffed. "Fat chance."

"It's that or military school," Fred said.

Though outwardly George was acting cocky, on the inside he was terrified. He knew his father. If John Müller got it in his head that military school was the only thing that was going to straighten him out, then come hell or high water, John Müller was sending George to military school.

And it wasn't like George hadn't had plenty of opportunity to change, and he knew that. He knew his father had little-to-no trust in him. Every time George had said, "That's it. I'm done. I'm never taking drugs again," it would be weeks if not days before he was back on the same track.

George's head fell in his hands. *Why can't I just be good?*

He didn't understand it. To Fred, being good was so easy. Fred would never understand how difficult it was for George.

Fred patted his brother on the back. "We're gonna do this, George. You and I. We're going to turn this around, okay? Make Mom proud, yeah?"

George swallowed. That was all Fred needed to say. Military school was terrifying, and George was keen not to go, but nothing was more convincing than those words. Make Mom proud. He would. Or… he'd do his best, anyway.

George nodded slowly, and Fred smiled a little. "Okay then. Come on. People are leaving, and we need to say our goodbyes."

Fay

George took a deep breath. "Okay."

The stars twinkled over George's head as he kicked a pebble into the gutter to his left. The streets of his wealthy neighborhood were mostly empty at this time of night, with only one car passing by every so often. Beautiful homes lined the well-kept sidewalks. George could still remember when they'd first moved in five years prior. He'd only been ten years old at the time, but he'd never forget how excited his mother was. She'd always dreamed of moving into this neighborhood, and after fifteen years of marriage, Dad gave life to her dream.

George loved the neighborhood for a while. Back then, he and Dad didn't really have any issues. It wasn't until he met a group of kids at his school about three years later that he started to get into sketchier extracurricular activities. Even then, it was another six months or so before Dad figured it out.

That was when their problems really began. Dad thought George was ungrateful and that his son spent all of his hard-earned money on video games and other "nonsense." This was technically true, though George didn't consider it nonsense. It got worse, however, when George began experimenting with weed and alcohol. He wasn't a troubled kid, and if anyone would've asked him back then why he chose to start drinking with the older kids at the school, he probably would've just said it was all for fun. He didn't have a good reason, but he didn't need one. Right? He was a kid. Kids were expected to experiment.

Evidently, Dad didn't think so.

It started getting bad when George turned fourteen. That's when he really got a backbone. Arrogance had a way of flaring up in his spirit, and he refused to back down from any fight. That led to a lot of groundings and a terrible relationship with his dad.

Fred didn't understand George's rebellion. In many ways, he was the typical older brother. He seemed disappointed in George and did everything he could to help him find a better path. For a while, George resented him for that. It made Fred seem "holier-than-thou," an expression George had heard his mom use when talking about some of the older ladies at her church. The phrase seemed to fit Fred, and George couldn't stand him for it.

Mom took pity on George, though. Every time Dad would banish George to his room, Mom would be there to rub his back and say, "Baby, your father is only looking out for you. This isn't the kind of life you want to lead, is it?" George never answered Mom. He didn't want to break her heart.

Mom was all that had made this fancy neighborhood in Greenville—this house—feel like home. Now that she was gone…he felt empty. That one string that connected him to his family had unwoven, leaving George feeling untethered and adrift in life. The only way he knew how to deal with it was to escape.

Beta's house was another one of his safe places, so it was no surprise he found himself on the front porch immediately after the funeral. The house wasn't as expensive as George's, but his mom had done an amazing job decorating it. The white home had warm, red shutters and a matching door. He knocked loudly. As soon as the door opened, he prac-

Fay

tically shoved his friend out of the way to get inside.

Beta Kelley had been George's best friend for as long as George could remember. He was tall and lanky with untrimmed, messy hair that dusted his dark brows and eyes. He was strangely proportioned, and it looked like his upper body hadn't quite caught up with the growth spurt his lower body had gone through, which made him look a little like a cartoon character.

Beta had always been a troublemaker, though he wasn't stupid. In fact, George would've said he was one of his most intelligent friends. He got the best grades and was smart about how he went about drinking and smoking illegally. He knew which crowds to stay away from—and which were safe. Though it would sound strange to say out loud, Beta was George's moral compass. If Beta said a drug was no good, George steered clear of it. If he condoned it, George would give it a go.

"What's wrong with you?" Beta asked. "And why are you in a suit?"

George looked down at himself. He probably should've changed out of his funeral clothes, but he hadn't even thought about it. He swallowed. "Mom's wake."

That sobered the clearly high Beta up. "Oh. I'm sorry, man. I would've been there if you'd told me."

George shrugged. "Wasn't really in the mood for company."

Beta nodded and took a drag from his blunt, then passed it to George. "You could probably use this more than me right now."

"Are you actually smoking in your entryway?" George questioned, snatching the joint. "Your parents are going to kill you."

"Nah. They're out of town. Trusted me to stay here by myself. By the time they get back to Greenville, I'll have killed this place with Dad's cologne. They'll never know." He nodded to the stairs behind him. "Come on. Everyone else is up here." Beta extended his arms wide in a show of dramatic flair as he backed towards the steps leading to the second floor. "Come escape your sorrows in a cloud of smoke and hedonism."

Clearly Beta had meant to look strong and majestic when he took his place on the first step with his arms lifted. In his current state, however, he looked more like one of the homeless than a member of the upper class.

George rolled his eyes. "Yeah, try not to trip in your stupor."

Beta jabbed a finger in his direction. "I'm offended…but I'm not *that* offended."

George playfully pushed his friend out of the way and headed up the stairs to the second floor where, sure enough, their friends were lounging on sofas and contributing to the heavy smoke that filled the room. They hadn't even bothered to open a window. This was exactly what George needed.

He told himself it was his "last hurrah." One more fun night before Fred "changed" him for the better…But deep down, he knew there wasn't a chance he was giving up this lifestyle. Not when these were the only people who accepted him.

There was no way Fred's plan to change him was going to work.

5 Years Later

Chapter One

The clink of two beer mugs clashing together was drowned out by the rush of sound pumping from the huge bass speakers that seemed to vibrate the entire fraternity house.

George laughed and drunkenly took a step back, looking down at the beer spattered all over his shoes. *Ugh,* he groaned. *These are my favorite shoes.* He soon forgot his annoyance when a pretty brunette sashayed up to him and passed him a red plastic cup filled to the brim with…something. Well, it was definitely alcohol, and that's all he cared about.

He looked back at his buddy and lifted his cup. "And so it continues," he shouted over the deafening music.

Across from him, his roommate Grayson snatched the other red plastic cup from the brunette's grasp and lifted it in unison with George's. "And so it continues!"

Grayson threw back his cup, and George followed.

The world was already spinning, so the dancing wasn't helping anything. He knew he'd have one helluva hangover in the morning, but he wasn't all that concerned. It was the first day of summer! Time to live it up, get drunk, and have a good time, and hangovers were sort of part of that process. *Gotta take the good with the bad,* George figured.

The college life was everything George had ever imagined: drugs, drinks, and parties every night. And as a twenty-year-old boy, you were expected to do that sort of thing. Not only that, but you were *encouraged* to do so. It was part of maturing and figuring out who you wanted to be.

It had been a while since George had been home in Greenville. The summer he'd spent with Fred the year his mother died had been amazing, but soon Fred returned to college. Things went back to the way they'd been before that summer, which was basically the way things were now: drugs, drinks, and parties every night.

His father didn't know what to do with him, but George suspected he'd gotten to the point where he had just given up. He no longer expected anything from his son, so even military school seemed like a waste.

George was fine with that. His father had finally accepted who he was and had stopped trying to change him, and that was the way it needed to be.

He still thought about his mother all the time, and truth be told, sometimes these thoughts sparked self-hatred. He hated that he wasn't there that night, and a sick feeling washed over him every time he remembered why he wasn't there. It never failed to put him in a dour mood…so he'd try to lift his spirits with drugs and drinking. It was a vicious cycle that showed no signs of ending.

Tonight was one of those nights. After his first two years experiencing the wild ride of college, it was time to go home and see the old man. He'd have to put on a show and demonstrate to his father that he'd been doing well in school—not that the prestigious lawyer didn't consistently check in. George would have to be on his very best behavior for the next couple of weeks. But tonight? Like Grayson said, it was time to live it up.

For hours music blared, drinks were passed, and games were played. George prided himself on being the reigning beer pong champ, along with a slew of other drinking games. His college buddies complained that he had an unfair advantage since he'd started earlier than most of them.

George wasn't obsessed with winning, necessarily, but he liked being recognized and seen. The best way to be seen was to be great at something; Dad had demonstrated that to him when he was very young. So George became infatuated with making himself look attractive in every sense of the word. He was charismatic, well dressed, well spoken, a good time, and extremely talented in just about everything he touched. Sure, maybe it wasn't all that healthy. He sometimes got embarrassed and angered over the slightest things that challenged the facade he'd created. Everyone loved him for the most part, so he was exactly where he wanted to be.

Friends cheered and hollered as George's ping-pong ball dropped into the last plastic cup with a splash while his opponent batted the cup away in frustration.

Some girl George had never met before jumped up and kissed him on the cheek.

Fay

"Way to go, George," she whispered in his ear.

George smiled and turned to get a better look at her, but before he could, his beer pong opponent was approaching from the side.

"Yo, George!" Milo, the opponent, called. He grabbed George and clapped him on the arm. "What the hell, man? You said you were gonna let me win one."

George laughed. "What can I say? Winning's an addiction."

"Well, I wouldn't know," Milo shot back. "Hey, speaking of addiction, got any grass on you?"

The term "grass" made George think of Beta. He was just about the only person George had hung out with consistently through high school that referred to weed by that slang. Most others just came right out and said it.

George was in no mood to share his victory pot with his opponent, but in the spirit of being the cool guy, he discreetly handed Milo a pre-roll. Milo gratefully pocketed the blunt and tipped an invisible hat.

"Much obliged, Georgie," he said. "So, what're the summer plans? Same old stuff?"

George shook his head. "I'm going back to Greenville."

"Gotcha, gotcha. Gonna see your pops?"

"Unfortunately," answered George. "All work and no play."

Milo scoffed. "Yeah, trust me, I'm in the same boat. My parents are *hella* religious so I gotta do my Hail Marys, and no, that's not a football term."

George cringed. "Sounds like a blast. Remind me never to visit your house."

"Eh," Milo replied. "I manage. Yo, is your pops still a lawyer?"

George nodded.

Milo whistled. "Bet it's nice havin' that income rollin' in. People always need lawyers. Economy's not exactly stable these days. My parents lost their jobs a long time ago. They were practically homeless for a while, but I guess their church or somethin' took them in. I dunno. But hey, they got new jobs, so here I am!"

The economy wasn't that bad, was it? George hadn't really been paying attention. His family had experienced their financial ups and downs in the past several years, but it'd never gotten bad enough for George to notice.

"Well, that took a dark turn. Not exactly party chat." Milo patted his pocket where the pre-roll was. "So if you'll excuse me, I'm going to go smoke my loss away. See ya in the fall, buddy."

George nodded. "Later."

Milo made his way through the crowd and disappeared amongst the heads of partiers. For a brief second, George felt sort of empty. It wasn't that he was just bored out of his mind at this party. It was more like for a moment he was struck with an unanswerable question: Why was he even *at* this party? What good was this doing him?

The brief moment in time passed, and before he knew it, he was back to being the beer pong champ and loving every second of it. He threw back shots—shots he knew he'd be throwing *up* later—and did what he hoped looked like an Irish jig on the dance floor before being waylaid by a group of giggling sorority girls.

Life was chaotic, exciting, and filled with every kind of vice he

Fay

could manage to fit in; and if he played his cards right and drank enough, he'd forget to wonder why he was doing any of it.

It wasn't until around five in the morning that George and Grayson finally began stumbling back to their own dorm. Unfortunately, being "honorary members" of a fraternity did not mean they were able to crash at the house. Their privileges were strictly limited to parties and drinks.

Even though George barely had the wherewithal to walk, he somehow found himself with his gaze skyward, staring up at the stars and the bright colors just at the edge of the horizon where the sun would soon begin to rise. For whatever reason, the stars reminded him of Mom. Like maybe she was up there watching over him. It didn't feel quite right in his gut, but he had to believe she was up there somewhere. Otherwise he'd go mad.

What's it all for?

"What?"

George tripped over his own feet but caught himself. Had he just said that out loud? Judging by the perplexed expression on Grayson's face, he assumed that was a safe bet.

"Oh," George stammered. "I mean, like, what're we *here* for? We're all just ants marching around on the planet with no purpose…"

Grayson scowled. "You're not a philosophy major, so cut it out. I'm too drunk to even *think* right now." He groaned. "And I can already feel tomorrow's hangover coming on. Quick, gimme a hit of your blunt."

George ignored him. He couldn't help but feel somewhat empty. If his mother wasn't up there watching him, what did that say about his life? Was this it?

It was a question everyone faced at one point or another, and George felt like surely men had to take those thoughts the hardest. Men needed a purpose…and George had none. Life's purpose was to get drunk, get high, throw a huge party, look cool, and then do it all over again the next night—all while maintaining excellence in school so that his dad didn't cut him off financially. Now, George wasn't complaining or anything. He really liked his life, but that didn't mean he was completely oblivious to the feeling of emptiness.

Grayson's continued complaints about his philosophical conjectures finally brought George back to the present—and to his own ringing head—so he let the thoughts drift away.

He and his roommate made their way back to the dorm where they realized they'd forgotten the keys at the frat house. Too drunk and exhausted to walk back, they took to the hallway floor and fell into a deep slumber.

It was the hangover from hell.

George spied his reflection in the window of the Greenville airport terminal as he made his way toward the escalators and baggage claim. His dark blonde hair was a mess, sticking out in every direction, and the circles under his eyes made him look like a raccoon. Time for the sunnies. He fumbled for his sunglasses in his backpack and put them on in hopes the light would seem less piercing.

He stepped up to one of the airport vendors and flashed the

cashier the most charming smile he could muster, along with a five-dollar bill and the water bottle he'd snagged. The cashier rang him up and slid his change back to him.

"Have a nice day," she said monotonously.

Swinging his backpack over his shoulder again, he unscrewed the bottle cap and took a long swig. His whole body felt like it was screaming for water. Good thing he'd done nothing but give it alcohol for the past twenty-four hours. He rubbed his temples. He had the feeling that last night's drinking fest wasn't the only reason for the pounding headache.

With Fred now away at law school like the oh-so-perfect son he was, it made returning home seem sort of pointless. George had somewhat kept in touch with the remnants of the family, but it wasn't like he and Dad were close. George had realized long ago that as long as he kept his grades up, made his teachers happy, and took responsibility for his "future"—or, if you asked George, lack thereof—his father would continue to put money in his pocket and wouldn't ask questions about his extracurricular activities. And sure enough, it was working in college. Still, it would be good to go home and make sure that he kept up the ruse with Dear Old Dad. Who knew? Maybe he'd even give George some extra pocket money for swinging by.

While George and his father hadn't technically "made nice," his father seemed to greatly approve of his *known* activities at school. He received the occasional text from Dad congratulating him on a good grade.

After the scare of military school put the fear of God—so to say—in George's mind, he did everything in his power to make sure he looked like the perfect son. He quit sneaking out when Dad was home and cleaned up his act for the sake of appearances. When Dad wasn't looking…well, that was another story. Beta had taught him during that time how to be sneaky, and it was one of the greatest lessons George had ever learned.

As he stepped onto the escalator, he became more convinced that his thinking was on point. Dad had always admired Fred—and why? Because he was driven, well-behaved, and got good grades.

After snatching his suitcase from the conveyor belt at baggage claim, he made his way outside and stood in a long line of people waiting by the "ride app" sign.

"George?"

He spun around. He'd recognize that voice anywhere.

Beta stood on the curb. George's jaw dropped. What were the chances?

After his mother's death, he and Beta had remained best friends throughout high school. They had gotten into all sorts of trouble together, and most of it ended in laughs. One summer, they even took a European vacation together. It was paid in full by George's father, who was under the misguided impression that George was on the straight and narrow.

They texted a lot when George first left for college, but as the months ticked by, Beta's responses stopped coming. George assumed he'd gotten busy at school or changed numbers or something. But seeing him again, it was like nothing had changed between them.

George quickly stepped out of line and pulled his friend into a hug before Beta could say a word.

Fay

"Man, it's good to see you," said George.

Beta laughed. "You too."

There was something different about him, but George couldn't quite put his finger on it. Until he stood back and took a better look at his friend.

Oh, no. Something was definitely wrong.

Beta's ill-fitting clothes had been replaced by a suit. It wasn't the finest suit, and there were definitely a couple of snags in the fabric, but Beta wore it proudly. He looked…presentable. His hair was cut nicely, he was clean-shaven, and he didn't even smell like weed. What in the world had gotten into him while George was away?

Beta beamed. "I heard you're doing well in school. Going to be a lawyer like your father?"

George could barely think. Beta just didn't make sense to him. When he finally remembered that he needed to respond, he managed, "Oh, yeah. Maybe. That's what Dad wants. How'd you know about that?"

Beta shrugged. "Your dad and I still talk occasionally."

That absolutely floored him. "What? You talk to my dad? About what?"

"Just to catch up, I guess. He sent me on a European vacation for crying out loud," chuckled Beta. "I just think it's nice to stay in touch."

George had a hard time believing his father would be into the occasional chat with George's stoner best friend. He'd never mentioned Beta's drug habit to Dad, but surely Beta's lifestyle made him suspicious.

"Dude, what are you doing here?" George questioned.

Beta nodded to the airport doors. "I'm picking up a friend. So how's school been?" he asked.

"Awesome, actually. You're missing out big time on the college life, dude. But don't worry, I'm keeping my grades up so my dad doesn't get suspicious."

Beta just laughed and said, "Same old George."

"Yeah," he chuckled. "Hey, how long are you in town? Let's smoke one for old times' sake."

Beta shook his head—and that was when George knew something was *really* off. "I don't do that anymore."

"You don't…smoke anymore?"

"Or drink," he answered. "Sorry, buddy. But if you're not too busy while you're here, I'd love to get lunch with you. I've been eating at Mimi's. I'm trying to support it because, you know, small businesses."

So he didn't smoke…and he didn't drink. He just ate at Mimi's. This was getting weirder by the second. "Umm…yeah. Okay."

And it was settled. Beta looked happy as he headed into the airport to collect his friend.

What the hell happened to him?

By the time George finally made it home, he'd forgotten all about Beta and his strange new behavior. He had a new problem on his doorstep… himself.

His father opened the door and saw him standing there outside the threshold, bags in hand. It probably wouldn't have hurt to call first to tell Dad he was coming, but last George had spoken to him, they were on

Fay

good terms.

A smile lit his father's face. "Welcome home, son."

George breathed a sigh of relief and stepped inside as his father helped him grab his luggage and carry it in.

The house had changed so much and yet not at all. New wallpaper adorned the entryway, and a new bench had been added where shoes were kicked off. It seemed so much homier than it did when George lived there just a couple years before. He guessed that Jane had finally convinced his father to get rid of the spartan, modern décor he'd always loved.

George heard soft footsteps around the corner in front of him, and the woman, herself, stepped in. Jane wore a bright smile and a yellow apron covered in sunflowers. The petite, delicate woman wiped her flour-dusted hands on the apron and then rushed in to hug George.

"George!" Her voice was high pitched and thrilled. She released him. "We didn't know you'd be coming back. Frankie's upstairs taking a nap! He'll be so excited you're here! I'll go get him."

With that, Jane hurried up the stairs in front of them and disappeared around the corner.

When his father had first remarried not long after his mother died, George had been furious. He'd hated Jane, and he'd hated Frank even more when he came along. Over the years his hatred of them faded, however, and he even grew to like Jane…a little. But she'd never replace his mother.

"How's college?" asked his father as they trekked up the stairs to his old room. "I've seen your grades. You're doing well there. And your professors praise you." He chuckled. "I never imagined I'd say this, but you've turned into quite the student, George."

A pang of guilt hit George's heart. But *just* a pang. What would it be like to really be able to accept his father's pride? His praise? George wondered if it would feel as good as he always imagined, and if maybe that feeling was the reason Fred had remained the golden boy his entire life.

"Thanks, Dad," he remarked.

Without warning, a torpedo of a toddler booked it out of a nearby room and tackled George with as much force as he could muster. George stumbled and looked down at the preschooler attached to his leg like an urchin.

Frank looked up at him with the goofiest grin on his face.

"Georgie," he shouted.

George chuckled. "Hi, Frank." He peeled him off his leg and looked at Jane apologetically. "Sorry, I…need to get unpacked."

It wasn't that he didn't like his little brother—he did. It was just that Frank was a constant reminder of the life George felt he should've had. Who knew? Maybe that was him when he was a toddler. Of course, that would mean *he* was the one who'd screwed up and made his relationship with his father as difficult as it was—and that surely wasn't the answer.

As his father led George back to his old room, George said, "I saw Beta at the airport."

"Oh?" Dad's demeanor brightened ever so slightly. "Good kid."

"Yeah…" George narrowed his eyes on his father questioningly.

Fay

Did he really think Beta was a good kid? "He seems to be doing well. Was wearing a *suit* at the airport."

Dad snapped his fingers. "Ah! Speaking of suits, I have something for you. Come on."

He hurried out of the room and rushed downstairs to his own bedroom, leaving George to do his best to catch up. When George finally made it there, he saw his father holding up a brand new, navy blue pinstripe suit. It reeked of success. It must've cost a fortune.

"Dad…" He couldn't believe it. His father bought him a suit?

Dad waved him over. "Come try it on."

George did. Everything fit perfectly, to the exact measurement. He turned and looked at himself in the full-length mirror and was astonished. He actually looked *good*…not like the pothead delinquent he knew himself to be.

"I figured that you're going into your junior year, then off to law school like your big brother. Nothing made me happier than buying this suit for you, knowing your future…"

George knew exactly what this suit signified and what it meant to his father. In the Müller household, there were few things as sacred as a good suit. Maybe it was just a lawyer thing. Dad prided himself on his suits and used to give George a dirty look if he'd even gone close to one of them.

To his father, this suit meant everything. Prestige, success, and a bright path forward. For George, it should've meant honor, pride, and acceptance from his father.

There was that guilt again. But this time, it wasn't because he wasn't being the student Dad thought he was…it was because as much as he loved the suit, he could never picture himself wearing it in boardroom meetings or in court where he was fighting for the rights of some murderer. Being a lawyer just didn't appeal to him at all. It took putting on the suit and seeing it through his father's lens to realize just how *not* cut out he was for this job.

He cleared his throat. That was nothing to say to his father now. "Dad, I don't know what to say. Thank you."

"You don't need to thank me. You've really proved me wrong, George. I…well, you know we've had our differences, but I'm so proud of the man you've become. You've truly applied yourself, and I couldn't be happier." He smiled again and patted him on the shoulder. "Now, what do you say we get some food?"

George nodded. As happy as it had made his dad to buy him this suit and imagine his future, it made George happier that his father even wanted to have dinner with him. That, right there, was a flying pig from a frozen hell, ladies and gentlemen.

George was late. It felt like he was always running late, except to classes.

"Sorry," he apologized to Beta as he slid into the wobbly chair at the family-owned Mimi's Restaurant. "Sorry, sorry, sorry."

"Hey," Beta said, holding up three fingers. "Only three things are certain in life: death, taxes, and George showing up ten minutes late."

George chuckled and looked around at the fading décor. "Can't believe this place is still here."

"I know. It was hanging on by a thread for a while, but I think they're doing better for the time being," Beta replied.

They perused the menu, but just as they'd done years before, they ended up choosing the same burger they always had.

After the drinks were placed on the table, George held up his mug of beer.

"To old times," he said.

"Old times," Beta said as he clinked his glass full of Coke against George's Bud. "And lessons learned."

George eyed his friend. *Lessons learned?* He thought. *What kind of lessons did we learn?*

They talked about innocuous things until the food came. The pretty waitress—"Sophie," her name tag read—flashed Beta a smile. When she walked away, George raised a brow at his friend.

"You should definitely tap that. She's hot," he said.

Beta cringed. "Get your mind out of the gutter, George."

That instantly threw him off guard. Since when did Beta start saying stuff like that? "Okay, is this some huge joke? Why were you wearing a suit the other day? Did someone put you up to this?"

At that moment, Beta's phone buzzed, and the screen lit up. He glanced at it and quickly turned it back off—but not before George caught a glimpse of the lock screen.

All things are possible if you believe.

- Mark 9:23

George almost came out of his chair. "What the hell, Beta? When did you become religious?"

Beta couldn't help but smile. George leaned back in his seat as if Beta had a contagious disease and George was afraid that he would catch it.

"Not religious," he explained. He eyed George. "But I did become a Christian."

George went silent for a few beats, a tangible divide falling between them. "I don't buy it. You're messing with me."

"No joke," Beta replied. "I know it's hard to believe, but George…it's just…I don't even know where to begin."

George laughed to himself, rubbing the back of his neck. This was real; his friend had really converted.

George sat silent, his hands gripping the well-worn, cool leather of his wobbly seat as if he'd suddenly been thrust into a tornado and was hanging on for dear life. His pulse quickened, and his head started throbbing as Beta talked. The next few sentences flew past him like debris.

"…ashamed of the way I used to act…"

"…my aunt Emily and her husband, Matt…"

"…Bible study at their house…"

"…Jesus *died* for me. Who else would do that?"

"…a better way…"

"Hold on just a damn minute!"

George realized he'd yelled because the two other patrons in Mimi's turned and stared at him. He lowered his voice.

"You're really telling me you're a…a…a—"

"Christian," Beta said.

"So…no more drinking. No more weed. No more fun," George

said.

Beta's smile lit the room. "I am having the time of my life! Never had more fun. I'm just sober now and can remember the good times."

George loosened his grip on his seat and ran an unsteady hand through his hair. "I just don't get it, Beta. This isn't…this isn't like you at all! You're telling me you went to a couple get-togethers at your aunt's house and now all of a sudden you're a changed man?"

Beta interrupted, his face serious. "George, I know it all sounds crazy. But you've got to believe me when I say that finding this peace and turning from my former life were the best things that ever happened to me."

George silently pushed his plate of unfinished food aside, having lost his appetite. He sighed heavily and stared off into the distance.

"Hey man, I didn't mean to offend. You okay?"

"No offense taken," George said. He shook his head in disbelief. "You're really being serious, aren't you? You're really into this stuff."

"Yeah," Beta said with a half laugh. "I'm really into 'this stuff.'"

A deep silence followed as George took that in. He didn't understand what had happened to Beta—or why he suddenly believed their teenage lifestyle was so wrong. Honestly it *was* a little offensive, even if he wouldn't admit it. I mean, this was his best friend who had taught him to do everything he'd been doing for the past two years at college—and all of high school. It was Beta who'd taught him that if he kept up his grades, Dad wouldn't suspect him of maintaining his druggie lifestyle.

So why was Beta now rejecting that lifestyle entirely?

There was a burning curiosity inside George. He needed to know what had changed Beta so much. So when Beta spoke up next, George was primed and ready for an answer he didn't expect.

"Would you like to come to a Bible study with me? See what it's all about?"

George scoffed, but he shrugged and said, "Why not? I've gotta figure out what this cult did to you. And if there's a magic spell to get you back."

That night, as sleep eluded him, he played the conversation with Beta over and over again in his mind. What stood out most was how happy Beta was.

Peace, Beta had mentioned. That's what it was. George would kill to have a little of that sometimes. It is what the drinking and drugs were supposed to give him. Unfortunately, that mellow was temporary.

The more these thoughts tumbled in George's head, the more he felt that unexplainable void in his own life—the emptiness he wanted nothing more than to fill.

Chapter Two

George was fully ready for this night.

"You nervous?" Beta asked.

George shook his head. "Not in the slightest."

He had to get to the bottom of this. Something crazy and otherworldly had happened to Beta, and George wanted his drinking buddy back.

Beta laughed. "Still think it's a cult?"

Before George could respond, the dark oak door opened and a slender, tan blonde woman stepped into the doorway. His mouth nearly gaped open. She stole his breath away.

There was something dazzling and captivating about her that snatched his gaze immediately. It was almost a presence more than an appearance. Her smile practically lit up the night as she threw her arms around Beta.

"Beta!" She greeted him. "Welcome home."

She turned to George. "This must be the young man you were telling me about. Such a pleasure to meet you, George. We've heard a lot about you. I'm Beta's aunt. My name's Emily."

George could only stare for a long moment, his brain temporarily leaving him at a loss for words. "Oh," George finally said. He fought an oncoming stammer. "Well…I hope my reputation hasn't been permanently damaged." He stretched out a sweaty hand to meet hers. "It's nice to meet you."

If this was the cult leader, maybe he'd be a convert too.

They walked down the hall and into an expansive great room. George counted thirteen…fourteen…fifteen people plus Beta and himself. He hadn't known what to expect, but this definitely wasn't it.

The group before him was a mix of rich and poor (if their clothes were anything to go off). They were diverse, but they were also all alike in that every one of them had a smile on their face as they joked and laughed with each other.

Emily stepped down into the area where the couches and chairs were, clasping her hands in front of her. Her golden blonde hair glimmered as it reflected the light fixtures above, and her light blue blouse seemed to sparkle as well.

She just had this ethereal glow to her that George couldn't help but notice. Something about her just radiated joy, peace, and *life*—something he'd sorely been missing.

"Everyone," Emily sang, "This is George, Beta's friend."

A tall man with a shock of blonde hair stuck out a hand the size of a ham. "I'm Matt," he said. "Good to have you here." He motioned to a chair. "Take a load off. Help yourself to some cookies and muffins. Coffee will be out soon." He turned to the group. "Let's get started. Anyone remember where we were last week?"

A smallish man with circular glasses adjusted his eyewear and said, "We had just begun reading the Gospel of John."

George didn't know where that was, but he faintly remembered hearing about it before on those few Sundays his parents had dragged him to church.

Matt took a seat next to Emily. "Let's dig in, shall we?"

The next hour blurred past. George kept quiet, but his brain was in overdrive. Some of the people knew their stuff, but others seemed as clueless as he felt.

More than anything, George thought these people were borderline psychotic (but not necessarily in a bad way, which was weird to think). They just seemed passionate about their beliefs and what they were talking about. It was kind of infectious.

He was so absorbed in trying to keep up that he didn't even hear someone calling his name. He finally tuned in and heard Matt's voice.

"George, what do you think?"

Caught unaware, George blurted out the first thing in his head. "This guy Jesus seems pretty cool if he can make that much wine for a party. I'd like to go to one of those parties."

He squeezed his eyes shut in horror. What did he just say? He waited for the reprimand.

The room erupted with laughter.

"Well put," Matt said. "A truly honest answer."

"That's George," Beta said.

George sputtered. "My bad."

"Don't worry about it," Matt said. "You just said what you were thinking."

The meeting—or whatever they called it—lasted about another hour. At the end, many of them stayed to talk and rehash some of the things they'd been discussing that evening while others stuck around just to chat with their friends. They seemed like such a tight-knit group of people that George felt entirely out of place as he tried to converse with them. He didn't have much he could contribute to the conversations, but his new friends were so welcoming that it was hard to feel like too much of an outsider.

George and Beta were the last two to leave Emily's house. As they headed to the door, Emily gave George a big hug.

"I hope you had a good time. You should come back next week! We loved meeting you," she said, and it made George feel warm all over. When was the last time someone actually and honestly wanted him?

The drive home passed without conversation. Beta played music and drove. George sat and thought.

Beta's beaten-up sedan bounced into George's driveway and idled for a moment before he killed the engine. George could tell there was something on Beta's mind, and he figured he had a pretty good idea what it was, so he tried to beat him to the punch.

"Hey, man, sorry about the party comment. I was out of line," he quickly said.

Beta laughed. "You kidding? You hit the nail on the head there.

Jesus was amazing at parties. No, I just want to clarify something I said at Mimi's the other day."

"Oh. Yeah, please do, because honestly I was too shocked to even know what the hell—*heck*—you were talking about."

Beta drummed his fingers on the steering wheel. "No, I get it. Remember when I told you about how Jesus died for us?"

"Yeah."

"I guess you just looked…confused. Or maybe it just rubbed you the wrong way. I don't know. I just wanted to talk about it."

George hesitated for a moment because he knew what he was about to say could definitely be considered offensive. But Beta was asking, wasn't he?

He adjusted his seat. "Yeah. To be totally honest, dude, I don't really believe that. Like, I kind of know what Christians say and all, but you're telling me a human actually died and was miraculously raised back to life after three days?"

More drumming. "I see," Beta said. "I understand the confusion, and it's difficult to explain my faith in it because faith is just that—*faith*. But it's not a blind faith, you know?"

George's head was whirling. Yeah, that wasn't making any more sense to him. "How is it not blind faith? Seems pretty blind to me."

Beta turned to face George. "Well, let me put it this way. The people who wrote the Bible were eyewitnesses to what happened during the days of Christ, and they weren't the only ones to record His teachings and the miracles that followed Him. I believe it, and I have *faith*, because even secular historians record His existence. Do they necessarily believe

He was 'resurrected?'" He shrugged. "Maybe, maybe not, but they can't explain where the body went…or why there were so many people who saw Him after his death."

Well, that at least explained why Beta believed it as much as he did. George would need to do more of his own research, of course, because he wasn't about to blindly follow someone. But if Beta was right, and it wasn't just blind faith…then wasn't that what George had been looking for?

"So how was He resurrected then?" George questioned.

Beta was quick to respond. "God's power. It's actually really interesting. There are all these theories about where Jesus went during those three days He was in the grave. Some say He returned to the Father, and others argue that he could've gone to Hell to carry out more of His Father's work. I'm not totally sure what I believe but—Yeah, anyway. Sorry. I could go on for hours."

Okay, that was a bit too in depth for George, but the passion was noted. He held up a finger. "Point of order," he said.

"Okay."

"You're calling God 'the Father,' right?" he questioned. "As in, Jesus' Father?"

"Yes," Beta said.

"If Jesus was the son of God, why did God let him die?"

A grin spread across Beta's face—small at first, then breaking into a gleaming smile. "That's the point," he said. "God did allow his son to die."

"Why in the world would he do that?" George asked.

Fay

"For you, George Müller. Jesus Christ, the Son of God, died for you."

That shook George to his core, in both a terrifying and awesome way. He didn't know what else to say to Beta, so he just reached for the door handle. When he stepped outside, Beta stopped him.

"Same time next week?"

Something was tugging at his heart. It was a different feeling from what he had ever experienced before. In one sense it was scary, but in another way, it was very comforting. At first, he wanted to fight what was going on, but then he decided to see where the tugging took him.

He nodded. "Sure," he agreed. "Same time next week."

So George went back to the Bible study the next week, and the week after that, and the week after that. There was something about the people and their presence that drew him there. He couldn't explain it, but there was something different about them. Just being in that room and reading those words written so long ago made him feel somehow more whole.

His lifestyle outside of the studies changed some as well. Though he'd only planned on staying in Greenville for a couple of weeks, he cancelled his flight back to college and decided to play the summer by ear. His college friends had their own busy lives to attend to, so they hardly noticed that George stopped texting in their group messages where they discussed fall plans.

It wasn't like he'd become a "better man" overnight, but he began to feel a tug at his heart anytime he drove by the homeless in the city, read about a broken foster care system, or listened to newscasters report the tragedies of the world on the radio in the morning. He began to wonder how Jesus would approach these situations. He no longer wanted to drown his thoughts with the burn of alcohol every evening. And a bonus: he and his father were getting along better than ever.

Emily and Matt became somewhat of a second family in those short, few weeks—a place where George could go to share his struggles and ask questions. He wasn't totally sure that God even existed, but if He did exist, George was sure He'd sent Emily to be in his life as an angel to watch over him in his mother's stead.

At the close of George's fourth bible study, Emily approached him. Her hair was piled in a messy bun on top of her head, and her pink button-up blouse only seemed to exemplify her cheeriness. She extended her hand, presenting something.

"This is for you," she said. "I tell most people to start in the Gospel of John. I just think it's the best place to begin. Then you can follow along with us as we continue through scripture."

George looked down at the small, leatherback book in her hand. "The Holy Bible" was printed in gold lettering against the royal blue cover. It was small, much smaller than any Bible George had seen the rest of the group read.

He stared at it for a long moment. Was this supposed to be a gift? He wasn't quite sure what to do with it.

"Uh...well...thanks," he began, a note of confusion in his voice. "How much do I owe you?"

"Our pleasure," she said as she gestured to the group, who were

Fay

deep in conversation with one another. "It's a gift from all of us. We all chipped in just a little bit."

George glanced around the room, noting the smiling faces.

"Just promise you'll read it," Emily requested softly.

He looked down at the cover. He knew he couldn't disregard the gift. And if he were being honest with himself, he'd even admit that he was a little curious. Now that he had the book in his hand, he actually had the desire to read it. Maybe it had some answers for him. Maybe it could tell him how these people had such peace and purpose.

Or maybe it's another one of their cult documents, a teeny part of him thought. Regardless, he needed to take a look.

When he started reading the Gospel of John, he wasn't sure he'd even make it through the first chapter. But as he continued, he discovered he was enraptured by the story that was unfolding before him. He wanted to know more about Jesus the miracle worker—"God" walking among man. George wanted to understand why Jesus was doing the things He was doing and why in the world he spoke in so many riddles. He'd be lying if he said he didn't feel better after putting the book down each night.

His relationship with his father continued to improve, and though he considered sharing what he'd been up to with his dad, George knew he wouldn't understand.

It wasn't that his father hated Christians or the Bible. In fact, Jane had convinced him to attend a few church services, mostly on holidays. It was more that George knew his shift in focus would anger his father. He'd see it as a distraction, and after all the money he'd spent to ensure George had a future…George just didn't picture it going well.

Chapter Three

"Not like college at all," George commented as Beta's car idled at a red light on the way home from Emily's house.

This was his sixth Bible study, and the more he went, the more he was captivated by the story on the pages and the idea of salvation through faith and repentance.

"What do you mean?" asked Beta.

"At school, if you ask something stupid, everybody in the class laughs at you and the professor ridicules you. Maybe not to your face, but you can see it in his eyes. You guys just answer the questions no matter how ignorant they are. And your eyes are always…kind."

"None of us have it down. We're all just trying to figure it out."

George shook his head as conflicting thoughts continued to filter through his mind. When the red light turned green and Beta hit the gas, it reminded George of all the times he and his friends had revved their engines and basically participated in illegal street racing. Now, Beta was following the speed limit, not even a glint of rebellion in his eyes. As interested as George was in learning more about this Christian lifestyle, *that* was the most difficult hurdle to get over.

"I don't get it," he finally said. "In two years, you went from a hell-raising party monster to this…this Jesus person."

"Thanks," Beta said. "Glad you noticed. But it wasn't over two years—it was almost overnight."

George recoiled. "Come on, man. You gonna tell me you had a vision or something?"

"Not at all," Beta said. "I had an awakening."

"Okay," George was getting borderline snappy. "Explain."

Beta seemed to consider it for a long moment before they pulled into George's driveway. Beta quickly killed the engine and swiveled to face his friend.

"Okay, man," Beta began. "I've held off long enough, but you literally asked for it. About three months after you went to college, I started getting stupid. I got into the hard stuff. Just popping pills at first. Big rush. Fabulous. I wanted more. Started shooting up."

George's eyes widened. Why didn't Beta reach out to him? He'd always been so cautious about what he took and had taught George to be that way too.

"Didn't think you were that stupid," George remarked.

"Oh, neither did I. I thought I was in complete control. I just snorted it—nothing in the veins. Felt great, but pretty soon, I was injecting between my toes."

George couldn't think of anything to say. Suddenly he felt like

Fay

maybe he didn't know Beta as well as he thought he did.

"Long story short, after a few months, I was a goner. One night, I OD'd. Died. EMTs brought me back with narcan."

Holy hell.

George had known plenty of people to OD, and in fact, Beta used to be the one *warning* him about it. He hated that for his friend, but he still wasn't seeing the full picture.

"So, you snapped out of it after that."

"Oh, hell no." Beta made a face. "I thought I was indestructible! So I did it again. And yeah, OD'd again."

"Jesus," George said.

"No, it wasn't," Beta said. "Furthest thing from Jesus. My thoughts had turned dark. I was in the grip, man."

"The grip?"

"Yeah, the grip of sin. Of my own nature. Of shoving that little voice inside that kept telling me to not do it as deep down as I could. I couldn't break free. Anyway, the second time, I woke up handcuffed to a hospital bed."

"What did you do?"

"I asked the nurse, 'Why? Why didn't you just let me die?' She said, 'Because God has a better life planned for you.'"

"And you believed her."

"I *wanted* to believe her," answered Beta. "I was stuck, caught in this vicious cycle, and I knew I was going to end up dead. I had finally understood that I was out of control, and that I'd never been in control. It was time to turn the reins over to someone else—someone who really could handle *anything*."

George let out a long breath. "I mean, I guess I can't blame you."

"Yeah," Beta continued. "Anyway, long story short, that's when I ended up reading the Bible. The nurse gave me an old, worn one to read and I had nothing else better to do…so I read."

George stared at his friend, then at his hands. "Beta, I don't know what all that means," he said. "I mean, I'm hearing what you're telling me, but I'm still not understanding the point of…all of it." He shook his head, sighing heavily. "Dude, you've got to remember I'm new to all of this. And quite frankly, I find myself having more questions than answers. You keep referring to 'sin,' but what even *is* sin? How can we define it? Everyone just defines it for themselves, so maybe what I'm doing *isn't* sin."

Beta shook his head. "You can't define sin for yourself. That's why having a relationship with God is so important. I used to think that the individual acts—stealing, constant drug use—were sin, but those are just symptoms. Like fever when you have the flu. Sin is something much more profound, more insidious, more cosmic.

"Let me make it simple. Okay, so fever is a sign of the flu. Sin is a sign that we are estranged from God. By that I mean we don't have any personal relationship with God. Remember what you read in the book of John? Jesus said, 'I am the way and the truth and the life. No one comes to the Father except through me.'"

"You've lost me," George said.

"Okay. Sin isn't simply us doing bad things. It's evidence that you don't have a relationship with God. But George, if you accept the gift of forgiveness and seek after a relationship, then God forgives your sin and accepts you as one of his children. Forever."

George broke in with a hesitant whisper. "But what if I don't want God?"

As soon as he said it, tears erupted from George's eyes. He knew that it wasn't true. And at that moment there was nothing that George wanted more than God. He wanted that relationship that Beta, Emily, Matt, and all the others had.

"Can you help me find Jesus like you and the others?"

Beta beamed. "Of course, George. Nothing would make me happier. You're my best friend, and at the risk of sounding crazy, I really feel like God told me to not give up on you. He told me you needed help to get here."

"It's...it's so strange," George replied, his voice raspy. "I knew when I was doing all the crazy stuff that I was doing...I knew deep down it was wrong. But I didn't know how to fill this void I've been feeling since my mom. But now..." he laughed weakly, tears spilling down his cheeks. "Now I know."

Beta's face cracked into a huge smile. "How about we say a prayer?"

George's voice wavered. He wasn't ready. The idea of trying to talk to a God he'd never really felt connected to was terrifying. But it wasn't that he didn't believe in God's existence anymore...it was that he felt unworthy. "No," he answered in an uncertain tone.

Beta was a bit surprised but just nodded. "Alright. I get it," he assured him, patting him on the shoulder. "Talk to Him when you're ready. And when you do, tell Him how you feel about your past life—how all those things you did never filled your emptiness and loneliness. And then tell Him that you trust in Jesus' death on the cross and resurrection to wipe away that past life. Tell Him you want to start a new life with His son."

"Yeah," George's voice was a whisper as he opened the car door and stepped out.

"Night, George," Beta called as George slammed the car door shut.

George was in a daze as he walked into the house. He'd never felt this way before. He was lightheaded, yet his entire body vibrated with energy. The hair on the back of his neck prickled as he walked up the steps to his bedroom. Somebody was watching him, and somehow, he knew it wasn't anyone earthly. He suddenly felt more aware of God than he ever had in his life, and he was appalled that a being so *perfect* had seen George at his absolute worst, bathed in debauchery and sin.

When he closed the door to his bedroom, he sank down the wall and let his head fall between his knees. The moonlight drifted through the open window, and a warm, summery breeze stirred his breaths. He looked up at the bright, reflective moon.

Did God really place that in the sky? He remembered how the Bible said that God had set everything in motion…and it all had a purpose: to serve Him.

George ached for that sense of purpose, and it frustrated him that even the *moon* had a purpose.

But I can have that purpose too, he remembered.

Fay

That's when it all clicked, and warmth filled him. He didn't want to live a second longer without accepting the love and purpose that Christ was offering him. He took in a deep breath and tried to remember Beta's words about prayer, but truth be told he hadn't really been listening. Instead, he just straightened his spine, looked up at the moon, and said, "Alright, God. You got me. I'm in."

So George made the biggest decision he had ever made in his life and took God at His word. He recognized that striving for lasting peace and happiness with his human nature wouldn't cut it. It had done nothing but led him further and further away from what he truly wanted in life. He made the decision to put all his trust in the Lord Jesus, and the moment he did, a real, true sense of relief washed over him. It was so powerful that tears welled in his eyes. He was horrified to admit that he'd cried more in the past few weeks than he had in the years since his mother's passing. Or perhaps in his entire life.

Wednesday rolled around, the night the Bible study convened at Emily's house, and George couldn't wait to tell his friends the news. He felt like he'd just won the lottery, and that *fire* he seemed to sense in them—that burning desire to talk, study, share, and witness (as they called it) to others—was now alight in his soul. He could feel the Lord's hand moving in his life, and he couldn't wait to be His instrument.

At the end of the evening, once they'd all closed their Bibles, George finally stood up proudly. "I...um..." Words failed him. Of course they did. Now that he *needed* them.

He cleared his throat and tried again. "I want to thank you all so much. You have no idea the impact you've made on my life. You folks have been so good to me. You have put up with my questions and my occasionally inappropriate outbursts."

Beta patted his friend on the back with a slight chuckle. "That's okay."

George smiled. "Well, I still appreciate it. If it weren't for you, this group, and of course Emily and Matt for opening their home to us… I wouldn't have given my life to Christ this summer."

Matt immediately let out a holler that instantly made George think Matt was *definitely* involved in some kind of fraternity in college.

"George," Matt said quickly. "We're so happy for you. That's amazing, brother."

George beamed. He felt like he was truly part of the family.

"Thanks, Matt," he answered. "But I have also made another major decision. I've decided to change my major. No more law school. When I declare my major in a few weeks, I am going to study Christian theology. Because I want to become a pastor of a church. I know you're shocked, but my life is so different now, I just want to help people find what I have found."

The group burst into applause and congratulations.

Matt broke through the chatter. "Alright, alright. Gather 'round and lay hands on the man. Let's ask the Lord to be with George on this next stage of his journey."

One by one, the members took turns talking with God. Each person mentioned George by name—each one asked for the Lord's blessing

Fay

in the future.

"Lord, we thank you for this fine young man. One who tells us he was once lost, now he is found. Lead him as he leads others. Speak through his voice, heal through his presence. Let all who meet him know the love and peace of Jesus, your Son and our Lord."

A chorus of "amens" echoed around the great room.

George fought the lump that was growing in his throat.

"You okay?" Emily asked.

George wiped his eyes self-consciously. "I feel…" he began, "I feel…I don't know…weird. Lighter somehow."

Beta threw his arm over George's shoulders. "It's the Lord's hand, carrying you. You are God's man, and you are going to change the world in His name."

As they walked to the front door, George trembled with excitement and an unexplainable energy he'd never felt before.

As Beta and George stepped out into the humid summer air, George felt as though he was stepping into his new life. And it truly did feel as though someone was going to be holding his hand and watching his back from now on. But it was more than that. He felt a profound sense of purpose and belonging, and he just knew that he was on the right path.

And then he remembered:

I gotta tell Dad.

Chapter Four

Sweat dotted his brow, and he swiped at it quickly. How was he already sweating?

It was nine o'clock by the time George returned home from the Bible study, which meant Dad would most likely be in bed already. It was fortunate, as George had absolutely no idea how he was going to manage this conversation with his father so soon. He needed time to gather his thoughts. No, he needed time to pray. To ask God how to word it best so that his father would understand.

"George?" His father's voice resonated throughout the house, coming from his study.

George stopped, one foot on the stairs. So much for Dad being asleep. "Yeah," he answered. "I just got home."

He steadied himself. His father deserved to know, and with George's flight back to college already booked, time was of the essence.

He found Dad sitting behind his desk, new reading glasses situated across the bridge of his nose while he pored over legal documents. George was yet again struck by the realization that he could never be like his father. These things—legal things—interested Dad, but George had no passion for them. He didn't feel drawn into that life at all. And the life he *did* feel drawn into was certainly not going to be the life his father had imagined.

His father looked up, and the little bit of courage George had mustered up immediately vanished into thin air. Dad smiled, and George thought, *How can I possibly ruin this?* They had just gotten to a good place, and for the first time in his life, Dad was proud of him. He showed his son off at fundraisers and events, presenting him as the next law school attendee to come from the Müller family. The man practically glowed.

It felt good, all of that pride directed his way, but George knew it wasn't right. He knew he couldn't keep lying to him.

"Oh, good," said his father, removing his glasses. "Take a seat. I have something to tell you."

"So do I," George answered. He swallowed as he sat down. "Where's Jane?"

His father chuckled. "Ladies' night. Can't get her away from them. One Wednesday out of the month. Personally I can't stand the women she hangs out with, but she loves them." He shrugged a shoulder. "What can you do? Anyway, about what I was going to tell you."

"Maybe I should go first."

His father must've understood the severity of whatever George was about to say because he just nodded. "Sure. What is it?"

George took a deep breath. "I know what I'm about to say is something you're not going to like, but I want you to know it's something I'm not doing on a whim. I've thought a lot about it. I've spoken to my college and...I've changed my major."

His father just blinked as the information sank in. "To what?"

Here's the kicker, George thought. "Theology."

Again, his father just stared at him. "Theology?" George could hear the venom seeping from his words. "Do you even know what that word means?"

"Yes."

"You're dropping out of pre-law school to become, what, a *pastor*?" He scoffed. "No. No. Why would you do this?"

"I've found something I truly believe in," George told him. "I've never felt this way about anything. Please understand."

He shook his head. "I don't. I don't understand. You've never done a religious thing in your life and now you decide you want to be a damn pastor? To commune daily with the 'God' that took your mother from us?"

"That's something I've had a very hard time coming to terms with," George admitted. "But I'm not mad at God anymore. I understand now that His plans are so far beyond mine that I could never comprehend *why* he allowed Mom to be taken from us." He saw his father start to speak, so he quickly continued. "Dad, I've never felt this way. I'd...I'd like to get your blessing on this. I think I've found my calling in life. I can't explain it or how I've changed, but I need you to trust me."

More than anything, George wanted to see a crack in his father's

Fay

hard exterior. He wanted some indication that Dad would accept the life he was choosing for himself—*no*, the life that he felt was chosen for him, that he had been *led* to—but his father's expression remained hardened. George had heard the term "hardened heart", and now he knew what it meant.

He waited for what felt like hours before his father set his glasses down on his desk and leaned back in his chair, way too calm. "What I was going to tell you…" his father began, "was that I've always wanted the best for you. You wouldn't know this, and as a father I shouldn't be saying it, but you were always my favorite son."

That floored George. *What?* He couldn't believe it. He'd been his father's favorite? But…what about Fred? Hadn't Dad always adored him? He was so proud of the older brother, the *golden* child.

Now, his father shook his head. "You *were* my favorite. I'm disappointed. It…it breaks my heart that you are doing this." He looked up at his son. "Why, George? *Why?* What in the world made you stray from the path I worked so hard to lay out before you? Don't you think I have your best interest at heart?"

"I know you do, Dad," replied George. "This just isn't for me."

His father swore. "No. Don't give me that nonsense. I worked my ass off for you. To give *you* a future. And this is what you do with it? How are you going to support a family on a preacher's salary? Huh? We're in the beginning of an economic crash. Do you know that? We're about to be facing another recession." He slammed a hand down on the table. "I need you to trust me, son. I'm giving you one chance. Go back to school and finish your degree. Who you pray to in your own private time is your own business, but no son of mine is going to become a Bible-thumping, self-righteous hypocrite."

George flinched. "Dad—"

"So, what's it going to be, George?" his father snapped.

George's hands were trembling. There was no way he could give his father what he wanted, and George didn't understand the venom behind his words. He knew his father blamed God for what had happened to George's mother years ago, but surely that wouldn't keep him from accepting George's decision now...would it?

"I can't go to law school, Dad," George answered timidly. "I can't ignore this calling."

John Müller chuckled darkly and raked a hand through his hair. He then looked up, and George knew what was coming. "Then no. You don't have my blessing. And if this is the path you've chosen to go down, then you don't have a house anymore either. I want your things out by morning."

The shock was immediate. "W-what?"

"You heard me, George," his father spat. "I want you out. And you can count on there being no money in your account by morning. If you want to pursue this life, then I'm not going to enable you any longer. Hopefully this will teach you a valuable lesson in the hardships of life."

George blinked slowly. Had he just been cut off? He knew his father would be upset, but *really*? Was he this mad? Did he hate God so much that he'd cut off his youngest son?

Somehow, George had the strength to simply nod and accept his father's wishes. He was hurt and confused, and he didn't know how to

Fay

process the loss of his father's support. As he went upstairs to pack his belongings, he prayed a silent prayer of frustration. *Was this really what God wanted for him?*

But there it was—that peace he'd been searching for. It covered his entire body like a blanket. Though he was deeply disappointed and discouraged, he felt he was doing the right thing. He took a deep breath and leaned into the love of God that he now understood was readily available to him. His father was rejecting him, but he knew that his heavenly Father loved him extravagantly.

By that night, George had packed everything. As he was leaving the house, he looked one last time at his father, who sat watching television. He hoped that he would see some sort of remorse, or at the very least, grief. Yet George saw nothing.

"Bye, Dad," he said somberly as he exited the home for the last time.

George was relieved that Emily and Matt gladly took him in for the remainder of his days in Greenville before he returned to university. During that time, he and Beta spent time helping those less fortunate than themselves. They joined their Bible study group in preparing meals for the needy and homeless, and they passed them out along the streets. George was grateful to Emily and Matt; he knew that if it weren't for them, he would be reliant upon the goodness of charities like theirs for his every meal. Yet he soon began to realize that, in a way, he *was* reliant. But not upon the Bible study group…upon God.

George had two years left at college, and he had absolutely no idea how he was going to pay for them. It wasn't like the particular school he was attending was cheap. But somehow, George knew it was going to work out. He was comforted in knowing that just as God had sent his study group to feed the needy, He would surely send someone to help George, if it was His will.

George continued his studies in scripture and was more and more encouraged by them daily. The peace, hope, and life he found in them gave him the will to carry on and strengthened him every day. And soon, George was sure he felt a renewed calling on his life. It was a calling he had never imagined for himself, but it was also one that excited him so much. The more he read of the biblical apostles, the more he felt a call to mission work. What greater call was there than to spread the Good News? His father's response hadn't changed his heart whatsoever. It saddened him, but the Lord had a plan in mind for him, and George was keen to listen.

When George's time at Emily and Matt's home grew to a close, Beta helped him pack his suitcases. The two couldn't believe the awesome summer they'd had. Emily and Matt were sad to see George go, but they were excited for him and the mission God seemed to be sending him on.

As George stood in the doorway of Emily and Matt's home, Emily kissed his cheek and said, "You've changed so much, George, and all for the better. Your heart for the needy is a *gift* that not many have, and I pray that you utilize it."

George knew she was right. He prayed the same thing for himself. "Thank you so much for opening up your home to me. It's been…hard since Dad kicked me out."

Matt looked at him, concerned. "Have you thought about what you're going to do to pay for school?"

Emily nudged her husband. "Why would he need to even put thought into it?" She returned her gaze to George. "Honey, if you're right and this is the path that the Lord has placed you on, then you already know that *all things are possible*. College tuition? That will be a breeze for Him. That isn't to say that you shouldn't work hard—you should—but don't fret. He will see to your needs."

A wave of comfort flowed over George because he knew Emily was right. After all, if even the sparrows in Matthew 6 didn't worry about tomorrow, who was George to worry?

"I know," said George with a smile. "I really don't fear the future. I know I should," he laughed to himself. "I'm a college student with zero ability to pay my own way, but I don't know. Somehow I just feel like… God's got this, you know?"

Emily nodded. "Yes. He does." She quickly wiped at a tear. "Okay, you two get out of here before you miss your flight!"

Beta started the engine, and George took one last look at the home he'd felt so welcome in. The home that he felt truly made him into the man he was meant to be—that God was calling him to be. Then he got into the passenger seat, and they drove off.

The ride to the airport was quiet, filled with an air of both hope and somber uncertainty. As they pulled into the terminal, George couldn't help but remember the last time he was here and the thoughts that had been going through his mind at the time. He was ashamed that all he'd been thinking about was draining his father's pockets for his own ridiculous pleasure. But he was more proud than anything—proud of the change and commitment he'd made.

He stepped out of Beta's car and took his luggage out of the trunk. When Beta stepped out, George immediately hugged him.

"Thank you," he said.

Beta laughed. "For what?"

"For being the example I needed," answered George.

Beta extended his hand. "I'm honored to have been able to help set you on this path, but you know I can't take any of the credit."

George accepted his friend's hand. "I know."

They shook hands. Though it was hard to say goodbye, they knew they would be in each other's lives for the long haul. George grabbed his luggage and bid his friend farewell as he headed inside.

Things were definitely changing in George's life, and he knew it. He was both thrilled and terrified. This new road he was walking down clearly wasn't going to be an easy one. He supposed he'd always known his life wouldn't be easy, but it wasn't until the rejection of his father that it really sank in. He knew things would change, but had complete faith. He didn't know exactly where this road would lead, but he knew the first thing he needed to do: boldly and passionately speak the good news of the Gospel wherever he went.

Chapter Five

The first of many lessons George was to learn on his new faith journey? God always prevailed.

Almost as soon as he arrived back on campus, George was offered work as a tutor and translator. If there was one thing John Müller had done right while raising his sons, it was making sure that they became bilingual. George's mother had insisted that the boys focus on German in order to honor their family heritage, and John ultimately complied with his wife's choice. Though George and Fred had sometimes resented having to take German lessons instead of play outside, George now appreciated his bilingual upbringing.

Tutoring didn't pay much at George's university, but he quickly learned that tutoring international students in English could drive in more income. Most of the international students he worked with came from wealthy families who were *more* than willing to pay George for his tutoring. The translation work George found also helped him make ends meet. With the help of a professor, George was soon connected with a job at a company that translated technical journals. George also made sure to apply for any government grants and university scholarships that his professors recommended, and he was shocked at how much he ended up receiving. The money flowing in was miraculously enough for him to afford his tuition, books, and living expenses.

To say that his new way of life was shocking to his friends would have been the understatement of the year. The first thing they did when he returned to college was throw a huge party with everything George loved—or used to love. There was drinking, loud music, and an insane amount of drug use. It just wasn't George's scene anymore, and he had no desire to attend, which absolutely stunned his friends. Like George when he first saw Beta again, their first thought was: *What happened to him?*

It was hard for George to explain his transformation, especially since it seemed to happen so quickly, but people around campus were soon beginning to notice the change. George was just *different*. The same things that used to appeal to him didn't appeal to him anymore. And even more of a shock? George was loving his classes.

He still spent time with his friends. He didn't participate in the drugs and alcohol, but he didn't want to write his friends off completely. He particularly didn't want to lose his friendship with Milo and Grayson, and he remained close with them even though they understood his transformation about as well as his father did.

While Grayson was no longer his roommate, the two still spent afternoons together, often with Milo.

"I just don't get it, I guess," said Grayson as he exhaled a puff of

Fay

smoke. He shrugged. "I don't know. It's just not for me."

George laughed. "Look, I'm not trying to convince you guys or shove anything down your throats. I get that it's confusing. I mean, my dad basically disowned me because of it."

Milo chuckled. "Yeah, that's rough," he said, leaning back in his chair so far that it almost tipped over. Still, he was absorbed in his video game. "I'd be losing my mind if my dad wasn't paying for my tuition anymore. Still, I guess you've managed. Maybe there is hope for me after all."

"So what's the plan?" asked Grayson. "I mean, after college. How do you plan to make money? What are you even going to do? Is it dumb that I don't know what a...what are you again? A clergyman? Is it bad that I don't even know what that *does*?"

"The plan is mission work," answered George quickly. "Or that's what I want to do, anyway. My theology professors are trying to steer me away from it for now."

"Why?" questioned Milo. "If you want to go to Africa and waste your time helping the 'less fortunate,' I say go for it."

George shrugged. "I guess I see what they're saying. I'm such a new believer; how am I supposed to teach when I'm still so new, myself? Anyway. How about you guys?"

"I dunno, dude," Grayson answered. "I'm sure not going into seminary. Not because it looks boring—which it does—but because... well, I guess I don't really think I'm a sinner. You know?"

Milo nodded in agreement. "Yeah, me neither. I feel like it's just propaganda to get you into churches."

"Seriously?" George shook his head. "Wait, so you're telling me you guys have never lied."

Grayson blinked. "Okay…guilty."

"You've never stolen? *Anything*?"

The boys exchanged a look. "Okay," admitted Milo. "Maybe that one time. Or those two times." He burst into laughter, but it seemed sort of uncomfortable. "Dammit, Georgie, why you gotta be bringing these things up?"

George threw his hands in the air. "I'm just saying. Don't shoot the messenger." He stood from his chair. "I've got homework to get done before class tomorrow, but if you guys want to talk…"

"Yeah, yeah, we know you're here," said Grayson.

George chuckled and left, but he didn't leave them to their own devices. He prayed for them on the walk back to his dorm. He had no idea if anything could get through to them, but he prayed anyway.

His prayers were answered sooner than he anticipated. Within days, something changed in his friends. Milo came around first, asking George countless questions. How had he come to find God? Why did he feel this calling on his life? Soon Grayson joined him, and George couldn't believe how a simple prayer had radically changed these boys' lives! In the same way Beta couldn't take credit for George's conversion, George didn't feel worthy of the pride he felt. He knew that the credit lay with God, but he was thrilled nonetheless.

After some months, Beta came and visited, and the four of them were able to spend time reading the Word together. Still such a new believer, George found the Bible to be an endless source of knowledge and insight. He read with the eagerness of a child.

While he enjoyed reading all of scripture, it was tales of the apostles that captured his attention. He wanted to do that—to walk on his own two feet and share what he knew. Of course being such a "baby" Christian, as Beta had called it, meant he wasn't yet suited for that sort of mission work, as much as he felt drawn to it. Now was the time to learn, he decided. Eventually he would be able to follow in Jesus' and the apostles' footsteps.

Milo seemed to be lapping up the biblical truths that Beta and George shared. He truly loved learning, and he shared with George that he'd never felt such purpose in his life.

"The world's gone to hell, man," Milo began, then his eyes immediately widened. "Shoot, I mean *heck*."

George chuckled.

Milo blew out a long breath, raking a hand through his hair. "For a long time, I'd sort of thought that God had abandoned us. We grew up Catholic, ya know? So I was taught to believe there was a God. I just didn't buy into some of the stuff my family believed in. But this?" He thumped the Bible in his hand—the one George had lent him. "This makes sense to me. It's *so* simple. And it's like…God doesn't ask that much of us—just that we believe and trust Him. And in return we get to live forever?"

George knew his friend was rambling. He finally understood how the members of his old Bible study felt. Rather than feeling annoyed and impatient, he was filled with a sense of pride and wonder that Milo was beginning to understand. And more than that, he was beginning to *feel* that same peace George had begun to feel.

"I know," George answered. "It doesn't seem like a fair trade."

"I guess what I'm saying is…with everything that's happening in the world today…it's nice to know there's a plan and to have someone to lean on."

George nodded. "Yeah. It definitely is."

While Milo took to the scriptures enthusiastically, Grayson's interest began to fade. It seemed there was some sort of bitterness preventing him from accepting anything George, Milo, or Beta tried to tell him. Grayson eventually stopped coming around. He was cordial and friendly when George and Milo would see him around campus, but he didn't engage much.

George had to believe he'd planted a seed. As much as he believed in seeing transformations through to the end the way Jesus and his apostles did, he knew that there was only so much he could do for Grayson in this stage of his friend's life.

But Milo? He didn't change his major like George, but that didn't mean there wasn't a definite difference in his life.

The summer after George's graduation, he was invited back to Greenville, where Matt and Emily offered to house him until he could get on his feet. He picked up some odd jobs here and there, helping a neighbor paint a fence or move furniture. It was enough to help pitch in with the groceries and some of the utilities around the house.

Beta had left town for the summer and was off studying under a rabbi. Though Beta's faith didn't entirely line up with the Jewish religion, he wanted to learn from those who had studied the Old Testament thoroughly, and he shared much of his studies with George. The two kept in constant contact, talking about their daily struggles and victories and discussing where they felt the Lord was leading them next.

After a few weeks, Emily introduced George to a schoolteacher who gave him an opportunity George had been secretly waiting for: the chance to preach his first sermon. The schoolteacher's name was Robert Miles, and he was a member of a small church in Greenville where the elderly pastor was struggling to continue his weekly sermons. As part of the congregation, Robert had taken it upon himself to help the pastor find a younger voice to speak on occasion and perhaps capture the attention of the churchgoers.

George gladly agreed to help; he was eager to share everything he'd been learning, along with some of the theories Beta had been sharing with him.

The nerves were insane. When he woke up that August morning, he was practically shaking. Feeling somewhat insecure, he'd ended up just finding an interesting sermon online and memorizing it…needless to say, it did not go well.

George stepped up to the podium and nodded to the congregation. From the looks of it, they'd already tuned out.

The church was an older style building with traditional pews. A piano off in the corner was the only instrument, and the pianist sitting on the bench looked like she was fighting a cold and was going to sneeze at any second. The most notable thing about the room was the lack of passion—the very thing that had brought George to Christ. He couldn't believe how lifeless the congregation felt, and he suddenly realized why Robert Miles was on the lookout for a new speaker to help the pastor.

Speaking of the pastor... *Where is he?* George hadn't met the man yet. He had been received by Robert that morning. He looked around the sanctuary, spotting the elderly pastor, and...yep, he was leaned into his cane, snoozing. Awesome.

"Hello," George began, and his voice cracked. Double awesome. He cleared his throat again. "My name is George Müller. I wanted to talk to you today about a study on the hypostatic union theology doctrine."

George could practically *hear* the boredom. Was the sermon an important one? Yes. Was it one that this particular congregation was going to understand? It wasn't seeming like it.

He immediately began to sweat and looked back down at his papers. "Umm...," he stammered, searching his mind for something else—anything else—to preach on, and it was suddenly as if God illuminated a lightbulb above George's head. He took a moment to gather his thoughts and then slowly flipped the papers on the pulpit.

He straightened his spine and looked up. "Who here has experienced hardships?"

Several eyes lifted, though no one raised their hand.

"Oh, come on," George said, stepping away from the podium. "Raise your hand if you've ever had a check bounce, or weren't sure if you could make that car payment, or needed something *desperately* and weren't sure how you were going to get it," he paused, considering. "Or... had a loved one die."

Fay

Hands slowly began to raise around the room. George nodded.

"It's scary," he admitted. "It's painful. Don't you think David experienced the same hardships? In Psalm twenty-seven twelve, David says, *'The Lord is my light and my salvation; whom shall I fear? The Lord is the stronghold of my life; of whom shall I be afraid?'* As believers, we are not exempt from hardship. In fact, it's practically guaranteed. But today I want to talk about David, a man who placed his enduring faith and trust in God despite the hardships he endured."

He spoke from his heart. He shared his thoughts on David's faith and the Psalms, and he explained what he believed they meant for modern Christians. The congregation seemed to eat it up, and when he was finished and opened the floor up for questions, many in the congregation began to engage with him.

He felt incredible. People *actually* respected him. He knew he wasn't to take any credit, of course, but it was hard not to. A bit of his sinful nature slipped back through the cracks, and he couldn't help but be thrilled that these people actually wanted to listen to what he had to say.

"They loved it," George told Beta over the phone as soon as he ran down the stairs of the small church. "I thought it was going to be an absolute bust at first. Serves me right for just downloading a sermon."

Beta laughed. "You have to find something you really believe the Lord has given you words to speak on, and it sounds like you did. Why did you choose that particular Psalm?"

George shrugged. "I'm not really sure. I guess because it was a powerful verse, and that type of life, purpose, and passion was what originally drew me to God. These people needed to be reminded of why they came to God in the first place."

"So are you going to continue preaching?"

George smiled. "As long as anyone will let me."

Chapter Six

George knew that didn't mean he was finished learning. He had so much more to discover in God's Word, so any time he wasn't preaching his own sermons, he spent at Emily and Matt's home at their Bible studies.

As the months ticked by and George continued to stay at Emily and Matt's, his financial situation began to weigh on him. It embarrassed George that he had to rely on them, but it was more than that. He hated being a burden on them. He could chip in for food, but it wasn't much, and Lord knew that Matt was worried about it because his job in real estate was absolutely *crawling* as the market began to take a dip.

Matt tried not to let on, but sometimes George could hear him and Emily talking about it. Matt loved having George there, but George knew it was difficult to support a wife and a friend who had nowhere else to turn. Yet Matt's attitude towards it was never concerned, and when George mentioned something to him, Matt assured George that they were fine and that they wanted George there. Still, his situation was a source of constant distress for George.

Emily had begun to notice, and true to form, she was quick and direct when questioning George on it.

"How's the job search?" she inquired as she leaned over the steaming vegetables cooking on the stove.

George exhaled roughly as he sank into a chair at the breakfast table. "Not good. Turns out I'm not exactly qualified for much of anything, and all I want to do is work in the ministry somehow."

Emily didn't seem concerned at all, which definitely annoyed George. She'd been sort of like a mother figure for him from the day they met, and weren't mothers meant to be *concerned* for their children?

She hummed thoughtfully. "You worry too much, George."

"Um, yeah," George replied. "I'm jobless and now parentless in an unforgiving economy where everyone is losing their jobs. I can't afford to be anything *but* worried."

"I'd argue that you can't afford to be worried," replied Emily. "Worry means you've lost faith in the Lord. Now obviously that doesn't mean you'll never worry ever again—we're human, aren't we—but it does mean that you have a choice *not* to worry."

George mulled that over but didn't see how he had any say in the matter. He didn't have a job; being jobless meant instability. Yes, he had people to rely on, but for how much longer? How long could Matt's commission support him without sacrificing their own needs?

Emily popped the sliced zucchini into the sizzling pan and placed the lid overtop before turning to face the whiner. "I know of a man. I've

Fay

never met him before, but his situation sounds similar. His story may resonate with you, and honestly you could use the life lesson." She rounded the granite island and went to her desk, where she shuffled through papers until she produced a business card.

"Here," she said as she handed George the card.

He read the name. "Anthony Groves," he said, then laughed. "Dentist?"

She nodded. "Go talk to him. He's not a dentist anymore. I think he'll have some insight into your situation."

George didn't see how that could be possible but decided that it couldn't hurt to go talk to the man.

George sat down that evening and emailed this Anthony Groves fellow. He spent quite a bit of time laboring over the email, trying to convey his position in the best way he knew how. When he finally sent the message, he also sent up a silent prayer that God would lead this man to accept George's random request to meet.

And almost immediately, Anthony Groves replied.

It was an answered prayer, and George didn't forget it as he walked up the steps to Anthony's house just a few days later.

He straightened his shirt and collar a bit self-consciously. He wanted to look presentable and respectable. He didn't know why, but he got the strange sense that he and Anthony were going to hit it off and that he just might be seeing him around in the future.

He knocked on the door, and a few agonizing seconds later, it opened.

"George?" asked the man on the threshold.

"Hi, yes," George answered, extending his hand to shake. "George Müller."

The man George assumed was Anthony smiled and shook George's hand firmly. "Pleasure to meet you, George. I'm Anthony." He waved him inside. "Come on in. Please excuse the mess," said the frazzled man as he stepped over a couple of children's toys. "We're in the process of packing everything up. Headed to India in just a few weeks."

"India? What for?"

"We have some sister churches I work with there," explained Anthony. "My family and I go to lend support and aid, plus we assist the rural dental clinics with our expertise."

Just as he said it, a young boy of about thirteen whipped past them, going way faster than George thought humanly possible.

"Hey," Anthony shouted after the kid. "Careful, Jonah! We've got a guest in the house."

A muffled "sorry" was returned before Anthony just chuckled.

Anthony led George to the sitting room and offered him a chair.

"If you don't mind me asking," George began. "How do you have the money to go to India? I'm sure it won't be an inexpensive trip for the family."

Anthony just shrugged. "I have a big God on my side. You know? I've never had to ask for a thing. Look around you. Everything you see, the Lord provided. I heard something powerful once: He doesn't call the equipped; he equips the called."

Fay

George just stared, that sentence bouncing around in his head.

"Does that make sense?"

To avoid looking like an idiot, George nodded.

Anthony chuckled, clearly knowing that George had absolutely no idea what he meant. "What I mean is I don't think God will only go to rich men and ask them to take care of the poor. I believe He could go to anyone, and if He truly has called you, then He will ensure you have what you need to make it on your road. Does *that* make sense?"

Make sense? It resonated with his entire being. He immediately thought of how God had provided for him in college when his father disowned him and how he'd been able to make the funds he needed to complete his education. He'd had *everything* he needed, and the Lord had provided it.

"Yes," George answered. "That makes absolute perfect sense."

Anthony smiled. "Good. So tell me, why were you so interested to meet with me?"

George settled in and explained the situation he'd found himself in, and boy did Anthony have a thing or two to say about it.

Anthony told George of his own experience while studying at Trinity College in Dublin. At a certain point, he became aware that he no longer felt the call to be at the school. Through a series of bizarre circumstances, God had confirmed that Anthony wasn't supposed to be there. He'd sent plenty of signs, and Anthony just had to learn how to interpret the signals. After that, Anthony had begun his mission work and had fully placed his trust in the Lord. He asked God for every meal, and his family never went hungry.

He told George of his own struggles to find jobs and explained how much more terrifying it was when he got married and started having kids. Anthony refused to lose his faith, though, and soon God placed him in a position in a small church where he was needed. Not long after, he began his mission work in earnest, and benefactors supported him to go.

"Now, here I am," continued Anthony, "living the life God has called me to live. And look around you. Sure, I don't have the nicest home, but make no mistake…God has provided everything I needed. Even things I wanted. We're so grateful. I think, if nothing else, I'd like to pass that along to my children. That absolute faith in God."

Okay. That was it. George was inspired. "Wow, I…" He shook his head. "That is incredible. I can't tell you how much that helps me. I've been struggling to figure out how I'm going to make it out here."

Anthony nodded slowly. "Trust me, I get it. But you're doing exactly what you're supposed to be doing. Just keep your ear to the ground—really *listen* for His voice. As long as you're following the path He's laid out before you, you have nothing to fear. Everything is going according to His plan."

George stood, extending his hand. "Thank you so much for your time, Anthony. I'm sorry I've kept you for so long when you should be packing."

Anthony shrugged. "Not a big deal at all, George. It's been a pleasure talking to you. Besides, I have help around the house. Five sisters."

George's eyes widened. "How many?"

Anthony laughed. "Yeah, I know. Trust me, it's a blessing and a curse. Oh," he paused, listening. "Speak of the Devil…"

Fay

George could hear footsteps rapidly coming down the stairs—two sets. Then, another child rounded the corner at top speed. Just before the young boy could reach his father, a woman stepped out and scooped him up into her arms.

"Got you," she said playfully.

George stared. She was *beautiful*. She absolutely glowed with brilliance.

Long, dark hair cascaded over her shoulders, making her jean overalls and white shirt look magically elegant. Her bright smile sent George's heart racing, and her green eyes were alight with childlike amusement.

She set the boy down, looking up at Anthony and George.

"Sorry," she said. "We got distracted."

Anthony glanced at George, taking in his rapt expression. "George, this is my little sister. Mary, this is George. He's a new friend."

"Hi, George," Mary said happily. She must have been several years older than George, but still she had this childlike air about her.

For a long moment, George couldn't say anything. Then, when it was starting to get awkward, he quickly said, "Hi, Mary. It's wonderful to meet you. Are you going to India too?"

"No," she answered. "That's my brother's calling. I guess I've yet to discover mine." She shrugged with a smile. "All in His time, right?"

George nodded, dumbfounded. "Y-yes…it is."

"Well," Mary said. "I'd better get back to those boxes. Nice meeting you, George." She waved as she walked off.

George shook his head and looked back at Anthony, who was just grinning. "What?" asked George.

"Mary is somewhat new to the area. Maybe she'd like to have another friend," suggested Anthony.

"You think?"

Anthony chuckled and pulled out his phone, typing something in. George got a notification on his own phone and looked down.

"That's Mary's contact information," said Anthony. "I'm sure she'd love to talk while I'm away in India."

"Thank you."

"Of course. It really was a pleasure getting to talk to you, George Müller. Stay in touch?"

Oh, George was *definitely* going to stay in touch with this family.

Chapter Seven

George took Anthony's words to heart, and he began to pray in earnest for the Lord's will to be revealed. He continued frequenting different churches, as there was no shortage of services to attend in the Greenville suburbs.

When Beta returned at the end of the summer, he was so full of life and had so much to share about his studies. George was thrilled to have his friend back, and he was now able to split his time between Beta's house and Emily's so he wasn't too much of a financial drain on either of them. He also continued helping out neighbors with odd jobs so that he would able to pitch in for his own groceries.

When September rolled around, George met a man named Thomas Milligan who was an elder at a church in Springfield. Springfield was a few hours away from Greenville, but the drive there and back could be accomplished in a day. The two were introduced by Anthony, who set them up to have lunch one afternoon. Little did George know that

Let the Children Come

Thomas was really using the lunch to interview him.

Springfield Community Church, the congregation Thomas attended, had been in need of a new pastor for some time. Knowing of George's desire to work in ministry, Thomas invited George to speak at the church for a while. George was beyond thrilled, and he gladly accepted.

Only two weeks later, George preached his first sermon at Springfield Community Church. Beta helped him come up with a passionate, life-giving sermon, and the congregation absolutely loved it. Thomas Milligan was thrilled, and George began to speak on a regular basis.

His car got him there and back each week, but it put a lot of miles on top of the already high mileage his car boasted. Beta said it was a miracle that his car was still running, but George wouldn't go that far. Finally, after months of prayer, the Lord placed it on the congregation members' hearts to ask George to be their pastor. And to offer him a salary.

If it wouldn't have appeared desperate, George would have fallen to his knees and thanked the Lord right then and there. Somehow, he managed to stay upright, send up a silent prayer of gratitude, and shake the hands of the elders in the church, accepting the position.

Soon after, George threw everything he owned into "ol' Betsy" and drove to Springfield to start his new life as Pastor of Springfield Community Church. One of the church members rented George a very small, one-bedroom apartment they owned. George filled it with cheap furniture from yard sales and flea markets.

George had never felt a stronger sense of conviction and purpose

Fay

in his life. He loved preaching. He would spend hours poring over scriptures before he decided which one he wanted to preach a message on. And he considered God's will in all things, because after all, it was His church, wasn't it?

George never lacked passion and zeal for teaching the scriptures, and it was part of the reason his church loved him so much. His young energy made him a fiery pastor, willing to talk about controversial messages and discuss tricky subjects while being open-minded to new ideas and interpretations should anyone in his congregation present them.

Admittedly, there were times when George didn't even have a sermon prepared. These were the days when his faith was put to work, and he would trust that the Lord had something He wanted to say to His congregation. There were plenty within the body that came and went because they didn't like George's preaching, but there were many more who flocked in, inspired by his honesty and true faith. George was amazed and humbled by it.

George's messages were heartfelt and geared towards a congregation of any education level. Soon there were a few homeless coming in from the streets, aching to hear the words of the Lord. And George knew so well how to communicate with them. But they weren't *his* words, and he made very sure that he wasn't saying anything that the Lord didn't want said.

In the early spring, several months after Anthony left for India, George sat down in his humble office at the apartment he was renting. He took out his phone and stared at the contact Anthony had sent him.

Mary Grove.

It had been such a whirlwind settling into his new pastoral role that he hadn't been able to focus on much else, but he had never forgotten Mary's infectious smile. He took a deep breath and...well, he chickened out on calling her and decided that texting was a better bet.

His text was direct. He inquired how Anthony's trip was going, told Mary that he'd been leading a congregation in Springfield, and asked if she had gotten her footing in Greenville yet. He told himself he wasn't going to sit around and wait for a reply after it sent but...yeah, he did. He definitely waited around.

He spent half the evening glancing at his phone. He'd alternate between cooking pasta on the stove—and nearly burning it—and checking his messages. Then he'd begin to look over the following week's sermon and check his messages again. It was exhausting, and honestly, he was pretty annoyed with himself. By now, he was a full-grown man. An *adult*. He shouldn't have butterflies like this, right?

Ding.

George scrambled across his study to where he'd left his phone on the arm of the sofa after telling himself he wasn't going to check anymore. He practically dove across the armrest to get it.

Mary had texted.

Hey, George! It's nice to hear from you. Yes, Anthony is doing well, but it's hard to talk to him much because of the spotty service. That's amazing that you've found a congregation! My

Fay

brother speaks very highly of you, so I'm sure they love you there. All my training in dance finally paid off. A studio in Springfield hired me as a dance instructor, so I actually just moved from Greenville to Springfield, too! I really love my students. I'm still in the process of looking for a church, though. Maybe I'll attend one of your sermons?

There were those butterflies again. Wow.

George was ecstatic to learn that Mary was now living in the same city as he was, but he tried his best to keep his cool and not seem *too* excited. They continued their texting conversation, mostly talking about how Mary liked Springfield and her new job at the studio.

As he closed his eyes to go to sleep that night, George started to pray about Mary. He had a feeling that she was going to be part of his journey, and he couldn't help but hope that he was right.

A few days later, George got up the courage to call Mary. He was nervous at first, but Mary's warm personality immediately put him at ease. It wasn't long before their conversation shifted away from small talk and became more personal. George even opened up about his past—the drugs, the drinking, and the death of his mother. He shared how being disowned by his father had affected him and how it had strengthened his love for his heavenly Father.

He felt so at peace when he spoke to her. Though they had only met in person once and had just had their first phone conversation, George knew that he really liked Mary. He didn't know what she thought, however, so he decided to proceed slowly. Even though they now lived in the same city, George told himself it was normal to get to know someone through text conversations and phone calls in this day and age. Truth be told, he was too nervous to ask her out, anyway.

Two weeks later, as George was closing his sermon, those butterflies popped up again.

George had made it a habit to make eye contact with those in his congregation. He wanted to create a personal connection with each of them. Now, with his congregation growing, it was difficult to really make that connection with everyone. It just so happened that one of the people he managed to spot in the audience was a face he'd been thinking of for a long time now.

Mary smiled kindly and didn't laugh when George momentarily forgot the closing words of his sermon. He somehow managed to conclude his message, and when he stepped away from the podium, Mary was there to greet him.

"I'm impressed," she said, startling George. "You actually display a lot of knowledge for someone so young. I guess I knew that before; it's just...different hearing your sermons."

"Really?" George asked. "Well, what did you think?"

"I think you're still learning, and that's your most admirable trait. Even though you're standing on this podium preaching, you don't think of yourself as more knowledgeable than anyone in your congregation. You seem to be constantly seeking God's will, and I think it's wonderful."

George relaxed, then finally gathered the courage he needed.

Fay

"Would you like to go out with me sometime?"

"Out?" asked Mary suspiciously.

"Yeah, like…" *To a restaurant?* No, that was lame. *A stroll in the park, milady?* What was he, living in the 18th century? He shook his head and laughed nervously. "I guess…" An idea popped into his mind. "A picnic."

She smiled. "Sure. I would love to go on a picnic with you."

George tried to contain his excitement. "Okay, then. I'll get it planned."

"Sounds good," she said, waving as she left. "Have a good day."

Chapter Eight

The second she left, preparations had to be made.

George spent what was left of his Sunday afternoon choosing the right park.

Then came the preparations for the picnic itself. He would be the first to admit that he wasn't much of a cook. In fact, he spent more time *burning* food than actually getting to eat anything. But he didn't want to just buy something anyone else could buy for her. If he was going to pursue her, he supposed he had better start putting his all into it.

When the day finally came, he ultimately settled on cold cut sandwiches—made with love, of course—and two slices of cake he'd made from a box mix. He didn't feel too proud of this picnic, but he hoped Mary would like it. He prayed nervously under his breath as he drove up to Mary's house to pick her up.

He waited for a few minutes outside before Mary finally came out. She was wearing a beautiful yellow shirt with white flowers. The col-

Fay

or made her dark, rich hair so much more vivid, and George could hardly look away. Somehow, he managed a gentleman's smile as he reached to open her door for her.

"Wow," she remarked as she slid into the passenger seat. "Chivalry isn't dead."

The drive to the park was filled with conversation, which was an absolute relief. He'd worried it would be awkward. After all, how long had it been since he'd been on a real date? On top of that, he knew he was still so young. She was thirty-two, and he was twenty-four. That wasn't a small age difference. What if she thought he was immature? Or that he was behind her in some way?

These worries faded to the back of his mind as they lost themselves in conversation.

Cherry Hills Park was a gorgeous nature reserve outside of the suburbs that George loved to visit when he needed to sit and reflect. He wanted to share it with Mary, hoping she would love it too. It was a nice get-away from the city, and George had a feeling Mary would appreciate time in nature. From the way Mary's face lit up when they arrived, he knew his choice was a hit.

Shadows danced across Mary's face as the sun shone through the canopy of trees overhead. George could barely keep his eyes on the road.

"This area is so beautiful," she commented. "It seems so untouched by the chaos of the world."

"I know," George answered thoughtfully.

When they managed to find a parking spot deep inside the park, George retrieved his little picnic basket (borrowed, of course) with an eagerness he thought he'd never find again. He closed the trunk of his car and led Mary down a path following an old stone wall.

The two were silent for a while, but it wasn't an awkward silence. Rather, it was one that George actually appreciated. It felt like they were just enjoying nature in silence. That was the moment that George completely fell for her. It was in that silence.

George found the perfect spot for their picnic—a grassy hill overlooking a small field of wildflowers—and immediately set to work. He laid out the blanket for their picnic and started setting out the classy but still plastic plates that he'd picked up from the grocery store a day earlier. Mary seemed to think he was cute, smiling as he went out of his way to make everything look perfect. When they finally sat down, George swallowed his pride and broke the news.

"So, I can't cook," he said. "Yeah, I'm pretty terrible at it. But I do pride myself on a darn good turkey and cheese sandwich."

He reached into the basket before he could gauge her reaction and offered her the Ziplock bag. He then dared a glance at her face…and the tension seeped out of him. She was smiling. Brightly.

"This is amazing," she said, accepting the sandwich. "I can't believe you actually tried to cook for me."

He shrugged and went for his own sandwich. "It's a first date. You've got to pull out all the stops."

She smiled, charmed. "Well it's all very impressive."

It was hard not to be joyful around her. Mary had this infectious laugh and a smile that seemed to shine brighter than the sun beaming down on them.

Fay

They spent the afternoon sharing about their beliefs, what led them to their convictions, and where they believed God was taking them. And Mary was by no means a bystander. She felt led to be very involved in a ministry of some sort; she just hadn't felt that she'd found the right one. And like George, she leaned on God for her every decision, including moving to Springfield.

One thing was for sure: Mary had a passion for children. In the few months she'd been living in the suburbs, she'd already helped organize activities for the youth in children's homes and was pushing others in her community to lend aid. She'd had little traction, so she'd done most of the work herself. She was everything George could have imagined, everything he could have wanted or needed. And it seemed like God was showing him that.

So the relationship did what it was meant to do: it progressed. They seemed to have so much in common, and they found that their differences strengthened each other. It really was iron sharpening iron, and George imagined that *this* was the kind of biblical, strong relationship that God had intended when he created Adam and Eve.

Over the next few months, they did everything together. Mary even began attending George's church. They refused to lose their love of adventure and visited the park whenever they could. George engaged in her passion as well, and he even led some members of his church to help Mary bring joy to the lives of kids in the inner city.

As the time passed, George only fell more and more in love with her. He couldn't believe how much he'd gotten to know her in only a few short months, and soon…well, he was pretty sure he knew what he needed to do. In fact, he'd known from the beginning. It had almost seemed like God had dropped her in his path and said, "Trust me, you're going to want to take a look at this one." He'd prayed long and hard about it, just to make sure he was hearing God's voice and not his own desires. And now he was sure.

Tonight was the night.

He looked at himself in the mirror. He desperately wanted to get Beta's or Emily's opinion on the suit he picked out, but he didn't have the time.

He straightened the collar of the jacket. Twice. Checked his shoes. They weren't new by any means and were covered in scuffs, but he'd done his best to polish them for the occasion. The suit? That brought back memories.

He stared at the pinstripes for a while. This was the suit his father had bought him the day he'd returned home for the summer that changed his life. The suit was a sign of trust and pride between them. He hadn't worn it until this point. He didn't know why…it was just difficult. But it was the nicest suit he had, and Mary deserved that.

He turned away from the mirror and headed down the stairs. Soon, the doorbell rang, and there were those nerves again.

He went to answer the door, and his jaw nearly dropped. Mary looked beautiful. She wore a jade green dress, elegant and sophisticated, and it only made George more nervous. It made her look so mature, so confident.

Fay

George was so much younger. He'd barely considered what that would mean. Did she even want to marry a man younger than she was? Would that be weird? What if she had no desire to marry at all? They somehow hadn't even gotten to that question. George had always assumed she did because of her love for children but…well, what if she just didn't want to marry him?

"George?" she asked.

He shook his head. "Wow, hi. So sorry, I guess I got a little caught up there. Please, come in."

She smiled and stepped inside. He kissed her on the cheek.

"Happy five months," he said, his voice still a little shaky.

She raised a brow curiously. "Happy five months," she echoed, but it sounded like she was a little suspicious of his nervousness.

He cleared his throat and escorted her to his humble dining room. "I'm sorry I didn't have the money to splurge on a nice restaurant. I wanted to, I really did, I just—"

"George." She immediately stopped him. "It's so sweet that you wanted to give me a nice dinner, but this is all I need. So, what do we have planned?"

He immediately relaxed some. He could get to the big question later.

"Well," he began. "I thought since I'm certainly no chef, we could make dinner together. What do you think?"

She was already going for an apron. "Absolutely."

The two immediately went to work. George mostly followed Mary's orders, but occasionally he would get the bright idea to throw in some "culinary artistic flair" in the form of seasonings that didn't complement the meal whatsoever. Mary would just roll her eyes and keep working. They joked some, talked again about Anthony and his travels with his family, and discussed what they'd learned in their studies of scripture over the week.

When they finally finished cooking, George brought the food to the modest table he'd found at a yard sale and set Mary's plate in front of her. There was nothing fancy or expensive about the floral arrangement resting in the center of the table, but Mary seemed thrilled anyway.

George took his seat uncomfortably.

She lifted her glass. "To another five months of happiness and encouragement."

George swallowed. This was his moment. He lifted his glass. "To forever."

Mary blinked. "What?"

George quickly stood, then questioned why in the world he stood. He set his glass down quickly. "Mary…I've been wanting to…" He cleared his throat again. "I've been wanting to ask you something for a while now. And I know this must seem so rushed, but I want you to know that I've really prayed about it and really think it's what God wants…and I think we should get married."

Wow. George wanted to slap himself on the forehead. What kind of proposal was that? Sure, he wasn't the most romantic—he was a guy, after all—but even he knew to do better than *that*.

She just stared. "Come again?"

George took a deep breath and prayed for the right words. He

Fay

stepped around the corner of the table and knelt down in front of her. *This*, George thought, *is how you're supposed to propose.*

"My darling, Mary. I am head over heels in love with you. I have adored learning about you and growing to understand your relationship with the Lord. You have inspired me to be a better man and have only encouraged my walk with God. I believe that together…we could do amazing things for the glory of God."

By now tears had formed in Mary's eyes, but her hesitation made doubt spring back into George's mind.

"I love you too," she began. "George, of course you know I love you. It's as if we were made for each other. And nothing would make me happier than to marry you…"

A pang of fear hit George square in the chest. "But…?"

She took a deep breath. "But, George, I'm eight years older than you. I know you don't care now, but you might care one day. In fact, you could resent my age one day. You should find someone your own age to give your heart to."

George was taken aback. How could she possibly think such a thing? Of course he knew that their age difference might play a role in her response, but he never would have imagined that she could be worried about being too old! He'd always worried that she would find him immature or beneath her somehow. His heart hurt knowing how she'd felt.

"How could you think that?" asked George. "That would never matter to me."

She wiped at a tear that threatened to spill over her cheek. "You say that now, but what about when I'm fifty and you still look thirty?"

"Mary, first of all, it's eight years, not twenty," George said with a roll of his eyes. "Secondly, I'm never going to care about that. I believe that we are meant to be together. I've prayed and prayed and prayed about this and you, and I know we are on the right path."

And that's when it happened. Her unsure expression turned sure, and she smiled so big it nearly knocked George over. "Then who am I to stand against the Lord's wishes?"

George barely dared to hope. "Does that mean…?"

Now it was her turn to roll her eyes. "Of course, George. Yes. I'll marry you!"

George shouted with joy and swept her up into his arms. He spun her in a circle, nearly toppling over the dinner table, but he didn't care. Mary laughed and held on for dear life.

This was it. He had found his life partner, and he couldn't wait to begin their new life together.

Chapter Nine

They say that when two people fall in love, it's hard to keep them apart. George wasn't sure who *they* were or what credentials they had to be providing this information, but he knew they were right.

Within a few months, Mary and George were married. They held a small ceremony together for close friends and family only. Fred and Beta were there, Matt and Emily were there, and two of Mary's sisters, Berta and Georgina, also attended. Mary's big brother, Anthony, had been unable to return from India due to some health complications, but he promised to congratulate the new couple in person as soon as he could. But George's father, who still refused to acknowledge him as his son, refused to attend.

The service had been beautiful, and George knew Mary was happy with it. It was an event he'd remember for the rest of his life. Seeing Mary walk down that aisle towards him? It meant everything. Hearing her vows spoken before family and God? It meant everything. That first dance? It meant everything. She was so beautiful. George could swear she was the most beautiful woman he had ever seen.

At the reception, Beta, Emily, and Matt congratulated George on the triumph of getting Mary to be his wife. George blushed as Emily and Matt recounted embarrassing stories of him and of how enamored he was with Mary after first meeting her. Mary seemed to find it endearing, though, and she just smiled, squeezing her new husband's hand.

"I'm so excited for you," Beta told George as the two stepped out for a breath of fresh air. "You've thrown yourself wholeheartedly into the ministry, and God is honoring that."

"Thanks, Beta," George answered. "It's crazy to me that not too long ago, I pictured a very different future for myself."

Beta snorted. "Tell me about it. Me too, brother." He stuck his hands in his pockets, staring up at the moon. "I'm going to be out of the country for a bit."

"Yeah? What for?"

"Ministry work in Haiti," he answered. "There's a project there that helps orphaned or abandoned kids."

Abandoned kids, George thought. The term didn't even seem possible. Who would abandon a kid? Of course, George knew how naïve a sentiment that was. There was so much sin in the world, and the abandonment of children was only a small portion of it.

"Wow," George said. "How long will you be there?"

"Not sure yet. I haven't booked a return flight, so I guess we'll see what the Lord has in store."

George's heart ached. He knew that meant he might not see his

Fay

friend for a very long time, and after spending the majority of his life with Beta, George knew it was going to be *very* different going forward. He couldn't be selfish with Beta, though. The Lord had great things in store for him.

"That's incredible, Beta," George encouraged. "You're doing what I've always dreamed of doing—mission work, truly helping the helpless."

Beta looked at him. "Why don't you come with me? From what I know of Mary, I'm sure she'd be on the same page."

George wanted to. With everything in him, he wanted to, but he knew that it wasn't his decision. "I don't think it's in His plan right now. I just have to be patient and wait."

Beta nodded. "Wise of you. I know too many men who would just jump at the opportunity, thinking that if it was a good cause, God would bless it. But if it's not His timing, it won't work."

"Exactly," answered George. He looked at his friend. "Well, I wish you the best of luck in Haiti."

Beta shook George's hand. "And you in your congregation." He pointed a finger at George. "But don't you dare think this gives you an out. You still have to keep in touch."

George chuckled. "Absolutely."

When that next fall rolled around, a problem arose: George had been praying, and he wasn't feeling comfortable anymore being guaranteed a salary from the church. Though he didn't think it wrong for pastors to take a salary, he felt like God was inviting him to take a step of faith with his finances. He wanted to ensure that money never motivated his ministry, and he never wanted to feel swayed or pressured to only speak the messages his benefactors wanted to hear. There had to be a better way.

Mary felt the same way. When George came to discuss it with her, he found that the Lord had laid it on her heart as well. She wasn't comfortable with it and agreed that a change had to be made. Knowing that he and his wife both felt so strongly on the matter made it easier, but it didn't completely extinguish the worry.

He told his church that he would no longer be taking a salary—his pay would now be on a donation basis only. He set up a website where donors could be anonymous, and he had faith that God would provide.

By that November, they had only forty dollars in their bank account. *Forty.* Because Mary was good with money, she was able to stretch it for groceries, but it couldn't last forever.

Being the prayer warrior that she was, Mary prayed daily that the Lord would provide for them, and George did the same. He spent hours kneeling in prayer, no matter where he was. He once spent nearly four hours on his knees in prayer on the hot pavement beside his car.

Without fail, God always saw to their needs and brought them through the difficult time.

Months passed, and the routine continued. Mary stretched money as far as it could go, and when it was needed, the Lord would answer their prayers and provide for their needs. The donations that had seemed so elusive before were becoming frequent, and God was quick to supply everything that George and Mary needed—and in *abundance*. Not only were they given enough to buy that week's food, but they were given enough to ensure that the next week was taken care of, as well.

It was an empowering experience for George. Though he'd seen the Lord's hand at work already, the consistent miracles and provision he was witnessing only strengthened his faith—and Mary's, as well.

Chapter Ten

"After the exponential decline in the stock market and yesterday's devastating dip, experts are warning that the US economy may experience a recession in the coming months," the clean-cut newscaster reported. He waved a hand to a chart beside him, shaking his head. "Look at all that red." He whistled low. "Dayna, what are your thoughts on this?"

To his left, a middle-aged woman dressed in a sharp suit looked into the camera. "Honestly, Reggie, I agree. Already we're seeing small businesses making changes, expecting the collapse that's bound to happen."

George had heard enough. He took the remote from the coffee table and switched the TV to a different channel. Mary, who was sitting on the couch, immediately turned and scowled at him.

"George, I was watching that," she said, reaching for the remote. "How are we supposed to know how to prepare if we aren't informed?"

George shook his head. "Aren't you the one always telling me that the Lord will provide?"

"Maybe He provides by placing it on my heart to watch the news so we're prepared," she suggested.

George chuckled and handed his wife the remote. "If you want to watch it, fine, but don't let it worry you."

George went about his day, trying not to hear the voices on the television talking about how dire the situation was about to get. He prayed that the whole thing would just blow over, but unfortunately it didn't.

Two weeks later, gas prices had dropped to just over a dollar. It seemed like everyone was out of work, and bored people who had nothing to pour their energy toward become antsy, which led to protests in the streets. George could never tell what exactly the mob was protesting. It looked like some were protesting the high tax rate while others just seemed to be protesting the economic collapse—as if protesting would help.

Mary was becoming more and more concerned by the day, but George knew better than to chide her.

One of the biggest changes George began to notice was the increase in homelessness. He often saw families sitting on the side of the road, the children holding up signs asking for money or food. George couldn't help himself; he always gave what little money they had.

With the economic situation becoming more dire, George's work at Springfield Community Church became all the more relevant and necessary. As more needy believers flocked to the church, George's donation-based income began to lessen. This was not because his congregation could no longer donate the way they used to. Rather, it was because George's heart was heavy for those less fortunate, and he often gave away more than he could afford to.

Mary was a miracle worker. Though George didn't like to admit it, he was actually grateful that she watched the news as much as she did. While George preferred to keep his mind on spiritual dangers, Mary kept her ear to the ground for the earthly dangers as well, which made her a fierce "watchman on the wall," just as the Lord had appointed to Israel in Isaiah.

She knew when to stock up, when to save money, and when they needed to spend it to prepare, which meant that while others were struggling to get by, George and Mary managed decently well. He didn't attribute it all to Mary, however; he knew that without the Lord's blessing, they would have nothing.

One afternoon, early in George's twenty-seventh year, he came home late from one of his prayer meetings. Before he even walked into the house, he *knew* he was in trouble. He and Mary had been planning a date night for weeks, and yet something had always forced them to put it off. Tonight was supposed to be another attempt at treating his wife to dinner, and he was late—very late.

"Sorry, hon," he quickly called through the small foyer. "I take full responsibility. I lost track of time and—"

And Mary was nowhere to be seen. George stopped dead in his

Fay

tracks as he looked into the kitchen. He'd expected her to be standing there, arms crossed, wondering where her dinner was, but the kitchen was empty.

"Honey?" he called.

"I'm up here," replied Mary's faint voice, muffled through a door.

He followed her voice upstairs to their bathroom and hesitated, knocking once. "Mary? Everything okay?"

He heard a sniffle behind the door. "Come in, George."

Truth be told, he was a little nervous. He deserved a tongue lashing, and Mary was known to deliver the best, so the fact that she wasn't yelling was disconcerting.

He opened the door slowly and peeked inside. Mary sat on the closed lid of the toilet, her knees tucked to her chest almost like a child. She clutched something in her hand, but George couldn't get a good look at what it was.

"Mary," he whispered as he knelt beside her. "Talk to me. What's going on?"

She blinked slowly and unclenched her hand, dropping whatever she'd been clutching into George's palm.

It took him a second to decide what it was. It sort of looked like a thermometer, but it was pink, and he'd never known Mary to willingly pick out anything pink. It wasn't until he spotted the two lines on the display that he realized what it was.

Pure excitement encompassed him as he leapt up. "Does this mean…?" he asked her.

She nodded.

He smiled and rubbed his face in disbelief. "Oh my word, we're having a baby…"

It didn't seem real yet. He never realized how much he wanted to be a father until he was staring at those two thin lines. It was the answer to a prayer he hadn't even prayed yet.

George looked back at his wife, and he immediately realized that he'd missed the expression on her face in his excitement. She wasn't excited—she was afraid.

"Honey, what's wrong?" George asked quickly.

Mary's lip quivered. "How can we possibly afford to pay for a child when we can barely afford our own cost of living?"

George knelt beside his wife and kissed the back of her hand. "We can do this," he whispered. "We have the Lord on our side." He touched her belly lovingly. "*This* is a blessing. A gift! He wouldn't have given us a gift without knowing that we could handle it and having a plan to provide for us."

She nodded, but George could tell she was still worried.

"I promise," he assured her. "We continue the work the Lord has laid out before us, and we continue to place our faith in Him. He's going to see us through this."

Mary took a deep breath and this time when she nodded, she seemed filled with the joy that only knowing God can bring. "I know," she said, opening her eyes. "I know, and I have faith."

A few months passed, and although the economic climate wasn't getting better, it wasn't getting progressively worse anymore. George was in a position to be able to help those in need again, and he thanked the Lord every day for that.

One of the men who had joined the Springfield Community Church congregation was an old acquaintance, Henry Craik.

George had met Henry shortly after his introduction to Anthony Groves, Mary's brother. Henry was highly educated for a twenty-four-year-old, and Anthony had hired him in the past to be a private tutor for his kids. At the time, he was somewhat of a new believer. Despite growing up in a church environment, it took a while for Henry to find a true relationship with God. He once told George that before he met and worked with Anthony, he'd considered himself "a religious man without God."

Henry was looking for a new congregation. He'd felt called to reach out to George. Henry was a brilliant man and was far overqualified for any of the positions available in Springfield Community Church, but George wanted to help. He brought it up to Mary, and as usual, she had the answer.

"Why don't you bring Henry in as another speaker for the congregation?" she suggested, barely looking up from the paperwork and expenses she was going over for the church. "He's a wonderful speaker, and it would be good for the congregation to hear from more than just one voice. He has a pastor's heart too."

"That's a great idea," George immediately answered. He'd been so dedicated to his church that he didn't even have time to work in other areas of the ministry.

So it was decided. George called Henry and invited him to come

Let the Children Come

to Springfield Community Church.

The first Sunday Henry was to speak, George prepared himself to go introduce his friend to the congregation.

Henry was athletic and tall with dark brown hair and matching eyes. George didn't know him all that well, but from what Anthony had said about him, George knew he was passionate about ministry and had a desire to grow in his teaching gift.

"Thanks again, George," Henry said. "I'm excited to be working together. I think the Lord can do amazing things through us."

George smiled. "I know he can."

"I'm going to go check on the wife," Henry said quickly. "Make sure she and Will are settled in. I'll be right back." He began to pass George, nodding at Mary with a smile before ducking out of the room.

Mary stepped up to George, stood on her tiptoes, and kissed him on the cheek. "I am so proud of you," she said.

George was taken aback. Mary rarely complimented him. Her love language was more along the lines of quality time. This rare praise made his heart jump and instilled a kind of calm within his spirit. Mary was a woman of God, and if she was sure of his decision, then it truly meant he was on the right path.

But Mary wasn't finished. "I fall more and more in love with you every day. With your faithfulness, your diligence, and your patience." She squeezed his hand. "I am your partner, and I am so excited to walk into this next portion of our journey together. Henry is going to be a great friend to have so close."

George didn't know what to say. He started to open his mouth

Fay

but then decided a kiss better expressed his gratitude. When he pulled back, he smiled. "What would I do without you?"

She giggled. "Flounder. Absolutely flounder, George Müller."

When Henry returned, he and George stepped out in front of the church and introduced their new part-time speaker.

On September 17th, while George was sipping coffee in his modest kitchen and going over that Sunday's sermon, Mary slipped into the chair next to him and put her hand on his arm to get his attention.

"Hmm?" He mumbled around a mouthful of coffee.

"It's time."

"Time for what?" he asked, hardly paying attention.

She squeezed his arm and laughed. "George, you never change. But please get me to the hospital immediately because our child is trying to get out right now."

George's head snapped up.

Now George had never been known for his levelheadedness, especially under pressure. Nor was he known for his constitution. The fact that he was able to jump up from the table, gather the necessities, and get his very pregnant wife into the car should be evidence of the Lord's provision.

It was a stressful night filled with labor pains, constant visits from nurses, and finally…a miracle.

In the early morning hours, Mary gave birth to a beautiful baby girl—breathing, crying, and *thriving*. Together, they named her Lydia.

When George took his newborn daughter into his arms, he couldn't believe it. He couldn't comprehend what he was seeing. How had *he* made this? It seemed like a culmination of all of his life. *This* was what life was about. This little, tiny human. This baby girl.

She grabbed his finger and squeezed and…well, that's when George lost it. He burst into tears, which almost seemed to make Mary embarrassed, but he couldn't help it.

A couple of days later, George, Mary, and their newborn Lydia returned home. George ensured that his wife and daughter were settled nicely into their house and had everything that they needed.

In those first couple of days, George could do nothing but praise God and spend time with his small yet mighty family. He admired how much they had conquered through the Lord's strength, and he marveled at the miracle of life.

Lydia was another answered prayer in what had been a stream of miracles…and God wasn't done with George yet.

Beta called from Haiti, where he was still residing and ministering. Honestly, George had been a little jealous of Beta's work, but after the birth of his daughter, absolutely nothing could squash his joy.

"I'm so happy for you, George," declared Beta over the phone.

George couldn't stop staring at his darling baby girl, asleep in her crib. "She's perfect, Beta. I wish you could be here to meet her."

"Maybe soon," he answered. "I'm trying to gather funding for some of the orphanages and group care homes in Haiti, so I may have some meetings with investors in the next few months."

"How are things there?" asked George as he turned out the lights in Lydia's room.

Beta's sigh echoed through the phone. "Heartbreaking. You wouldn't believe some of the things I've seen…or what some of these children have gone through. It's unspeakable. But I've made some connections within the US immigration system, and we're hopeful that eventually we can establish a program where these kids are brought into the United States and placed into group care. The idea would be to educate them with degrees and/or trades so they can go back to Haiti and really help the country."

George was astounded. "Beta, that's wonderful!"

"Well, it would be," he answered. "Surprisingly, government officials are willing to listen. It's just that there are no facilities in the US willing to take them. They're all privately funded, and since resources are so scarce right now, they're wary about taking on a group of Haitian children."

George spotted Mary in the hallway, and she gave him a confused look. He mouthed *Beta* and pointed to the phone before ducking onto their front porch.

"I have no doubt you'll figure it out," George answered. "The Lord seems to be blessing this endeavor, and if His hand is on it, nothing will stop you."

Beta chuckled. "Your enthusiasm is refreshing. I'll let you get back to your family. It was good talking to you, George."

"You too," he answered before hanging up the phone.

For days, he couldn't get those Haitian children out of his mind, and he wondered if other missionaries were struggling with the same issues in Guatemala, Belize, Honduras, and other developing or third-world nations. He brought up the subject to Mary, and together they prayed that the Lord would guide Beta's hands, as well as their own.

Chapter Eleven

The misfortunate had always weighed heavily on George's heart. The goal "to help" seemed far too broad, however, so George decided to narrow it down to education. All children were required by law to attend school, but how could they do that when they had no home, no food, and no one to look after them?

The first thing George needed to do was understand who needed help the most, and how to help them. So he began doing some research.

With the economy being as unstable as it was, and the threat of a recession looming, foster care systems were struggling to keep up with demands. Because the government was focused on other areas of the economy, federal funding had slowed. Stimulus checks for American businesses and households had come to an almost complete halt, and this had a dramatic and negative ripple effect on child care systems. There were rumors that foster care systems were now so completely overrun that some children were slated to wait up to two years for a placement.

Makeshift shelters had been created in the meantime to house children who were waiting in line for a home.

George wanted so desperately to help, but he still didn't fully understand the situation. After all, he'd known nothing of the foster care system while growing up. Mary, however, had done volunteer work with foster care organizations before and had contacts within the programs. She reached out to one of her old friends and arranged for her and George to spend time with the children to better understand their needs.

When George arrived at the government facility that housed kids waiting to be placed in the foster care system, he couldn't believe the conditions. It wasn't that they were being abused by any means, but these concrete walls and lifeless caregivers weren't suitable for a child who needed to be nurtured. Of course, Mary had an idea.

"We'll have one day out of the week where the kids can come out to the house, and we'll spend time with them," Mary suggested, bouncing a toddler on her knee in the playroom of the downtown foster care facility. "We can get permission from the case workers. I know they are overwhelmed and need the help. They can probably help us through the paperwork quickly. We could take three or four at a time. Cook them dinner, uplift them, and show them a real family environment."

George loved that idea, but was it enough? He shook his head. "We have to be able to do more."

"George," Mary whispered. "You know I would give anything to help these kids. But look around you." She gestured to the room overflowing with kids placed into the foster care system. "We don't have a facility like this." She placed a hand on his. "For now, let's just start out

Fay

with a few kids a week. It'll be good for Lydia to be around other kids as well."

George nodded. He knew she was right, but he felt this yearning to do *more*. These kids deserved that.

As if she could sense his inner turmoil, Mary stroked her husband's cheek softly. "We'll pray that the Lord will reveal His path for us. For now, let's do all we can with what we've been given." She smiled at the toddler in her lap. "Isn't that right?"

The toddler giggled, smiling broadly at Mary. Even the children loved her.

"Alright," George conceded.

Mary worked it all out, and soon they were taking in many from the foster care system for field trips, dinners, and outings. They even brought those who wanted to go with them to their church. They became the unofficial aunt and uncle of the system, and word was spreading of their compassion. George prayed that the Lord would give him an opportunity to help more than just these few children.

As the weeks turned into months, George and Mary cultivated relationships with the children in the foster care system, as well as with the case workers. Henry and his wife Sarah had even hopped on board and were now acting as an aunt and uncle to these neglected children by taking them on outdoor adventures, teaching them to cook, and even bringing them to church activities.

The more Mary witnessed the system, the more she began to see systemic shortcomings, which she continued to bring up to George.

"I know," he would say. "I told you. I want to do more."

"So how do we do that, George?" she asked genuinely. "We have no money."

"We don't need it," George answered. "Well, we do, but I mean we don't need to worry about it. Perhaps the Lord will—"

George's cell phone began to ring. He stared at it for a long moment before Mary said, "Aren't you going to get that?"

"Right," George said, picking it up and answering.

"George, it's Beta," said his friend quickly over the phone. "How are things in the great city of Springfield?"

George smiled, glad to hear his friend's voice, and he quickly put Beta on speaker so Mary could hear as well. "Things in the Müller household are going well."

"How's Mary doing?"

In the background, Mary called, "I'm doing well, Beta, thank you."

"Oh, you're on speakerphone, by the way," George added.

"Well, it's good to hear your voice, Mary," Beta replied. "So George, remember how I was telling you I'd be coming to the States to secure some investors? Well, it looks like I'll be coming in next week. I have several meetings scheduled, one of which is near Springfield. I was hoping you'd be in town and I could swing by and say hello?"

"Absolutely," he answered immediately. "We'll be here. We'd love to see you."

George and Mary couldn't wait for Beta's arrival. They spent most of the week preparing for him and made up a bed in their spare room for him to stay in while he was in town.

When Beta finally arrived, George felt like he was embracing his brother after years of being apart.

He didn't look the same at all. He'd completely buzzed his head, which he said was to ward off the Haiti heat, and he had definitely lost some weight, which Mary remedied by feeding him more food than he could stomach. But his attitude, personality, and love for the Lord hadn't changed in the slightest.

"I hear you're working with kids in the foster care system," Beta said as they were cleaning up dinner.

"We are," Mary answered. "And Lydia *loves* it. Isn't that right?" Mary asked in baby talk to the toddler sitting in the high chair. Lydia just giggled and clapped.

"So what's next for you in that world?" asked Beta.

"We're not sure yet," replied George. "You know me. I want to do more. I have this crazy feeling that we're supposed to be helping so many more kids than this. It's really been on my heart recently."

"That's not a crazy feeling, George. That's the Lord's voice speaking in your heart," Beta encouraged. "Listen to it. He'll open doors for you if that's the right path."

George nodded in understanding. "How did your meeting with the investors go?"

Beta sighed. "Poorly, but I have faith we'll find the right people to work with. On the bright side, members within our organization in Haiti have finally broken through the government's red tape and we're in the process of creating a program that allows kids under the age of fifteen passage into the United States if they come from sanctioned organizations in third-world nations."

"What?" George's eyes widened. "That's incredible!"

Mary smiled. "Congratulations, Beta. I know you've been working on this for a while now."

"They'll get a path to citizenship too if that is what they want?" asked George.

"Well, that's the next step. Hopefully," Beta said, rubbing the back of his neck. "That's where things get tricky. But our representatives think we have a good shot at passing this program and yes, eventually granting the kids who are given asylum citizenship. Provided that they stay out of trouble."

George squeezed his friend's shoulder. "That's incredible. I know there isn't much I can do, but if you need anything…name it."

Beta came with George and Mary to Springfield Community Church the next morning, and after the sermon, George gave Beta an opportunity to share his ministry with his congregation. Many in the church offered donations. Though small, George felt that they were the beginning of something miraculous.

Months ticked by. The more time George spent with the children in foster care and the more calls he received from Beta regarding the kids in Haiti, the more he felt a stirring in his heart. He began to believe he was definitely called to do something about this neglect and injustice.

Children within the foster care system rotated out and went to families, and this gave George the opportunity to minister to many different kids, but he knew that wasn't how it was supposed to be. Jesus had called His followers to make *disciples*, not converts. George didn't like that every time he seemed to be getting somewhere with one of the kids, they'd inevitably be placed into a family unit—and many times they'd come back a little bit more damaged. He wanted to be able to minister to them long term. He wasn't sure how yet, but he had faith that God was working in miraculous ways, and that He would reveal His plan soon enough.

Chapter Twelve

Before February of the year George would turn twenty-nine, he'd never heard of August Hermann Francké. Soon, however, Francké's autobiography would change George's mission and life forever.

Francké was an amazing Christian scholar and philanthropist who had a unique approach to ministering to the poor. In November, George began to read Francké's autobiography. He wasn't entirely sure why he was so drawn to the book, but he felt like he had something important to learn from Francké's life.

As George was reading one day, he received a call from Beta, who wanted to catch him up on everything happening in Haiti. Despite gaining the Haitian government's approval for asylum program, they still hadn't found facilities in the United States that were willing to take on the influx of children they'd have to receive. It broke George's heart, and he wondered how many children were suffering due to neglect, bodily harm, or sicknesses in these nations…and he was helpless to save them.

Fay

That's when it hit him. All of a sudden, it felt like the Lord was saying, "*Finally*, you've figured out what I've been trying to tell you all along."

Francké had done so much for the homeless and orphaned, and he did it all through faith—trusting God to provide for all the financial needs. George had felt called to do the same. Now it was time to put that into practice.

He nearly burst through their bedroom door, where Mary was reading a book in the corner of the room. Beside her, Lydia was playing with her toy horses.

"Mary," he gasped. "I have an idea. It's going to sound crazy at first because you're right, we have no money, but I firmly believe the Lord is moving us in this direction."

Mary set her book down and turned to face George. "Okay. Let's hear it."

"Beta's program is up and running, but they don't have any group homes willing to take in the kids in America. There are fifty of them who are in the program right now, going through the process of being accepted into the United States. But when they finish all the paperwork, they'll have nowhere to go."

Mary's green eyes lit up, and the vitality she'd lost over the past few months returned in full force. "You want to help."

"Yes," he answered. "I believe the Lord wants us to be the program that receives them. We could teach them about Jesus and show them the love that He has shown us." He hesitated. "An Academy for Christ. What do you think?"

Mary bounded from her chair and threw her arms around her husband's neck. "Nothing has ever felt so right." She said, her voice filled with laughter.

"Momma, what?" Lydia asked, tugging on the hem of Mary's shirt.

George swept Lydia into his arms and kissed her cheek. "We're going to do this. But if we're going to do this, we have to make sure it *is* God's will."

"Agreed," Mary replied. "Let's talk to Henry about it. He'll want to help, and he's such a prayer warrior." She squeezed his hand. "If this is what the Lord wants, He will open the doors."

The first thing to do was speak to Henry. He didn't even want to get Beta on the phone until he was sure the Lord was with them on this project.

Henry's response was an emphatic *yes*. He was with his wife, Sarah, who adamantly agreed that this was the way to go. Even still, they all wanted to be sure they weren't allowing their passion to save these helpless kids sweep them up in the heat of the moment, so they took three days and fasted together, asking the Lord to reveal His plans. When the four reconvened after three days, they all had a unanimous answer: this was what the Lord was calling them to.

And so George set about his work. The next thing to do was to announce to their congregation that they would be starting a children's home—which they would call "Cherry Hills Academy". George liked the idea of calling it this, as it would serve as a perpetual reminder of his first date with Mary at Cherry Hills Park. He hoped this would be a home

Fay

where the kids would learn and grow as disciples.

George prayed that his congregation would find it in their hearts to support the endeavor, and support it they did. After the meeting, George was handed fifty dollars to begin his work. It wasn't much, but he had faith that the Lord would provide the rest.

In the following days, more money was given, and one member of his congregation even volunteered to work in the academy, desiring to live like he and Mary did—depending on the Lord for their every need. Some offered donated clothes, others offered furnishings, and those who could afford it offered funds. By the 31st of December, George had received almost thirty thousand dollars in donations.

Once George knew it was possible, he called Beta and told him the good news, rendering him absolutely speechless.

"George, I…" Beta stammered. George had never heard Beta stumble over his words before. "This is an answered prayer. Truly. We didn't know what we were going to do."

"It's an answered prayer for me as well," George responded. "Mary's been talking with the foster program we've been volunteering at and they are considering sending us some of the kids they have to turn away."

"You have no idea the incredible impact this is going to have," Beta assured him. "How soon will the academy be ready?"

"We've gathered most of the funds, and now it's just time to find the building. I'm thinking maybe six months to a year."

"That's perfect." Beta replied. "We have the funding to transport fifteen kids right now, so we'll have time to raise more money." He paused. "Thank you for stepping up. Many men would pretend they didn't hear this calling on their life and would opt for safer ministries."

George smiled. "I've got a good support team here, and I serve a big God. You can count on us, Beta."

The academy—a large house George had rented in a subdivision cul-de-sac—opened the following year, when George was to turn thirty-one. It was a nerve-racking experience for everyone involved.

The foster care group that Mary had been in contact with immediately sent seventeen kids their way. These kids were ones that had nowhere else to go. The foster care system was so overpopulated that government facilities were struggling to keep up, partly due to government cutbacks in funding, and partly due to the fact that many parents just felt they couldn't adequately provide for a child in their current situation at the present time.

Beta's kids were the next to arrive. It was a day of celebration when sixteen children stepped onto American soil for the first time. George, Mary, Henry, and Sarah were there to receive them at the airport when they arrived, and they showered them with affection, encouragement, and prayers.

George set all of the kids up in their shared rooms he let them decorate themselves. The first few weeks were rough, as all of the children tried to learn to trust the Müller family. They'd been so abused in the past and, in the case of the foster children, had been abandoned so many times that they were skeptical that this academy would be their *home*. But over time, Mary's nurturing kindness and George's fatherly advice and encouragement began to win them over.

Fay

George brought on enough staff to ensure that all of the children's needs were met. He brought in caregivers, schoolteachers, nurses, and therapists to help the kids adapt. Some of them worked full time and received a salary, while others were volunteer workers from George's congregation and around the city.

Cherry Hills Academy was a dream come true—George's vision fulfilled by the Lord's hand.

More children would come, especially as Beta's program began to grow across Central America, but George wasn't worried in the slightest. God had seen them this far, and He would continue to see them through.

As the months passed, the Lord continued to meet the needs of the academy and those involved. Because George wasn't very good with numbers, he asked Mary to keep track of their expenses and donations. She wasn't a particularly high-strung person, but this job definitely made her anxious.

Henry was as involved as George was in the ministry of the academy, and soon he suggested that they rent a second academy building—this one for homeless mothers and their infants. Much thought and prayer went into the decision to rent a second large house in the same cul-de-sac as their first property. Soon, however, the two determined that it was the Lord's will and acted upon it. By the third week of October, the "infant" academy building was rented, the facility was ready, and George had hired a senior caretaker along with many volunteers and staff members.

George's faith had never been stronger. God had answered his prayers and proven that George's faith was not in vain.

In response to the Lord's continued provision, George placed his trust in Him yet again. When a third house in the immediate neighborhood came available for rent, George knew it was time to establish another facility, this one for children over the age of seven. The third academy building was generously funded by a friend of Henry Craik's, who donated fifty thousand dollars as "seed money" to its establishment.

Beta's program continued to work miracles, sending children into the United States for asylum. These kids were rescued from child trafficking, abusive parents, gang-ruled areas, and other unspeakable horrors that George had barely realized even existed anymore.

While George looked after their wellbeing, Mary worked with Beta over the phone to secure these children's home in America permanently. This meant going through stacks of paperwork so high it overwhelmed them and making calls to the government officials who enforced policies surrounding citizenship.

The Samuel Project. The program's name was George's idea, as he'd always loved the story in the Bible of Hannah trusting in the Lord and giving her son, Samuel, to be raised by the prophet Eli.

Members of Springfield Community Church continued to volunteer and donate to the children. Despite the demands of Cherry Hills Academy, Henry and George never failed to continue ministering to their congregation, evangelizing, and supporting missionaries around the world.

Fay

As more children joined Beta's life-giving program, George's expenses grew. Every new child who was accepted into the academy brought their own needs to be met. In addition to the kids rescued from difficult situations through Beta's Samuel Project, George and Mary had continued their volunteer work with the foster care system, which brought even more children to their doorstep. Often these kids were the ones deciding to move into the Cherry Hills Academy rather than hop from home to home in the foster care system.

Additionally, many homeless families had begun to send their children to the academy, similar to how wealthy people might send their children to boarding school. George and Mary had made allowance for this when they realized how many children fell through the cracks of the system because they had parents but no consistent housing. They also gave the parents of these children the opportunity to visit the academy anytime, provided that they were sober. The Springfield Community church was instrumental in finding jobs and homes for these parents. They also provided showers, clothes, computers, internet access, charging stations for cell phones, and a mailing address. George and Mary were amazed at how huge this need was, and they were grateful to be able to meet the need in such significant ways.

Despite the abundant blessings the Lord had bestowed upon George and Cherry Hills through caregivers, government favor, and faith, funds were low, and George had been pleading to the Lord to seemingly no avail. But George refused to lose his faith and gathered many of his employees to discuss the financial situation. Blessedly, they understood the situation and prayed with George that the funds would find them.

Let the Children Come

It was a difficult time for George's faith. Mary was his rock, his true warrior. She constantly reminded him of his past, the fire that he had walked through to reach the point he was at, and his Lord who was holding his hand and walking beside him the entire way.

"You're only human," she said kindly. "You are prone to fear, worry, and apprehension."

George knew this, but it still felt as though he were failing. He wondered if somehow his lack of faith was the reason for their financial situation. Yet he knew that God's testimony was at stake, and he just needed to continue to trust in Jesus Christ.

His wife sat beside him on their old couch and said, "It's natural to have moments of weakness, George. You can choose to give yourself over to your weakness and let it drag you down, or you can learn from it and use it to become stronger."

Had George ever mentioned how much he *adored* his wife? She had a way of getting to the root of the problem.

"Thank you," he replied.

She squeezed his hand and winked. "No problem, darling. Any time you're feeling a bit lost, I'm here to guide you back to Him."

Chapter Thirteen

In late December, nearing Christmas, something extremely out of the ordinary happened.

George's phone began to ring in his pocket. He held a finger up to Mary, who sincerely did not like being shushed when she was in the middle of a story.

"Sorry, just one second," he said as he glanced at the screen. His eyes widened when he saw the name.

It was his father. The father he hadn't spoken to in years.

George's heart ached at just seeing the caller ID. He missed his father, something he never imagined he'd think to himself. Things had never been the same since his mother died.

He stared at his phone as if it were a snake about to strike.

Mary glanced between his white-knuckled grip and the ringing cellphone. "Aren't you going to answer that?"

George nodded and cleared his throat. He stood from his chair abruptly, which made the chair topple over backwards. *Wonderful,* he thought. *It's been years, and I still get nervous when I talk to him.*

He turned away from Mary so she couldn't see the anxiousness on his face as he brought the phone to his ear. "Hi, Dad," he began, his voice wavering uncomfortably. "Is everything alright?"

He knew the answer to that question before he even asked it. Things hadn't been good between them for years—in fact, they were bad more times than they were good. If he was calling now, something had to have happened.

"Hi, George," his father answered, and George decided that no, everything was *not* alright. His father's voice was weak and strangled, as if he could barely force the words from his mouth. "I'm…I'm so sorry to call like this. I hear you're running a home for children?"

George still wasn't sure what to think. "Three."

"Three." His father sounded shocked. "Wow. I guess…I guess people really do change."

Was it just George, or did his father sound just as uncomfortable as he was?

"Dad…why are you calling?" George wasn't trying to be rude or disrespectful. Despite his apprehension, it was good to hear from his father. He'd learned to forgive him long ago and often wished he'd gone back and asked for his father's forgiveness.

George knew he'd been a hellion as a child and that his father had put up with a lot. He didn't handle it very well, but George still felt that he was owed a certain amount of respect. Being a father himself, George understood the incredible responsibility it was, and he could imagine how guilty his father must have felt when George acted the way he did.

He must have been so ashamed of me, George thought, embarrassed. *He must have been heartbroken that he'd failed.* Because that was how George would have felt.

His father cleared his throat, reminding George that he was still on the line. George was about to open his mouth to apologize—to remedy his regret—but he didn't get the chance.

"Fred has passed away."

George's thoughts immediately tripped over those words. He couldn't have possibly heard his father correctly. Fred was a thirty-five-year-old healthy man. It had been a few months since the brothers had spoken, but last they talked Fred was doing well! He was enjoying his career and seemed to still have a good relationship with their father.

No, George thought. Dad must have been wrong. Fred wasn't dead.

"What do you mean?" George asked.

"What's so difficult to understand?" barked his father, almost angrily. "Your brother is dead."

George felt a twinge of anger rise up in him as well—that bit he got from his father. *How dare he be angry with me? Or take his anger out on me?* George thought.

Mary came up beside him and placed a hand on his shoulder, looking up at him. Her gentle touch brought him back, and he gratefully clamped a hand over hers.

"What happened?" he asked, willing himself to be calm amidst his father's anger.

There was a moment of quiet on the other end of the line before his father said, "There was an accident…" He took a deep breath. "He was involved in a car wreck. Some moron in a truck ran a red light and slammed into the driver's side of his car. He was dead before they got him to the hospital."

George shook his head and held Mary's hand tighter. "This can't be happening," he said under his breath, more to himself than anyone else.

It was just…unbelievable.

George had always thought that the word "unbelievable" was thrown around a lot in life. People said that the cake they ate was "unbelievable" or the deal they got on a house was "unbelievable." But this? There was no comparison.

"I'm sorry, George," his father said, and he actually sounded soft for a moment. "I wish…" His voice cracked on a sob and frankly George was close to tears as well.

Mary, with her incredible intuition, somehow knew and leaned her head against George's shoulder, comforting him.

"It's okay, Dad," he answered. "We'll leave early tomorrow morning and be there by nightfall."

George had always hated funerals and had barely wanted to attend his own mother's, but he'd grown out of that. He wanted to be there for Fred, and more than that, he wanted to be there for his father. Despite John Müller's cruel attitude the majority of the time, George knew his dad. He knew that this was killing him and that he'd never admit it. He

Fay

needed George more than ever, and George refused to let him down.

"Okay," his father answered. "I'll see you tomorrow night."

"Hang in there," George said as he ended the call.

The second he set it down, the floodgates opened. He collapsed into Mary, who held him close.

"George, talk to me," she urged.

"It's Fred," was all George could muster before dissolving into more tears.

She guided her husband to the couch where they both sat. He buried his face in her shoulder, and she wrapped her arms tightly around him.

"Oh, George," she said, emotion thickening her voice. "I'm so sorry."

He clutched her tighter. Wrapped in each other's arms, they grieved the loss of his brother.

Heavy snowflakes landed softly on the mahogany casket raised just a few feet above the ground. Flower petals adorned the ornate casket, and they looked strikingly out of place against the blinding, snow-laden ground.

"In the name of Jesus Christ, our Lord and Savior…amen." The pastor closed his worn Bible.

"Amen," echoed the procession surrounding Fred's casket.

George stood beside Mary and Lydia. Lydia clutched her mother's hand tightly, and George wondered if she truly comprehended what was happening.

Let the Children Come

To his left, George's father stood like a statue, staring at the place where his son would be lowered into the ground. While everyone else held umbrellas just in case the snow turned to sleet, John Müller stood with one hand in his pocket, the other holding a cigarette, hardly paying any mind to the overcast sky. He took a long drag of the cigarette, and George wondered when he'd picked up that habit. He certainly wasn't a smoker when George was a kid.

Beside George's father stood Jane and Frank. Frank looked just like his mother, though he had his father's height. The two wore all black, and tears freely fell over Jane's flushed cheeks.

The pastor made his way to where George and his father were, shaking hands as he went. When he arrived in front of them, he took George's hands and clasped them between his.

"George," said the pastor. "I want to express my deepest condolences for your loss."

George nodded. "Thank you, Pastor."

"Mr. Müller," continued the pastor as he turned to George's father. "I know it seems hard to believe right now, and you must be filled with questions, but the Lord's ways are not our ways. They are beyond our understanding. Your son is in a better place now."

George wanted to laugh. *He* was having a hard time understanding it—he couldn't imagine how his father was doing. Still, his father nodded slowly as if he'd accepted that, then turned to walk away. Jane and Frank quickly followed him after a quiet "thank you" to the minister.

The balding, elderly pastor looked back at George. "I have heard of what you've been doing with The Samuel Project." He set a hand on

Fay

George's shoulder. "Don't lose your faith, brother. It is a testimony to all of us. We need that."

George nodded. "Thank you."

He took Mary's hand, and she looked up at him. Snowflakes had landed on her eyelashes, and he could see she was fighting tears—but not for herself…for George. She hadn't spent much time with Fred, but she must've known how difficult it would be on George, and since he had to be strong, she was allowing herself to be weak for him.

He smiled and kissed her on the forehead, then gave Lydia a big hug. "Let's go."

Mary nodded and took the umbrella from him. Together they followed his father to the line of black cars rented for the family.

It was difficult to come to terms with what had happened. George wrestled with it for days, even as they spent time with his father, who—until now—had no idea he had a daughter-in-law and a grandchild. With time, prayer, and Mary's help, George began to accept what had happened and was able to set aside his anger.

Mary had wiped the tears from his eyes, kissed his cheek, and assured him that God's plans are mysterious to men and that they weren't *meant* to understand all of them. George had nodded with a small smile and accepted the great kindnesses the Lord had given him in his wife and beautiful daughter. When he looked across the room, then, and saw his father—shattered and alone—he decided then and there that the next step in his journey would be to pray ceaselessly for the salvation of his father's soul.

His father was having trouble letting go of his anger, and like many men, he directed all of it at God.

"Why Fred?" asked his father, as he nursed a glass brimming with whiskey. "Why not any of the people who do horrible things? Like murderers? Why did it have to be your brother, who tried to do the right thing all of his life?"

George didn't have a great answer. Wasn't that the question of all questions? Why do bad things happen to good people?

He knew there was nothing he'd be able to say to his father. Words would be useless right now, especially those words that *everyone* said at funerals.

"It'll be okay."

"He's in a better place now."

"It all happens for a reason."

Even though George did believe all of those things, that didn't necessarily mean that people who were grieving needed to hear them. He certainly didn't. Right now, all his father needed to hear was that his only remaining son was with him, and that it was okay to grieve.

"I don't know," George replied softly. "All I know is that he'll be greatly missed."

Dad scoffed, unsatisfied, and to George's sorrow, he seemed to fall into an even deeper anger. George just sighed and knew that truly all he could do for his father was pray. Until John Müller let go of this anger and opened himself up to the Lord, there was no way for him to accept

Fay

Fred's passing, or that the only one at fault was the truck driver.

George knew that his time with his father was short. He had duties to attend to back at Cherry Hills Academy.

"I have to leave soon," George continued with a heavy sigh. He set his hand on his father's shoulder. "I'm going to keep in touch. Alright?"

His father just shrugged. "Do whatever you feel is best. I've been through this before with your mother. I know how to get over someone." But he still sounded angry.

He was right. Time was the great healer of wounds; George had learned that firsthand. But his father would still need someone to talk to. Otherwise, he would let his anger fester, and the results would not be pretty.

"I'm here, Dad," he assured him. "I know we never had the relationship you did with Fred, but we can have that now." He hesitated for a moment, considering his next words carefully. "I wanted to apologize to you in person. I wasn't the son you deserved or needed, and I'm sorry that I did everything in my power to disrespect you when I was growing up. I understand now how wrong that was of me, and how much it hindered me in life.

"I want to start fresh with you," he continued. "I want to make amends."

His father took a long swig of whiskey. "I get it," he said, his voice twinged with irritation. "I'm not an easy man to get along with. But your brother never had any issue." He took another drink.

George watched him, his heart aching. It wasn't forgiveness, but it might be as close as George was going to get for a little while. At least he'd said what he wanted to say.

George slowly stood. "Love you, Dad. I'm always here."

"Yep," he answered curtly. "Me too."

George nodded and went to collect Mary and Lydia. As he went, he sent up a prayer asking that the Lord would soften his father's heart so that George might have the opportunity to receive forgiveness and lay that part of his life to rest.

Chapter Fourteen

In the early spring, Cherry Hills Academy began preparing for a very special visitor.

Since its founding, Beta had managed to secure places in George's academy for kids from three countries: Belize, Guatemala, and Haiti. He was working on opening doors in other countries, though George had his hands full with the children he was *already* housing.

Beta hadn't done it alone, of course. Mary had a way with people and had been instrumental in the creation of the program. Even George, with all of his other ventures, took the time to help The Samuel Project along.

It seemed like years since George had seen Beta last, so when his friend arrived at Cherry Hills, George maybe hugged him for a few seconds too long.

Beta laughed and clapped George on the shoulder. "It's good to see you."

"You too," answered George as he walked Beta to his office. "How was your flight?"

Beta rubbed his face. "Longer than I remembered." He took in the sight of the academy's interior. "You've done a great job here. It feels like a home."

George looked around. He didn't exactly agree with Beta. There were so many things about these old, rusting buildings he wished he could change. He hated the smell of mustiness in the showers and that the kitchens permanently reeked of sausage. There wasn't a floorboard that didn't squeak, paint was peeling, and the kids had no room to play outside. There was a public park about a mile and a half away, and the older kids could go there by themselves, but the younger ones needed supervision, which meant they didn't get to go as often.

Regardless, he was happy to be here as long as the Lord willed it. He was grateful for the space they had been given, even if it was a little rough around the edges.

Beta stayed for a couple of days and got to interact with some of the kids he'd been working with in Haiti. He also told George of all the other kids just waiting for a place to open up in George's academy. That crushed George. He'd known that more kids would need homes, but they were rapidly running out of room. He refused to let that get to him, though. After Beta left, George brought it up with Mary, and the two decided to stay in prayer about it until a solution was found.

On April 7, George received another harrowing call. His phone began ringing, and he looked down to see the name "Frank" illuminating his cellphone screen.

"Frank?" he asked when he answered.

"George?" He sounded terrible, as if he'd been crying all morning.

George felt his heart sink. He hurt for his half-brother, knowing that something was troubling him, but he also suspected that this *something* had to include him, otherwise he wouldn't have been calling him.

"Is everything alright?"

"It's Dad…" began Frank. He took a deep gulp before continuing. "He died in his sleep last night."

George immediately felt a knot form in his throat, too big to swallow. He had to take a seat in the academy sanctuary before his legs collapsed from under him. "What happened?"

"I don't know," Frank continued. "I don't know. All I know is that when Mom went to wake him up this morning he wouldn't wake up… and then she screamed and now no one will tell me anything so I have no clue what happened…"

He was rambling, his words getting caught on tears. His voice was thick with pain and worry, and George knew he was still so young—not younger than he was when his mother died, but young nonetheless. He couldn't imagine how Frank must have been feeling.

George nodded slowly, allowing the words to sink in.

His father was dead. That was that. He wondered idly how many times he'd prayed for his soul in the previous months. Had his father made a change? They hadn't spoken much, and George's heart was heavy with that knowledge, but he knew that he'd done all he could to make amends with his father.

"It's going to be okay, Frank," George insisted. "I know it doesn't seem like it right now, but everything is going to be alright."

Frank choked on his words. "Okay."

"Just sit tight," said George. "I'll be there very soon."

"Okay," his half-brother echoed. "Thank you, George."

George hung up the phone and felt a hand land on his shoulder. He looked up and saw Mary standing there in the hallway of the academy, a sad smile on her face.

"Your father?"

George nodded somberly. He had to admit that Dad's death hadn't hit him the way Fred's had. He supposed it was because with his dad, part of him was always expecting something like this to happen. George knew he was getting older, and after the death of his first wife and his firstborn son…well, George imagined that would take a toll on anyone.

Mary squeezed his shoulder. "I'll go get Lydia and pack the bags."

"Thank you," answered George with a rueful smile as she turned on her heel and set out to get everything ready to leave.

As she walked away, George turned and looked at the cross—the focal point of the room. He thought again of his prayers about his father and considered for the first time that perhaps God didn't answer all of George's prayers the way he wanted Him to. It wasn't that he didn't pray hard enough or had sin in his life that would prevent him from getting his prayers answered. He knew that wasn't the good news of the Bible! He simply had to recognize that God's will and understanding was not always

Fay

George's to know.

With that knowledge, George stood from his seat in the pews and made his way out of the academy chapel.

George and Mary helped Jane with the funeral preparations. It was a sad affair for everyone, and Jane was increasingly worried. She seemed to rest a bit easier when the will was read and she knew what she and Frank would have to be able to rebuild their lives with.

Surprisingly, some of John Müller's will was made out to George, and though George was at first uncomfortable with accepting anything from his father, he came to the understanding that this was yet another way that the Lord was providing for him. After much deliberation and prayer, he determined that he would accept the inheritance. After discussing it with Mary, they determined that they would keep a very small portion of it for themselves—only what they needed to cover the next few weeks' expenses—and put the rest to use in the academy.

George did what he could to minister to Frank while he was there. He knew that right now what he needed wasn't a pastor—he needed a brother. He needed a shoulder to cry on, so George became that.

They spent over a week together, though Henry Craik wanted George back at the church and academy to deal with the ever-present problems. George knew that this was a catalyst in Frank's life, and he couldn't convince himself that it was alright to leave so soon.

Frank was a good kid—way better than George had been at his age. He was still into some things that George now knew to be vices, and

George did what he could to sway his half-brother away from them. He was careful not to push too hard or to come across as pious, though. He made sure to build a strong relationship with Frank over the days following their father's funeral so that Frank might reach out to George should he ever have questions or just want someone to talk to.

When it came time for George and his family to leave, it was clear that Jane and Frank wished they didn't have to go.

Jane smiled sadly and embraced George, and he could tell she was fighting tears.

"George," she whispered. "I want you to know that even though I'm not your real mother, I've always cared for you as such." She released him and did nothing to wipe the tears from her eyes. "I know your father wasn't good at expressing his feelings, but he loved you *so* much. I wish he weren't such a stubborn man," she whispered, mostly to herself. "But after you left Fred's funeral, he talked about you constantly. Eventually he was *glowing* about you and your work. I'd give anything to go back and insist he call you and tell you so…"

George just stared.

What? His father was *proud* of him? He'd felt his father's pride before, but back then it was clouded with shame and remorse, coupled with the knowledge that he didn't deserve that pride. Now it was different. His father had been proud of him for something he'd truly done… something truly worth his father's approval.

He was dumbfounded, so Mary had to step in. She hugged Jane tightly.

"You have no idea how much that means to George," she told his

Fay

stepmother. "Thank you so much for sharing that."

Jane sniffled. "Of course. You are family. Please, *please* keep in touch." She reached for her son. "We both love you all so much."

Mary kissed Frank on the forehead. "It was such a pleasure seeing you again, sweetie. I just wish it weren't under such difficult circumstances."

George knew he'd have to thank Mary later for stepping in during his moment of speechlessness. He extended his hand to Frank.

"Take care of your mom, okay?" George said, clasping his half-brother's hand. "And never forget that I'm always here for you. Always."

Frank nodded, clearly trying to be strong. He'd been handling the death of his father so well, though George suspected it still hadn't totally sunk in. "Thanks," he answered. "I really appreciate that. And I'll definitely take care of Mom."

George and his family packed into their car and waved goodbye to Jane and Frank as they backed out of the driveway.

A peace fell over George as he began to drive down the road, away from the home he'd grown up in. Tears stung his eyes as he repeated his gratitude to the Lord over and over again in his head.

He'd always had this special sense of knowing when he prayed. He just *knew* that the Lord had heard him and that his prayers would be answered in His way and in His timing, even if they weren't answered for years.

Having his father's respect and pride wasn't the answer George had been expecting, but it was the one the Lord had given him, and he was more than willing to accept it. As he drove, he sang silent praises to the Lord for allowing him to find peace.

Chapter Fifteen

Though George's records could show him the numbers of those currently in the academy, he'd never truly know the number of lives touched through those kids who left his ministry and went on to disciple others.

George not only fed, clothed, and educated the kids, but he also ensured them a future by helping them to find jobs when they were ready. He was tireless in his efforts to create better lives for them than they had been living, and all the while the economy was still floundering—even though the economists said they saw "green shoots" of recovery.

In spite of the optimism in the economic forecast, it seemed the foster care system was still keen to send any children they couldn't take in to George, and many of the kids actually requested it. Some of the children were brought in from all over the country. When their guardian died or when they were removed from a toxic environment, they'd ask to be brought to *George's academy*. Every time George heard his name associated with the academy his blood pressure went up a bit. Mary would say, "Now George, everyone knows it is the Lord's and not yours. It's only a reference."

Beta's program continued to send children to the academy, and it was difficult to keep up with all of them. Unfortunately, not all of them got to stay for very long. There were some who, try though they might, George and Mary couldn't teach. Some kids had such hardened, rebellious hearts that they endangered the academy and constantly got George in trouble with the law. Stealing, dabbling with drugs, arson, and breaking and entering were just a few of the crimes some of the kids committed. Since he'd grown up partaking in some of the same things they were doing now, George showed leniency and mercy as long as he could. Mary gently reminded him that they couldn't permit these actions or allow consistent run-ins with the law to endanger Beta's program and the academy.

Soon, it was decided that the academy would have a "next to zero tolerance" system when it came to illegal activity. George was forced to remove some of the children from the program and send them home. If the kids could maintain good behavior, they would be able to continue on with the program and have the opportunity to pursue citizenship. Many, however, had a deep desire to go back to their home country and engage in leadership there.

Through the constant roller coaster of circumstances, George, Mary, and Henry never feared or worried for their academy. Somehow, some way, God always provided for their needs, and they never doubted Him.

Although George's work was entirely for the benefit of those less fortunate and for the glory of the Lord, neighbors still complained. About what, George had no idea.

All of the children under George's care lived in one of three large-ish houses George rented monthly. They weren't all right next to each other, but they were in close enough proximity that they all had the same neighbors…and many of these neighbors were unhappy. The neighbors of these properties had filed noise complaints to the city, along with reporting a myriad of other issues. Regardless of George's feelings on the matter, it was becoming increasingly evident that they were no longer welcome in the area they had been occupying.

If they were able to move into a location with more space, the children might be able to have room outside to play on a bigger playground or learn to garden and cultivate plants in a garden. George had also been wanting to move the children farther into the countryside for some time. The benefits of this would be absolutely astronomical. The healing that nature could provide was unparalleled and could truly help these little ones who had lost their parents, homes, and ways of life at such young ages.

The more he thought about it, the more moving seemed like it would be a necessity. Although he was *furious* when he first received the complaints, he was eventually able to cool off and see it from his neighbors' perspectives. He was still irritated that they couldn't see past their own comfort, but he was also horrified that the ministry he'd created for *good* had actually done harm to others in some small way. Romans 14:16 truly seemed to sum it up: "Do not let what is for you a good thing be spoken of as evil."

Let the Children Come

With this in mind, George began his search for a suitable piece of land in the proximity of Springfield. He needed the land to be close because his home was fixed, as were the homes of the employees and volunteers who helped him run the academy.

He spent months looking for land and gathering the funds to purchase it. Some were selling land at a ridiculous price that the academy couldn't afford, and others simply weren't an option because of location.

It wasn't overnight. The Lord didn't drop a huge pile of cash on George's doorstep, much to George's chagrin. The move required an enormous amount of prayer, faith, and—of course—listening for God's direction as to where he was leading.

About two months into their search for a new plot of land for the academy, donations began to roll in. While small at first, they began to pile up overtime, and soon George was certain that they'd have the money they needed. In addition to that, an architect named Tom Foster offered to volunteer his services to help build the new academy buildings. With those pieces in place, it just came down to finding the right plot of land.

In February, George learned about a piece of land that was relatively inexpensive. He felt a draw to this particular piece of land. Though the February conditions were brutal, the weather was biting, and the landscape looked bare, somehow he knew that lush, green fields were just around the bend. He looked down at his boots in the soil as he stood next to the wife of the landowner and thought, *Here. This is where the Lord wants us to build the academy.*

"When will your husband be home?" asked George.

"Around eight o'clock," answered the wife. "What do you think of it?"

"I love it," George answered, and he truly did. He could imagine the children growing up here on this land. He could imagine the springs, summers, and beautiful autumns. He could almost see it now—piles of leaves, stacked pumpkins, and steaming cocoa resting on the porch rails. Yes, this was definitely the place.

As they walked back towards George's car, he agreed with the woman that he would return after her husband got home from work. He thanked her for her time and immediately began to think about the great work God would do here.

"Pastor Müller," the wife called out as he started to get into his car.

George looked up. "Yes?"

"Do you mind telling me what you'd like to use the land for?"

George smiled and took the opportunity to tell the wife about the academy he'd begun and their struggles to get to this point. In a brief, two-minute explanation which did no justice to the whole story, he told her of the children and his desire to ensure their safety. He told of their need to vacate their current facilities and how this land could very well make many of their dreams come true.

When he tried to come back that evening to meet with the couple together, the husband had still not arrived home. Though the woman he had spoken with earlier was extremely apologetic about this, it was hard not to be a little annoyed. George knew that the Lord would solve the problem as He saw fit, so he resolved himself to be patient—or persistent, as the situation sometimes called for. And this was just one of those situations.

The next morning, George returned to the home and managed to catch the husband on his way to work. The husband didn't seem surprised at all to see George, as the pastor jumped out of his car and rushed up to the man to speak with him.

"Hi, you must be Philip," George said, hand extended.

"Hi, yes," the landowner answered. "Pastor Müller, I take it?"

"George," he answered. "I'm sorry to drop by unannounced like this—"

"No, actually I'm thrilled you stopped by," Philip replied. "I'm sorry I wasn't able to meet you last night. Got held up at work and…" He shook his head. "Anyway, my wife told me about your offer."

"Oh, she did?" Secretly, George was hoping she might. Surely it sounded better—a man needing land for an academy.

"She did," said Philip. "I have to tell you…I'd been planning on selling this land at twenty thousand dollars per acre. But I woke up in the middle of the night and just couldn't sleep. Miranda told me about your academy and the children you were purchasing the land for…honestly, I couldn't get the thought out of my head." He took a deep breath. "I'm willing to sell the land to you for twelve thousand dollars per acre."

George couldn't believe his ears. He immediately shook the man's hand. "In that case, I'll absolutely be buying the seven acres from you."

Philip laughed, and the deal was struck. The two put the agreement on paper soon after. The following day, George spoke on the phone with the architect, and together they began to get the ball rolling.

Without delay, the architect, Tom, came and took a look at the land to see what he was getting himself into. He was thrilled to see the space he had to work with. He was confident that they could build exactly the type of academy George had always imagined—the academy that God could truly work through. George knew that God could work through a hut if He needed to, but he believed God had something a little bit bigger than a hut in mind this time around!

The past summer, Lydia had fallen into a bad crowd and had developed some "anger issues." At least, that was what Mary had called it. George would've said his now teenage daughter was just throwing a temper tantrum. It didn't take long, though, for Mary to recognize the source of the issue: neglect. Not meaningful neglect, of course. Somehow, in their pursuit to love on abandoned children, they'd occasionally forgotten to spend quality time with their own daughter.

As soon as they recognized their flaw, George and Mary set out to rectify the issue. They implemented a weekly movie night as a family, and they began spending more intentional time around the dinner table. With these small changes in place, Lydia became steadily more pleasant to be around. She began to blossom in her own passions and giftings, and it became apparent that she had a knack for interior design. When the opportunity arose, George asked Lydia to help him with designing the academy. It took some prompting, but pretty soon she was on board. And when Lydia was on board, it was full steam ahead.

Every hour that she wasn't at school, she was working on sketches and bringing them to George. He had to admit they were pretty good. She even voiced an interest in architecture, and Tom, the architect, gladly took her under his wing and showed her how his job was done.

Everything was falling into place.

When the time came to announce to the orphans that they'd be moving, George anticipated quite a bustle, but he didn't realize they'd practically start a riot. The kids were bouncing off the walls with excitement at the prospect of having actual land to run around on, along with all of the other joys George was praying the Lord would provide them with.

By August of the next year, the construction was underway.

Chapter Sixteen

The volunteers were working hard—if not harder than those who were being compensated for their work—and George was endlessly grateful to them for their sacrifices of time, energy, and resources. Slowly but steadily, the Cherry Hills Academy was beginning to take shape. It took time because George refused to take out any loans, and he insisted that they use only the cash funds the Lord had provided them. This meant that the construction stretched out over a long period of time.

The August of George's forty-third birthday marked a little over a year since the construction had begun. By this point, the building itself had been fully constructed and was almost entirely roofed in. Some of the inside plastering had even been completed.

By the end of February of the next year, construction was finally coming to a close. With amazement, George realized that not only had the Lord supplied them with the means to accomplish the task at hand, but that they would have money left over. The thought was almost inconceivable.

Finally, it was time for Mary to see the near-final product they had been so diligently working on together. She had been handling the paperwork and payments from afar and had seen it several times during the construction, but she'd been so covered up dealing with the current facilities that she hadn't been able to see it in a while. George was beside himself with excitement and giddy like a child when he finally managed to drag her away from her desk.

"Okay, okay," she finally conceded and followed him to the car.

George couldn't shut up as he drove toward Cherry Hills. He told her about how beautiful the building was and what he imagined the kids could do with it. Mary humored him because he was hard to control when he had this much bottled-up excitement inside him.

As they neared the construction site, George couldn't help but grin at Mary's wide eyes as she took in the whole picture. She leaned forward in her seat, mouth agape.

George smiled. "This is where our children will live now. They'll have all the space they need, without any neighbors to complain about the noise."

Mary huffed with a roll of her eyes. "Grudges don't become you, George."

"Grudge?" he asked. He shrugged. He wasn't holding a grudge. He was just…mildly peeved, he supposed. But still…*look* at all that God had accomplished in spite of those complaints. No—*because* of those complaints. This new building, this new location, was beyond either of their imaginations.

As they stepped out of the car, Mary sidled up to her husband and wrapped her arms around him. "This is all because of you, George."

"Me?" He shook his head adamantly. "No, this is all God. I couldn't have done any of it without Him."

"I know that," laughed his wife as she squeezed him. "But without you to put it into practice…it never would've happened. Your faith in the Lord and your love and desire to help these children is what made all of this possible. Now stop arguing with me, and get used to the idea that I'm not going to change my mind. Without you, this wouldn't have happened."

George slowly nodded and smiled fondly.

A loud shout drew their attention back to the construction site, and that's when George realized it was a bit busy for a Saturday afternoon. Trucks were driving in and out, the rumble of machinery filled the air, workers raced back and forth, and the foreman was shouting things left, right, and center. Was this really Saturday?

When the construction had first begun, George had wanted to tell the foreman to ease up and treat his people with more respect. However, he soon realized why he was so loud. Once construction was truly underway, George was beyond shocked by the sheer volume of noise these machines produced. Did a backhoe really sound like that? You wouldn't be able to hear yourself think, let alone talk at a normal volume.

It turned out that the foreman—Roger Nielsen—and his men, despite their loud and crass ways, were all true believers in Christ. They willingly worked longer hours than usual and even came in on weekends without charging George overtime. George was amazed at how God had inspired them. Even Tom Foster, the architect, commented that he had never seen such dedicated workers.

Mary's insistent tugging dragged him out of his own thoughts. "Come on," she said with a grin. "Let's have a look inside."

"Hang on a second," George answered, then looked to find the foreman. Once he spotted Mr. Nielsen, George shouted, "Is it safe for us to come inside?"

Mr. Nielsen cupped his ear to hear George over the noise then just shook his head and stomped down the steps. He made a quick, jerky motion to one of his men with a power saw to cut the noise before he approached the couple.

"Welcome back, Mrs. Mary," said Mr. Nielsen. "Lovely to see you again, my dear."

George was astounded. Nielsen had never spoken to him that way. Leave it to Mary to bring out the kindness in people.

"I was hoping to take her on a walkthrough," said George. "She hasn't seen it in several months. Is it okay to come inside?"

"Yeah, of course. Come on." He waved them toward the door, and Mary practically bounded after him. "There's a little work left to do on the interior, but it's mostly cosmetic," continued the foreman. "Most of the work being done right now is on the grounds."

George and Mary ascended the steps, and Nielsen opened the front door to reveal the mostly finished interior. Mary stepped inside and looked around in awe.

Fay

"They really did do a great job, didn't they?" asked Nielsen.

Mary was dumbstruck, and George wondered if he'd ever seen his wife speechless before.

George had seen the inside already. He'd been meticulously inspecting it. It wasn't that he needed to ensure that the orphans got the best—though he wanted that—but he was just so enraptured by the process in general. He was too excited to just wait around at the house. He needed to be on site.

The view seemed to stun him yet again. Everything was perfect.

Though still covered for protection, George knew the floors beneath the tarp were a beautiful, warm mahogany, and the walls surrounding them were soft cream. He had wanted the building to have a warm, welcoming feel to it because it was so much more than an academy. It was supposed to be a home. It was why the building itself looked more like an oversized house than a heartless block of apartments.

When Tom and George were first designing the structure, Tom had informed him that it would be much more economical to design something that looked more along the lines of a standard apartment complex. George was conflicted when he heard it would cost approximately five percent more to get the homey feel he wanted, so he took the time to ask for God's guidance. After extensive prayer, it became clear to George that he was to give these children the home they deserved. This is why the new academy resembled one of the manor halls of old that dotted the English countryside, complete with a sloping roof, much more so than the boxy, cold apartment buildings Tom was suggesting.

Lydia had suggested warmer tones for the interior colors, and she'd gone above and beyond when designing each room. The rooms designated for the younger children were painted in bright, vivid hues, while the common areas were a pale yellow or cream.

"Look at it," Mary crooned. "Isn't this adorable? I'm sure the kids will love this!"

George dragged her on to the rest of the tour. The rooms were not as large as most expected because they had decided against taking the usual bunkhouse-style approach that had been traditionally used in group homes. Still, they needed a way to fit 120 children into one building. When Tom had first come up with the plans, Mary had immediately vetoed the idea of putting twenty children in one room together. She was afraid that after living with only two or three in the same room, it would be an uncomfortable shift. She also didn't want them to feel like they were being treated like cattle. In what way was that healthy for a child? Naturally, George had agreed with her. The end result were rooms large enough to house between four and six children.

Mary surveyed another room, running her hand along the decorated windowsills. "The large windows will help with sunlight." She smiled as rays of said sunlight flickered through the spotless glass.

"Mm-hmm," agreed George. "I wish we could've made it even homier, but—"

"George, stop worrying," his wife chided. "You've managed to do more than this whole country has ever done for these children. Can you imagine where they would be right now without this academy?"

George smiled. He took his wife by the hand and led her out to see the other rooms.

Fay

The building had been laid out so that the bedrooms were all on the upper floors, while the ground floor housed the common areas, which included a large dining hall, study rooms, a library, a gym, and more.

The dining room was large and had French-style doors that opened up to the lawn, and George hoped the children would choose to take their dinner outside on warmer evenings. It was a way to encourage them to go out and play after their meals.

Outside, they'd set up areas for a soccer field and a basketball court, and they had begun building fully equipped playgrounds for the younger kids. There was also an area set aside specifically for gardening so that the kids could learn agricultural skills and the academy could have its own supply of food to a certain degree.

As they were making their way to one of the annexes that was meant to house the kitchen, they were waylaid by Mr. Nielsen.

"George, there's someone here who wants to speak to you. He says he runs an IT company or something like that. Says he wants to talk to you about helping out," said Mr. Nielsen.

George turned to Mary with a questioning look, and she just shooed him away. "I'll be fine," she said with a laugh. "I promise I won't get lost. Go. See what he wants."

He nodded and followed Nielsen back outside where a man was waiting for him.

He didn't look like much. He seemed quite young, and his jeans had surely seen better days, as had his flimsy T-shirt. He had a warm look in his eyes and a wide smile on his face.

"George Müller?" he asked.

"Yes, that's right," answered George. "And who might you be?"

The man extended his hand. "My name is Richard Jones. I run a network design company. One of my favorite blogs posted an article on your academy. I know this is a bit strange, but when I read about it, I had to come out here and see it for myself. And thank you."

"Well, I'm thrilled to hear a blogger has mentioned our Academy, but…I'm sorry, why are you thanking me?" asked George.

"There are very few people who think about the kids who don't have anyone left. I'd like to help if I can, so I thought maybe I could donate a computer lab."

A computer lab? Not only would the kids love that, but it would teach them some really valuable skills—and it surely couldn't be inexpensive. The Academy probably wouldn't have been able to afford one without the donation.

George smiled broadly. "Well, I don't like to speak for the Lord, but I believe that everything we've accomplished was only made possible by Him. And we'd really appreciate your help and donation."

"I wouldn't doubt that the Lord has helped you with everything thus far," he replied, "but it seems so few are actually willing to listen to His direction."

He hesitated for a moment before continuing. "I grew up in foster homes," he said finally. "It wasn't a great time for me, but I was lucky. My computer teacher at school saw something in me. She really turned me into the man I am today. If it weren't for her…well, the Lord only knows where I'd be. I'll always be grateful to her, and I'd like to pay it forward in any way I can. So, with your permission, I'd like to donate the

Fay

computer lab *and* volunteer my services and the services of some of my employees to come out at least once a week to teach your children what we can."

Immediately, George knew that this had to be the will of God. There was no doubt that this man had been inspired to not only donate his equipment but also his knowledge and time as well. Already, George could think of several of the children who would particularly benefit from this program.

Chapter Seventeen

Flowers bloomed, and the grass around Cherry Hills Academy grew greener as April bled into May and May bled into June. You could feel the excitement buzzing in the air like electricity when you walked through the doors of the soon-to-be-vacant houses. Kids were vibrating with jitters as they frantically packed their bags weeks before the move-in date just because they simply couldn't contain themselves.

George and Mary spent every bit of spare time they had ensuring that the Cherry Hills Academy was in tiptop shape when the children arrived. This meant stocking the pantry (which required considerable donations) and testing all of the games and toys. This was a task which George particularly enjoyed after a long day of paying expenses, budgeting costs, and dealing with paperwork.

Lydia graduated from high school that May, and she dedicated her entire summer to helping around Cherry Hills. She was eager to continue to help when the fall rolled around as well, since she'd been accepted into a local college and was planning to study interior design.

Eighteen, he thought. He couldn't believe she was eighteen. It seemed like just yesterday she was trying out her first words.

Working at the academy seemed to revitalize her and restore her purpose in life. She was no longer as quick to anger as she once was, and though George wanted to take credit for that and say that it was because he'd spent more time with her, he knew the credit lay with the Lord and with these children. A lot of prayer and love had been poured into her life, and she was now thriving.

George couldn't believe how much she resembled her mother, both in character and appearance. He could hardly tell them apart from a distance as they graciously ordered employees around and corrected mistakes before they became an issue. They were both excellent troubleshooters, able to solve even the most complex problems quickly and efficiently.

Mary seemed just as excited as the children, and he loved to see that. She *hummed* now. He wasn't sure he'd ever heard her hum before. But as she went through the kitchen, shining dishes and instructing the staff on how to operate the new kitchen appliances, she was practically dancing.

Soon, the home would be filled with the sounds of laughter and children—and probably the smashing of plates and other fragile objects.

Days passed, and the excitement grew exponentially until June 18th—the long-awaited move-in day. George hadn't been expecting a single-file line with all 120 resident children moving in an orderly fashion, but he wasn't quite prepared for the pandemonium that ensued.

"Hey," George shouted, trying to get everyone's attention as they practically started a food fight in the cafeteria. "Hey!" Again, nothing. Finally, he took a page from Nielsen's playbook and let out an ear-piercing whistle.

The children perked up. That got their attention. *Thank you, Mr. Nielsen.*

"Okay, thank you," George continued calmly. "I need everyone to pay attention. Everyone is going to have to follow instructions and listen to their teachers, or we are never going to manage this move. Now…Mr. Nielsen will be here soon, and we can't waste his time, so those of you who *haven't* packed weeks in advance, I want you packed up by the time he arrives. I also want the older children helping the younger ones so that we can move as quickly and *quietly* as possible. Sound good?"

All the children nodded in unison. Fortunately, they truly did seem to get the message. The day continued fairly smoothly, even when Nielsen showed up.

The kids flocked around Nielsen, who looked as though he was uncomfortable with all the attention. Many of the girls expressed their gratitude for his assistance, and some of the older boys even mentioned that they were interested in joining his team. They were a bit young for something like that at fourteen, but Nielsen humored them, and George suspected that Nielsen even relished that idea.

It took four whole days to complete the move. Of course, there was a little more chaos once they reached the new building. The kids were screaming with excitement about their new home, and George really couldn't bring himself to call them to order too soon. He let them explore, ripping and racing around bends. He occasionally called to them to

Fay

be careful, but it was too amusing for him to do much else.

The most entertaining part was watching the kids learn how to play basketball on their new court. George laughed as they figured out the sport. They looked a bit like wounded giraffes. Since they'd all grown up under George's care, they'd never had a basketball court before. And George imagined he wouldn't look much better if he tried to play.

Suddenly, someone grabbed George's hand. He looked down to see ten-year-old Faye watching the boys as well.

She looked up at him. "Is this going to be our home forever and ever?" She sounded almost fearful, as if it was a dream too good to be true.

George's heart broke a little, as it did every time he interacted with these children. Some had no one left in their families, and many had been treated poorly before coming to the academy.

George bent down on one knee and smiled at her. "Yes, Faye. This will be your home forever and ever." He didn't have the heart to tell her that one day she'd be old enough to want her own life and would want to move away. All she needed to know was that Cherry Hills Academy was here for her as long as she needed it.

After spending so many years in the original buildings, it was a little strange settling into the new academy facility. Things were a bit awkward for the first couple of months as the kids grew accustomed to their new home, but they never complained. To say that the Cherry Hills home was a step up from their previous buildings would be an understatement.

The Lord had spared no expense when providing for His children. Though George hadn't spent the money frivolously by any means, he'd ensured that the kids had their every need met at Cherry Hills Academy.

The summer months led to water fights in the yard and suntanning on the roof (which George was particularly worried about, considering it was slanted!) Mary just seemed to find it amusing, however. The kids really did seem to be thriving here in their new home. George was right; access to nature was doing wonders for their health and attitudes. And another huge plus? No neighbors complaining about noise.

Because they'd built the Cherry Hills Academy from the ground up, it would be years before anything needed to be repaired. Well, theoretically. George imagined that with all the wear and tear the building was going through as it housed growing kids, repairs might be necessary a little sooner than expected.

Chapter Eighteen

George was often struck by how quickly time seemed to pass. He felt that it was as if he'd just blinked and another year had gone by. They would soon be nearing their second anniversary of moving into the new Cherry Hills Academy, and in honor of that momentous occasion, Lydia created a blog where they could record the miracles they'd witnessed.

As of May, the Cherry Hills Academy now housed 275 children from Haiti, Guatemala, and Belize, but the majority of its residents were from the United States. They had 33 staff members, raising the total number of souls in the new Academy to 308 people, plus dozens of volunteers. From when they'd founded the academy to date, they had cared for a total of 443 children. And the number of kids only kept growing. By December of the same year, the Cherry Hills Academy was caring for over 300 youths.

Their new home was rapidly filling up and reaching maximum

capacity. For a few months, George was thrilled. He felt that he had truly achieved his goal—his academy was *full!* It was a little cramped, but that didn't matter to him. He was caring for 300 children who had nowhere else to go and no one else to turn to.

The joy faded, however, when Beta began to request more room for children and George was forced to turn him down due to a lack of space. He turned away five, then ten, then thirty, then seventy-eight children. It killed George to have to turn them away, especially knowing how difficult their lives were and how unlikely it would be for them to find suitable care elsewhere.

There wasn't anything *wrong* with the foster care system; he just felt it could be better. Once a child was stuck in a small family unit, there simply weren't enough people in the social system to check up on them and see how they were processing the change. Not to mention the unscrupulous people who were just looking to benefit from the system. That didn't mean there weren't wonderful people who took these children in—there absolutely were—but George felt called to offer another solution. Plus, homeless families were sending more children to Cherry Hills for care and boarding.

George knew he couldn't take in every needy child in the world, but with the Lord's help, he would be able to do more. Of that he was convinced.

In the fifteen years since George had begun to take in orphans, he had learned one thing for sure: he served a very big God.

Rather than jumping in head first, George humbled himself and began to pray fervently to determine whether or not the construction of

Fay

another Academy was an action God wanted him to take. He could practically feel the spirit of doubt and uncertainty surrounding him, but he prayed it away.

George was desperate to begin building an additional building on the property. His soul seemed to be crying out for it, and with every child they had to turn away, the need to begin construction seemed to grow stronger. Still, he knew better than to act outside of God's will, so he remained faithful and continued in his prayers.

By January of his forty-sixth year, George was still conflicted.

There were obstacles he had to consider as well. He had to wonder if he wasn't "tempting God" by planning to build another academy building. The funds they were currently receiving were barely enough to supply them and keep them afloat for the next month. But…hadn't that always been the way of things? When they only had twenty kids to feed, God provided for the twenty. When they had 200, he provided for the 200. When they needed funds for a new Academy, he provided them generously. Would it not be the same if George felt called to build an additional building to house more of God's children?

The issue of financing was no small concern. To construct and furnish another large addition to the Cherry Hills Academy would take more money than George had ever received. More than that, he would have to look beyond the building itself. He would have to provide for the new kids who came in. If he planned to build a structure large enough to house 1,000 children, he'd have to have the funds to meet their needs on a monthly basis.

When compared to the miracles, George's worry seemed silly. To him, anyway. The Lord had provided for them for the past fifteen years; what made him think He would suddenly *stop* providing for them? This is how faith grows—it builds upon previous experiences of faith.

The more he considered the prospect of establishing an addition to the Cherry Hills Academy, the more at peace he felt. By March, George was all in. He knew that this was the next step in his journey.

In May, George revealed his desire to Lydia and Mary as they sat around the dinner table. Lydia had dodged the college cafeteria to come over for dinner, and it was the perfect opportunity to get their thoughts.

"Took you long enough," Lydia joked.

"Wait, really?" asked George.

"Of course," Lydia laughed. She looked at her mother. "Mom and I have been wondering when you'd make up your mind about that for a while. You know, you're not very good at hiding your thoughts."

Mary smiled. "It's true."

"So, you think it's a good idea?"

"I do," Lydia answered. "I've prayed about it a lot, honestly. I think it's a great idea."

"Okay then," he began. "It's settled. We'll build another academy building at Cherry Hills."

"And I want to help," Lydia interjected. "Not just with the construction… but forever."

Mary straightened in her chair and looked at George with a sly grin, like she'd known all along.

"Really?" George couldn't believe it. "No, I couldn't ask that of you, Lydia. This is my calling. I don't want you to feel obligated to con-

Fay

tinue a work that you don't feel the Lord has called you to."

"But maybe this could be my work," she answered wholeheartedly. "I feel the same calling, Dad. I want to devote my life to this."

George dropped his fork. "Lydia, nothing would make me happier." He fought back tears. "I just…"

"Dad," she said, though he could tell his tears softened her.

"I know," he quickly said, swiping at a tear. "Sorry, I know I'm the most emotional one in the family. Which is weird since I'm the only man in the family."

At that, Lydia and Mary laughed. Mary laid a hand on her husband's arm.

"It's because you care," she said softly.

George nodded. "You both are indispensable. Really," he assured them. "Mary, the way you've deciphered all of my notes…"

George had written down all of his thoughts during his time pondering the expansion and…well, let's just say they were not entirely legible. Mary always had this ability to decipher his handwriting, though, and she was able to turn the stack of papers into an easy online filing system.

At the end of the dinner, George was more confident in his decision than ever. He knew that it was time to build another building at the Cherry Hills Academy site.

By the month's end, they'd had to turn more children away. In total, 170 kids had been sent away by the academy due to lack of space, which tore at George's heart.

Though small, George continued to receive donations from people around the world he had never heard of. They were evidence of George's positive presence and impact and of the Lord's continued provision.

Many people could hardly understand George's confidence in the Lord. He prayed every day for a year straight for the same thing, never lacking in dedication or faith. While most would have quit after not having their prayers answered within the first few days or weeks, George had so much trust in the Lord that he never gave up, even when it seemed like an impossible task.

Chapter Nineteen

As George continued to feel the call to expand the facilities so he could help more children, he knew he would need to take on more assistants. One of those assistants was a man named James Wright.

The day the young man came in for his first interview, Mary had immediately endorsed him, and George couldn't blame her. He was a respectful, brilliant believer originally from the southern United States, which meant he referred to Mary as "Mrs. Müller" and "ma'am." Though she didn't particularly like the way it made her feel older, she did appreciate the respect.

There was something about James' kind, blue eyes that made him seem trustworthy, and he'd received glowing recommendations from his former employers. George couldn't imagine anyone better to help run the place. So, after a couple more interviews and plenty of hours in prayer, he finally shook hands with the man and welcomed James Wright onto the team.

In his forty-ninth year, George received enough donations towards the building fund that he felt comfortable beginning the process of the additional build. He hired surveyors who informed him that there was enough space on the land for another building, so they wouldn't need to look elsewhere for more property.

Assembling the plans was easy and quick, especially when you had a team like George had. Once Tom Foster completed the design plans, it was just a matter of completing the preliminary arrangements. Of course, George couldn't help but envision a third building as well. What it would be used for, he had no idea, but it didn't matter. They didn't have the funds for a third building yet, so that particular dream would need to wait a little longer.

With all of the pieces in place, construction on the new building began. Roger Nielsen had since moved out of the state but had offered to refer George to another foreman he knew and trusted, a man named Gino. Gino looked and sounded like he could've been Nielsen's long-lost twin, and since George had liked Nielsen's work so much, he was happy to hire someone his previous foreman had suggested.

Gino gathered his crew and showed up on time every day. They put in the same amount of work that Nielsen and his men did, if not more.

Tom Foster again donated his time and expertise to the construction of the second facility. He'd reached out to George without ever being contacted. He offered his services free of charge to the academy, and together George and Tom designed a home that would be a true heaven on earth for the needy kids. Finally, in late fall of George's fifty-second year, it was time. The new academy building was finished, and four hundred new kids were given the opportunity to move in and begin a new life in Cherry Hills' second building.

Chapter Twenty

Beta's program continued to thrive, and though he and George kept in touch as often as they could, they found that they were becoming too busy to stay in constant contact. To ensure they had an opportunity to connect, Beta decided to plan a trip to Cherry Hills.

When Beta arrived, he was yet again received by those who remembered him from Haiti, and George was thrilled to have his friend home again. Beta had definitely aged since George had seen him last. He'd let his beard grow out unusually long, but George thought it was a good look on his friend.

Beta stayed for two weeks before having to return to Haiti. By then, he'd shared enough news from Haiti that George was convinced they'd need even more space in the coming months.

It took over a year of faithful prayer, but in September of George's fifty-third year, he was able to purchase eleven acres right next to the other academy buildings.

Fay

The land was just as beautiful as the seven acres they'd purchased before, and it had so much more space. As soon as he purchased the land, he called Tom Foster, who somehow already knew the purpose for George's call.

Tom agreed to take a look at the land, and Lydia emailed him the topographical and cadastral maps of the lot. On Friday morning, Tom arrived bright and early. Together, George and Tom walked the land to see what could be accomplished. When they were finished, they sat in George's office.

"Okay, I know the initial plan was a building for three hundred orphans, but after seeing the land, I'm convinced we can put up a building for four hundred. Maybe even four fifty," Tom explained.

George's eyes widened. "What? Really?"

"Yes," said Tom with a nod. "Of course, it would cost more, but we'd be making the most of the land, as you put it."

"No, no, that's excellent news," said George, his voice bubbling like a laugh.

"Do you want me to get started on the plans?"

"Yes, absolutely," George said, standing and shaking the architect's hand. "Really, Tom, I can't thank you enough."

Tom shrugged sheepishly. "It's my tithe to the Lord. I'm happy to help."

On December 9th of George's fifty-fifth year, they celebrated the twenty-fourth anniversary of the ministry to children in need. It was a day of praise and rejoicing in what the Lord had done for them. In that time period, they had received and helped a total of 1,129 children from the United States, as well as Haiti, Guatemala, Belize, and now Honduras. Of those, 469 had come to them in the past two years alone, indicating both the increase in need and in their ability to provide. And as of that day, they were currently caring for over 700 orphans at the Cherry Hills Academy.

The day after the anniversary, George received a grateful message from Nico, a boy who had aged out of the Academy. Nico had been given the opportunity to take on an apprenticeship under a local electrician George had befriended. The electrician had taken it upon himself to provide Nico with room and board until he was able to afford his own place. So far, many of those helping the "graduated" kids had offered similar arrangements. It seemed that most who came in contact with George's ministry felt touched by the Lord and inspired to help in some small way, whatever it may be.

George was just sitting down to eat lunch when his phone *dinged* loudly. He glanced down and saw the email from Nico and smiled. Despite the large number of kids attended to by the academy, George still remembered every single one, and Nico he remembered fondly. He opened the email.

> *George,*
>
> *I'm writing this email with incredible feelings of gratitude and thankfulness for all the kindness you showed me under your care. I also cannot express my gratitude sufficient-*

ly for the apprenticeship you arranged for me, which means that I will be able to earn a decent living in the future.

I once again wish to thank you for finding these amazing people who took me in and are teaching me a valuable trade. But I also wished to thank you for the education you provided me, for the shelter, the food, the clothing, and for taking care of my every comfort.

However, above all else I wish to thank you for the instruction in God's Word, because it was under your roof and in the happiness I experienced at the academy where I came to know Jesus as my Savior.

I pray that I am able to prosper in my trade so that I might be able to repay some of the kindness you showed me while I was under your care. I also pray that you remain hale and hearty for many years to come so that you are able to care for more poor, destitute children like me.

You should know that I consider my time in the academy as the happiest time of my life, which is more than most kids like me can say. You gave me a real chance at life. I regretted to have to leave, but thanks to you, I have a future to look forward to.

Blessings,
Nico

Okay, tears *may* have welled in George's eyes, even if he didn't want to admit it. He sniffed and tried to quickly close the email but of course, his eagle-eyed daughter missed nothing.

"What are you reading? What has you so emotional?" She rushed over to take a look and practically tore the phone from his hands.

As she read it, she too found herself sniffling.

Through every trial and tribulation, through every test the Lord saw fit to bring upon them, *this* was what kept them going. This was what prodded George and his family along. Every letter, every message, every note was an inspiration and boosted their determination to move forward.

Though Cherry Hills Academy was a place where children could have their physical needs met, George also ensured that it was a safe place for them to explore and grow in faith in Jesus Christ. As a result, there seemed to be mini revivals and spiritual awakenings taking place all the time at Cherry Hills. At one chapel service in July, countless students experienced the tangible presence of God in a powerful way, which lit a fire in them to read the Bible and learn more about Jesus. Their curiosity and questions reminded George of his own conversion years before. About eleven months later, thirty-one of these students were fully confident in their salvation, while others continued to work out their faith slowly.

The second revival happened at the end of January of the following year, leading over 70 students to accept Jesus as their savior. In many cases, the children found peace in their faith. Some even came to George and Mary and asked if they could lead their own Bible studies and prayer meetings amongst themselves, which only led to *more* revival.

Fay

The spread of God's Word was contagious, so George and Mary had many reasons for their continued gratitude. Of the 700 children they were caring for at the time, there were 118 kids who they were fully confident had been saved, with many more either moving toward that direction or experiencing this spiritual awakening to some extent. No other year had seen such a great wave of God moving in the young hearts, and no other year had given the Müllers a greater cause to give thanks to the Lord for His spiritual blessings.

Chapter Twenty-One

That spring, in George's fifty-fifth year, work finally began on the third Academy. Once again, he relied on his previous foreman, Gino, for help.

It took a little over a year for the construction to be completed, but in George's fifty-sixth year, he was finally able to receive another 450 orphans, just as Tom had promised.

The third academy building was everything George had imagined, teeming with life. Cream-painted bricks made up the exterior, and dark, wooden shutters dressed the windows, through which children could be seen eagerly choosing their bedrooms. A quaint stone pathway led up to the wrap-around porch where crimson rocking chairs swayed gently in the breeze.

James came out the front door and jumped off the porch, quickly walking up to George. "Everything's in order. It's a bit…hectic in there right now."

Fay

George shrugged with a smile. "It'll be chaotic for a few days. But that's what you're here for, right?" he joked, slapping James on the shoulder.

James laughed uncomfortably. "Right."

George stepped away from James to examine the grounds and see what all they had to work with.

Since most of the kids coming into this facility had no prior experience with George, he made sure to spend as much time as he could with them for the first couple of months. He wanted to be sure they knew they could trust him.

It helped having the other two buildings so close by so that kids could intermingle. The kids who had been around for a long time *loved* the Müllers with every ounce of their being, and when the new kids saw that, their own adoration for the Müller family grew.

These children would now have a safe haven and a place to learn and develop. George was proud to say that the education they offered in their academy didn't just rival public and private schools—it even surpassed them.

The need for more space was ever present. As the children grew, so did their need for greater privacy and more room to move. The boys were especially difficult to contain, since they seemed to end up breaking something fragile on a daily basis. There were just so many of them—and boys will be boys.

They *needed* a larger facility. George had a habit of taking in more children than he could comfortably house because he knew of the conditions they had been living in. This meant that with every passing day, as the children grew, the current facilities seemed to get smaller and smaller.

It wasn't until October of George's fifty-ninth year, upon receiving a donation of five hundred thousand dollars from one individual, that he felt the time was right. With three million dollars in the building fund, he felt confident in beginning his search for a new plot of land for another facility.

Well, *search* was a strong word. In fact, George had been eyeing a piece of land near his property for quite some time. It was eighteen acres and, like the others, wasn't lacking in beauty.

Unfortunately, the peace and excitement he was feeling about the potential new property wasn't going to last.

George stared out the window, watching the violent, dark clouds roll towards them. They'd be over Cherry Hills Academy soon. His fingers twitched at his sides. He should be there, protecting the children, rather than hiding in his own house.

"I'm going to—"

"Don't even think about it," Mary stopped him in his tracks without even looking up from the weather channel. "Look at that, George. High-speed winds, temperature changes. This very well could be a tornado. You're staying right here."

"What about the children?"

"We've taken precautions for a reason. They'll be fine. We just

Fay

need to sit here and wait it out."

He didn't like that idea in the slightest, but somewhere deep down he knew his wife was right.

He couldn't sleep at all. The storm sounded like a jet engine firing up. But it wasn't the noise that kept him awake—rather, it was the uncertainty. He knew that God had His hand over the children, but it didn't comfort him enough to sleep soundly. Should he have done more? *Could he have?*

By the time the sun rose the next morning, the storm had temporarily quieted. George had gotten in maybe thirty minutes of rest before Mary woke him. Along with Lydia, they went to check on the buildings. All three had major structural damage. Roofs had lost slates, leaving gaping holes in the ceiling, and many windows had shattered.

George was both relieved and disheartened to see the damage. None of the children had been injured, so it could have been much, much worse. Still, there was a lot of damage. With the weathermen predicting more storms rolling in, they had very little time to get the situation under control.

George's footsteps were muffled in the wet grass, only making a sound when he stepped on the scattered, broken twigs and glass lying in a chaotic array around the courtyard. There was a slight sense of unease in the air. The winds were restless again and picking back up. The trees bent and shook underneath the gale, their once strong leaves trembling and falling to join the others on the ground. There was something so powerful about thunderstorms like this. Despite their destructive capabilities and the carnage they often left behind, the air always smelled cleaner after the storm rolled through.

The children's toys in the yard were completely gone—washed away by the rains and blown away by the winds. The basketball net had fallen over, balls were nowhere to be found, and much of the grass was littered with debris from the academy. It wasn't a pretty sight.

James rushed up behind George as he surveyed the mess left behind.

"I have the reports," said James. "Do you want to look them over now or later?"

George sighed. "Later. Just leave them in my office, and I'll take a look at them."

"Sure thing," said James. "I just spoke with the repairmen, but they won't be able to make it out here until Monday."

Monday. Two days away. With the new storms rolling in, the children could very well be in more danger than before.

George refused to panic. He just nodded and said, "Thank you, James. Let's get them scheduled for Monday."

When George returned home, Mary was already seated in front of the television with Lydia. They were watching the weather report carefully.

"Any good news?"

Lydia turned around and shook her head. "Unfortunately not. It looks like the rains are definitely on their way. What did the roofers say?"

"They can't get to us until Monday," George answered.

Now it was Mary's turn to look back at him. "Monday? Are they serious? We have kids in those homes!"

Fay

"It's the only time they can make it," George replied. "But don't worry. I'm going over to the church to meet with Henry. We are going to pray that God protects the children and holds off the rain until the roofs are fixed."

George, Lydia, and Mary spent the rest of the afternoon with bowed heads and in fervent prayer, asking that the Lord send aid, whether it was by withholding the rains or sending the repairmen sooner.

George was reminded of a passage in James in which the apostle spoke of the prophet Elijah. James recounted that "Elijah was a human being, even as we are. He prayed earnestly that it would not rain, and it did not rain on the land for three and a half years." George by no means would compare himself to the great prophet Elijah, but he did believe in the power of earnest, dedicated prayer—not for himself, but for the children who had been entrusted to him.

The Müllers spent hours in their living room, their voices a symphony of praise and pleading being lifted to the heavens over the roar of the wind outside.

After nearly four hours, as George was thanking the Lord for His constant provision and reminding Him of His promise to look after His children, George paused to take a breath…and noticed something. The wind was no longer a high-pitched whistle behind him.

At the same time, Mary and Lydia looked up, noticing how quiet it had become. The three of them quickly stood and rushed to the window, drawing back the dark blue drapes.

Rays of sunlight had fought their way through the dark clouds, and though the trees' leaves still trembled, the trunks stood strong against the gale, no longer shuddering with every gust. From the looks of it, the worst of the storm was over. A brilliant rainbow caressed the dark sky, and a colorful sunset slowly crested the horizon.

Lydia's eyes widened in disbelief. She'd witnessed so many miracles around the academy—just never one this massive.

Mary grabbed his hand and squeezed it tightly. "The rains will hold for now."

While it wasn't surprising at all to George that God answered his prayer, it never ceased to amaze and humble him. George never failed to give God thanks and glory with a grateful heart.

The rains and winds held until Wednesday, giving the repairmen plenty of time to see the job done right. And then the skies opened again.

Chapter Twenty-Two

Sarah was uneasy.

She'd always been a worrier. This was something that endlessly annoyed Henry, but deep down George knew Henry appreciated her concern. She repeatedly called Mary with concerns about her husband's health. George worried as well. Henry hadn't quite been himself as of late. It was hard to keep up with his health when they both had such taxing schedules.

One afternoon, Sarah called Mary again, and this time she was desperate.

"He's in a lot of pain," Sarah relayed on speakerphone. "He won't go to the hospital either. I just…I don't know what to do. I'm worried sick."

Mary looked up at George. He nodded, just as concerned.

"Okay, Sarah," Mary answered. "We're on our way over."

The two jumped in the car and drove to the Craik's home, where they found Henry propped up on the couch. George could tell right away that he was in pain. His jaw was clenched tightly, and a light sheen of sweat misted his forehead.

It was strange to see him like this. When George met Henry, he was the picture of health, and George had even briefly envied his physical strength and athleticism.

"I'm not going anywhere," Henry stated mulishly the moment he spotted George coming through the doorway.

"Why are you being a stubborn old goat?" George demanded.

"It's just a stomachache," answered the goat. "It'll pass."

"If it's just a stomachache, why are you afraid to go to the hospital?" George pressed.

"Afraid? I'm not afraid," Henry retorted. "I just know what they'd do. They'd give me more painkillers—which I'm already taking—and tell me that it's a stomachache and it'll pass."

More painkillers? George thought. If he had already taken painkillers, then the fact that he was still in pain wasn't a good sign.

He glanced up at Sarah, who gave him a *See? What did I tell you?* expression. George finally nodded and went to Henry's side, grabbing him by the arm.

"Hey!" Henry shouted.

"Time to go. It's my time we're wasting, and I don't mind wasting it, so we're off to the hospital."

There wasn't much Henry could do or say to get out of it. George, Mary, and Sarah helped him to the car, even as he griped and complained.

Fay

When they arrived at the hospital, it took forever for someone to actually take the situation seriously. It seemed like doctors asked the most ridiculous questions for hours before someone finally decided that an MRI was in order.

When the results came back, the doctor who delivered them looked all too calm.

The doctor was older, probably around George's age. His hair was graying, and the green eyes that perhaps once sparkled with a brilliant luster now seemed dull and lifeless.

"Is he okay?" Sarah questioned immediately.

The doctor reached to shake Sarah's hand, his posture impeccably straight. "Mrs. Craik, I'm Doctor Fields. I was the one overseeing your husband's MRI test. We've found something troubling in the scans."

Mary put her hand on Sarah's shoulder. "What is it?" George's wife asked.

"We've found a mass growing in his stomach. A tumor…" continued Doctor Fields.

Sarah paled. "What?"

"It will need to be biopsied immediately to know if it's benign or malignant. Let's not panic until we have to; rest assured that your husband is in capable hands." The doctor tore off a piece of paper from his notepad. "I'm referring you to an oncologist from here. He's a good doctor."

Sarah just stared blankly as she shakily took the piece of paper. "Okay."

The news sank in slowly for George, though he imagined Sarah was not in a place to truly receive it either. They all knew what a tumor meant, even if it were benign: surgery. And for someone Henry's age, it also meant a long, hard recovery.

Lord, George prayed softly. *Give him strength. Give us all strength.*

Evidently, getting the *name* of the oncologist wasn't even half of the battle.

It took just two days to get an appointment with Doctor Redmond, who then decided to do another MRI to confirm the previous doctor's diagnosis. After the results came back, Doctor Redmond scheduled Pastor Craik for a biopsy that very evening, which meant Henry wouldn't be leaving the hospital.

Sarah was beside herself, and George barely knew how to help. Mary was a lifesaver, coddling her the way she would have had it been Lydia in Sarah's shoes.

"Sarah, love, breathe," Mary insisted. "I think it's time to call Will, don't you?"

George's heart ached at the thought. Their son, Will, had always been a close friend of Lydia's growing up, though they hadn't seen him much in the past few years since he began working in finance.

Sarah shook her head adamantly. "No, Will is away on business. I can't interrupt him."

"Sarah—"

"What if it's nothing? I don't want to worry him for nothing. You heard what the last doctor said. Let's not worry until there's something to worry about, okay?" Sarah sounded as if she didn't believe the words coming out of her mouth.

George sat beside Sarah. "Have you told Will anything?"

"Henry didn't want him to know," Sarah replied, voice trembling.

Mary sighed, shaking her head.

The three waited for the biopsy to be completed and tended to Henry once he returned to his room. Then it was just a waiting game. It took several days for the results of the biopsy to come back…and the news wasn't good.

"Stomach cancer," Sarah repeated the words back to Doctor Redmond.

Mary gently held her hand, glancing at George, who stood across the room beside the bed where Henry lay.

"I'm afraid so," replied the ruddy-faced doctor. He must have been desensitized to delivering this sort of news; there wasn't a bit of sorrow in his features.

"I just…" Sarah couldn't seem to finish the words.

Henry was in complete shock, just as much as his wife. He seemed to hardly register the words, which was difficult for George to see. Pastor Craik had always been such a steadfast man, one with an incredible faith, yet it seemed as though he'd been temporarily broken.

"Sarah," Mary tried. "It's time to call Will."

Sarah nodded, still dumbfounded.

"Don't, Sarah," Henry pleaded. "I don't want him to know. He can't see me like this."

Tears streamed down Sarah's face as she bit her lip.

"Henry," George said, laying a hand on his friend's shoulder. "Don't let your pride get in the way. Don't rob your son of knowing what is going on. He deserves to be here."

Henry's gaze flickered between George and Sarah, and after a long moment, he finally nodded his head slowly. "You're right," he whispered. "Sarah, call Will."

Sarah didn't need another word. She ducked out of the room, phone already in hand.

George cleared his throat. "Doctor Redmond, would you mind waiting to give us the options until their son arrives?"

"Of course," replied the doctor. "I'll be back tomorrow to check in."

As expected, Will was on the next flight. George couldn't imagine the panic he must have been experiencing. He was the first to meet Will in the waiting room since Sarah refused to leave Henry's bedside.

George had always thought Will looked more like Sarah than Henry. He was shorter and thinner than his father, but he held himself with the same courage.

The first words out of Will's mouth were, "Is he going to be okay?"

It pained George not to be able to give an answer. He looked at Will, who seemed shattered. His eyes were rimmed with tears and bloodshot after what was likely a sleepless redeye flight from Los Angeles to Springfield.

George answered the only way he knew how. "Let's go see your dad."

Fay

George brought Will upstairs and found that the doctor had come in while George was gone. Though Will looked like he wanted to run up to his father, he first turned to the doctor.

"I'm the son, Will," he introduced, shaking the doctor's hand.

"Good to meet you, Will. We've been waiting for you. I'm Doctor Redmond, your father's oncologist." He glanced up at Sarah. "Would you all like to hear the treatment plan now?"

Sarah nodded numbly as Will came to sit beside her, clutching her hand.

Doctor Redmond turned to Henry, who George thought was looking weaker by the minute.

"Mr. Craik, I'd like to surgically remove the tumor immediately. From there, we can proceed with chemotherapy treatment."

Henry scoffed. "That's not happening."

Sarah burst into tears, and Henry's harsh expression softened.

"Sarah, dear, I don't want to spend what little time I have left in a hospital room!"

"Dad," Will pleaded. "You have to be here to fight this. If you come home, this cancer is going to take you out."

Henry sighed. "If it's the Lord's will, then it's the Lord's will."

Will jumped from his chair while his mother continued to cry. "Maybe the Lord's will is for you to stop acting like a pious, ignorant man and take your medicine!"

Henry seemed shocked, and Lord knows George was. Seeing that, Will softened.

"I'm sorry…I shouldn't have said that. It's a lot to take in." He took a deep breath. "Please, Dad. I'm begging you. We're begging you. I'm not ready for this. Please give this a chance…"

Sarah's crying lessened, and she looked up through watery eyes to see her husband's reaction. Henry inhaled deeply and slowly nodded. He was giving in. Sarah's tears returned, but this time they were filled with relief as she hugged Mary close.

George watched the interactions between Sarah and Mary and Will and Henry, and he sent up a silent prayer that this wouldn't be the last time any of them saw Henry in good health.

Henry went in for surgery shortly after, and the doctors removed the growth in his stomach. The recovery from the procedure was long and difficult, especially when coupled with chemotherapy treatment. It was hard to watch his friend go through a treatment that seemed so barbaric in nature. It seemed to be weakening him more than the cancer was.

Mary was Sarah's rock and strength, just as she'd always been for George, and George was more than happy to lend her to the Craik family as long as Mary could comfort them. Will spent every second at the hospital and even started ignoring his work calls. It was George who convinced him to put in for a leave of absence due to family matters, and Will did so, freeing his mind up to truly be with his father. Lydia came a few days later. She'd been tending to the academy in George's absence, afraid that James couldn't handle it all on his own.

Months ticked by, and though the world seemed tipped out of orbit, things carried on somewhat normally. George was able to return to his duties for the most part, including visiting his congregation, who faithfully prayed for Pastor Craik's recovery on a daily basis. He also maintained a strong presence at the academy, seeing to the children's every need.

Lydia and Mary practically lived at the hospital with the Craik family. True to form, Lydia mirrored her mother in her strength and faith.

James came to visit as well. Although he wasn't close with Henry, he'd seen the man around the academy and had also read some of Henry's former academic works, including a couple Hebrew translations. Sometimes, however, George wondered if James wasn't there more for Lydia's sake than anyone else's. The few times that James did stop by, George would catch him and Lydia talking quietly in the hall.

The time George spent at Cherry Hills Academy gave him a much-needed peace. Even James' nerves couldn't rattle him; hearing his assistant share about issues that had popped up was a helpful reprieve from focusing on his friend's declining health.

Within the month, Henry's health took a turn for the worse. His breathing became shallower, and his energy levels plummeted. Sarah tried to remain positive, but Will's understanding of the situation was keen. The only person who was shocked when the doctors came to report bad news was Henry's wife.

"I'm very sorry, Mrs. Craik," said Doctor Redmond in his usual callous way. He turned to Henry. "I'm afraid all we can do is keep you comfortable. I wish there were more we could try."

"No," Sarah said adamantly, stealing the attention of the room. "I want a second opinion."

"Sarah," Mary whispered softly, tenderly. "Doctor Redmond is the leading oncologist in the area."

"Then I want to go to another area," Sarah insisted. "We don't stop until we find someone who can beat this."

"Sarah, my love," Henry choked out, his voice strained. "The Lord is calling me home."

Tears fell over Sarah's cheeks, and she shook her head firmly. "I haven't heard Him say so. Will, have you heard Him say so? No, I didn't think so."

"Mom." This time, it was Will who spoke. "It's okay."

That's when the tears really began to fall. Sarah practically threw herself onto Henry, sobbing into the hospital blanket as Henry stroked his wife's back.

"It'll be okay, love," Henry managed.

Doctor Redmond cleared his throat. "I'll give you some time. A nurse will be in shortly to administer your medication."

George nodded. He knew it would take time for Sarah to come to terms with everything and even longer for her to find peace with it.

It was a painful time, filled with the anticipation of great grief—but also the celebration of life. George spent what little time he had with Henry reminiscing about all of the good times. Of how so many had doubted them when they wanted to start the academy, and how the Lord had proved all the naysayers wrong. George cracked jokes and retold stories of Henry that had him in tears he was laughing so hard, and Henry would've been in stitches if it weren't for the fact that…well, he was in *literal* stitches.

George often found himself having to step out of the room and catch his breath. He felt like his chest was collapsing in on him. He was losing his closest friend. It took much prayer for him to understand that this was the Lord's will, and it helped that Henry was so at peace with what was to come. Still, it didn't make it easy for anyone involved, George included.

At night, when the three Müllers would return home from the hospital, Mary would have to comfort George as he mourned the coming loss of his friend. Both Mary and Lydia had their hands full comforting those who would be most affected.

The end of the year came and went with no improvement from Henry. Sarah's strength had returned to her thanks to Will's encouragement and assurance that he would help her through this time, and there seemed to be a peace surrounding the whole situation.

George had just spent the entire day with Pastor Craik, doing all of the talking since Henry had grown too tired to speak. When the sun began to set, George slowly stood, nodding silently to Sarah across the bed. He was about to leave when Henry's voice stilled him.

"Could you stay?" His voice was weak and every word was a struggle. "I just want to look at both of you."

George returned to his seat, and together they sat by Henry's bedside until he fell asleep. Once he was peacefully resting, George quietly stood and gave Sarah a hug before leaving.

That evening would be the last night George saw Henry Craik alive. The next morning, Mary received a call. Pastor Henry Craik had passed away.

Let the Children Come

It was a strange time. George wasn't sure how to continue on without Henry. They had both known the Lord for a little over forty years and were both barely over sixty years old at the time, but George's beloved brother and friend had finished his course ahead of George, and he'd finished well.

One of the biggest losses was that of Pastor Craik's faith and wisdom. George had often come to him and sought his counsel on various matters in his own life. It would take George a while to break the habit of reaching for the phone to call him.

The memorial service was held at Springfield Community Church, and the immense crowd that gathered was a fitting testimony to the loss that the entire Christian community felt with Henry Craik's passing.

Chapter Twenty-Three

Mary and George kept up with Sarah as much as they could, and Will had done as he promised and taken a leave of absence to help his mother through the difficult time.

Eventually, though, even grief begins to fade. George still felt his painful loss, but life had to continue. With his pain serving as a catalyst, George began construction on the fourth facility at Cherry Hills Academy. Everyone needed fresh hope, and he knew that Henry would have wanted him to drive full force ahead with the project. As he anticipated, the new building project greatly raised morale within their community, and the congregation rejoiced in the work the Lord was doing through George Müller.

Construction began as planned and continued to progress quickly throughout the year. George had again hired Gino, who was practically a miracle worker in the way he was able to accomplish projects.

At the end of the year, they received an incredible donation of

$750,000, allowing them to begin construction on the fifth building, as well. Accustomed to the building process at this point, they eagerly began construction on this new building in January.

George rejoiced at this huge gift, of course, but not any more than if it had been ten dollars. George rejoiced when a multimillionaire came to understand that it is more blessed to give than to receive. And he also rejoiced when a poor person trusted God for their daily bread and gave the ten-dollar gift, which may have been all he or she had.

George was nearly completely preoccupied with the progress of the new Cherry Hills Academy buildings. *Nearly.*

Still, he couldn't help but notice that Mary had been losing an abnormal amount of weight. Her energy levels had dipped significantly. Whenever he brought it up to her, she just laughed it off and reminded him that she was sixty-eight years old, and her weight and energy levels were bound to start changing.

After the loss of his best friend, George wasn't comfortable leaving the topic alone, but his wife urged him to drop it. She insisted that all was well, and since George couldn't possibly argue with the woman, he agreed to temporarily drop the matter.

In George's sixty-third year, just two years after they'd begun construction, they were able to open the doors of the fourth Cherry Hills Academy building.

When George stood back to take a look at what Gino and his men had accomplished, he couldn't help the little bubbling laugh that

Fay

erupted from him. If you'd asked twelve-year-old George Müller what he'd be doing in his early sixties, he never would have imagined this. In fact, he probably would have dog cussed anyone who suggested it. Yet here it was. And the work wasn't even complete—they still had one more building to accomplish.

It took another year before the fifth building was completed and ready to open its doors, but it was well worth the wait.

A strange feeling washed over George as he stared at the two new buildings. In just a few weeks, Beta would be sending more kids, which meant George would be caring for 2,000 children. The responsibility was enormous and humbling. He'd accomplished what he'd set out to do all those years ago. He'd proved that anything could be achieved through unconditional faith and prayer.

Though Lydia had moved out of the house years ago and was renting a place several miles away, she still dedicated the same amount of time she always had to Cherry Hills Academy, if not more. It was inspiring for George to see his daughter starting her own life, yet her heart was so captured by these kids that she didn't stray far, and never for long. True to her word, she seemed to want to carry on her father's work with the academy after his retirement, and Lord knew they'd need the help.

The added costs of the new buildings brought the total expenses to an all-time high. George wasn't worried, though the same couldn't be said of his colleagues. While James had witnessed many of the same wonders George had with regard to the academy, he also had the burden of watching the finances. Naturally, he'd endured his fair share of stress during his time as George's personal assistant.

The added stress had also fallen on Mary's shoulders, and George noticed. Only a year ago, these added responsibilities would have been nothing to her, and she'd have laughed if George dared ask if she was managing alright. But now? He was worried.

He hadn't wanted to press before, but he'd begun noticing that she couldn't sleep at night. Like with her weight loss and lack of energy, she played it off and made George feel silly for daring to ask anything. And at the time, he'd *felt* silly. Here was this marvel of a woman, this oak in the midst of a thunderstorm, and he was worried about her? Truth be told, the thought wouldn't have even crossed his mind years ago, but now he was beginning to wonder if something wasn't wrong.

Chapter Twenty-Four

A cold, winter breeze sliced through the open window just before George had a chance to close it, and it felt like it chilled his bedroom at least fifteen degrees. He shivered against it and went back to the closet, tugging his warmest coat from the hanger.

He hurried down the stairs—well, he didn't so much "hurry" as he did attempt to hurry. Sometimes George forgot his age, and in his head, he was still a nimble and lithe thirty-year-old man.

He reached the bottom of the steps and smelled the dinner that Mary was making. He glanced in the kitchen on the way to the door and saw her pulling something from the oven. There was something about her movement that was off—like her arm was giving her trouble. She shook it out and set the dish on the stove.

"Mary?" he called. "Everything alright?"

She glanced over her shoulder. "Oh, yes. I've just got a bit of back and arm pain. It's nothing. I just took some ibuprofen so it should relax here pretty soon. Where are you headed in such a rush?"

George sighed. "James called. There's an issue with the computer lab. I don't know what he thinks I'm going to be able to do, but Lydia is meeting me there, so perhaps she can help solve the issue."

"Home for dinner?"

"Should be," George kissed his wife on the cheek. "I'll see you soon."

As promised, Lydia met him at the academy to figure out what the problem was. Lydia, the tech-savvy genius that she was, realized that the WIFI was simply down. She restarted the system, and the computer lab was back online within minutes. Now, James was an intelligent man, and George knew there was no way he hadn't noticed the simple issue. Lydia, however, was oblivious to poor James' attempts to spend more time with her.

Lydia came over for dinner, and the three shared a nice meal, complained about the chilly weather, and thanked the Lord for His daily blessings.

The next morning was Sunday. When George awoke, he saw Mary putting on a jacket out of the corner of his eye, and something was definitely off. Whatever pain she'd been experiencing yesterday must have intensified because she could barely manage the small movement.

George sat up in bed and rubbed his eyes. "Mary? Are you still in pain?"

She flinched a little but shook her head. "It's not a big deal."

"Maybe we should call Doctor Pritchard." he insisted.

She laughed. "It's the cold, George. The cold always does this to my joints."

Really? George had never noticed that, and by now, he knew that Mary was a master of deflection.

"Come on downstairs," she offered. "I picked up bagels yesterday. Easy, quick breakfast so we can get on to the service."

Despite her persistent denial, George felt that something wasn't right. He didn't bring anything up until the next day, though her pain was clearly increasing. This time, when George suggested calling Doctor Pritchard, she agreed.

George dialed the doctor's office and waited somewhat uncomfortably while it rang.

"Doctor Pritchard's office, this is Patricia speaking. How may I direct your call?"

George breathed a sigh of relief. "Hi, Patricia, this is George Müller. I'd like to—"

"Oh, good morning, Pastor George," exclaimed the overly cheerful receptionist in a lilting, southern accent. "I just finished reading your latest blog post yesterday. It's always so inspiring to see how God moves in your life. I don't know. I guess it sort of just makes us think that He's always watching out for the little guy—even me!"

George couldn't help but be slightly impatient. "That's lovely, Patricia, thank you. I need to speak to Doctor Pritchard. It's urgent."

"Doctor Pritchard is with a patient at the moment, but I'll have him give you a call as soon as he's finished."

George wanted to argue and remind her what "urgent" meant, but Mary gave him a look, and he shut his mouth. "Sure, thank you." He hung up the phone. "He's with a patient."

"That's alright," answered Mary with a shrug. "I'm sure it's nothing serious."

George hoped the same. He picked up his phone again. "I'll tell James to postpone my prayer meeting."

"Don't be ridiculous," Mary laughed. "Go to your congregation. I'll be just fine."

"I don't want to just leave you by yourself, Mary."

"I'll call Lydia," she assured him. "She can go with me to run some errands. I'll be fine. A few hours won't make a difference."

George still didn't like it, but he reluctantly nodded. "Okay. Call me if anything changes, please."

"Of course." She stood gingerly and kissed him on the forehead. "Have a good prayer meeting. I love you."

"Love you." He kissed her back and grabbed his bag as he headed for the door.

Though George felt uncomfortable the entire drive there, the Lord gave him some semblance of peace so that he was able to lead the assembly without being anxious. When the meeting was concluded, George said his goodbyes and went to retrieve his phone from his jacket.

His heart plummeted.

A text message from Lydia illuminated the screen. She'd had to rush Mary to the emergency room.

George broke every speed limit on his way to the hospital. He couldn't stop himself from imagining the worst. Even still, he chanted in his head, *The Lord is good and does good; all will be according to His own*

Fay

blessed character. Nothing but that which is good, like He is, can proceed from Him. If He pleases to allow this, it will be good, like Himself. What I have to do as His child is just be satisfied with what my Father does, that I may glorify Him.

He double parked in the parking lot, but he was obviously preoccupied and couldn't bring himself to realign the car. He ran into the waiting room, where he found Lydia wringing her hands.

"Dad," she exclaimed. She ran into his arms and hugged him tightly.

"Where's your mom?" he asked.

Lydia pulled back. "The doctors are with her now. They're running more tests. They're saying something about rheumatic fever with severe damage to the heart?" She shook her head. "I've been doing my research, but I don't know much. All the doctors have said is that it's rare in this day and age, but serious, but they won't tell me anything else."

George tried to process everything she was saying. "Okay. Have you spoken to Doctor Pritchard?"

She nodded. "Yes, I called him to tell him what was happening. He's looking into it to find out what's going on, but they aren't saying much to him either."

Over Lydia's shoulder, Doctor Pritchard materialized from one of the hallways. George spotted him and stepped around his daughter.

"How's Mary?" George quickly asked him, practically shouting it across the waiting room.

Doctor Pritchard had a bit more decorum and waited until he didn't have to shout to say, "She's stable for now, but they think she has rheumatic fever."

"They think?" What kind of doctors only *thought*?

"They're waiting on a few more tests to confirm the diagnosis."

George raked a hand through his hair. "How long will that take?"

"Probably a few more hours," replied Doctor Pritchard.

George nodded. "Okay, Lyds…settle in. Looks like we're going to be here for a while."

Doctor Pritchard returned to Mary's room while George and Lydia remained outside in the waiting room. The hours seemed to drag on, and Lydia's eyes didn't leave the clock as they waited for the test results to return. George found himself pacing at one point, so to take his mind off of his worry, he began to repeat the same thing he'd chanted to himself in the car.

The Lord was good. He was always good. He could only do good. And if He chose to bring Mary home, then it was all a part of His good, pleasing, and *perfect* will.

When George saw Doctor Pritchard walk through the doors at the end of the waiting room again, he knew he was just going to keep having to repeat that mantra if the look on the doctor's face was any indication.

"It is rheumatic fever with severe heart damage as we thought," confirmed the doctor.

George's shoulder's slumped greatly, and all of the breath seemed to depart from his lungs. His head felt light and a sharp pang erupted in his chest—a physical pain. He didn't know much about rheumatic fever—it's generally a third-world disease, but he could tell from the doctor's tone that it was not good.

"They want to admit her for treatment. They're worried because they've also found congenital problems with her heart. She's had these problems for a while, which makes the situation that much worse."

Lydia began softly crying on George's shoulder, unable to contain her worry any longer.

The Lord is good and does good. Nothing but that which is Good, like He is, can proceed from Him.

George had so many questions, but he couldn't verbalize them right now. He attempted to find his voice. "Thank you, Doctor Pritchard."

Lydia stepped up when her father couldn't. "Could you stay?" she asked. "We've met some of the doctors here and…they don't know us like you do. You've been our family doctor for a long time, and you have always taken such good care of us." At Doctor Pritchard's concerned expression, Lydia insisted further, saying, "Please. I know it's unorthodox, but maybe they can give you permissions in this hospital or something? You're a doctor too. You should be able to stay here."

George squinted his eyes shut. "Lyds," he whispered. "It's not about getting permission. Doctor Pritchard has other patients and a practice of his own to tend to. He—"

"Would be honored," Doctor Pritchard interjected. "George, your family has been close to my heart for years." He turned his gaze to Lydia. "Lydia, I'll ask the hospital for permission to stay and help on Mary's case. My other patients will understand." He set a hand on George's shoulder. "But for the time being, I think you two should head home.

They've sedated Mary, and she won't be waking up until tomorrow."

George wanted desperately to stay, but what good would it do? The doctors weren't going to let him in to see her, so he would be of no use to her there. That didn't stop him from feeling entirely helpless and useless as he drove home with Lydia. He wished he could be with his wife to wait by her side and comfort her, but he couldn't.

He dropped Lydia off back at the house and made a beeline for Cherry Hills. There, he practically slid into the gravel, causing a few of the children to sprint to their bedroom windows to see what all the commotion was. He avoided their inquisitive eyes as he made his way to Mary's office, where he immediately closed the door and sat down in her chair.

The feeling that washed over him was one of extreme emptiness and loneliness. He'd never been in her office before without her being there. It felt wrong, somehow. For the first time in the years they had been building Cherry Hills, Mary wasn't there.

On her wall, he noticed a calendar that she'd put up somewhat recently. She called it her "silent comforter," and the day's text was from Psalm 119:75. It read, "I know, O Lord, that your judgements are righteous, and that in faithfulness you have afflicted me." George read the words over and over again, willing them to sink into his soul and for his heart to receive them.

His head fell between his shoulders and into his hands as he mouthed the words over and over to himself. He needed to be strong, now more than ever, and he had a sense that a difficult time was upon him.

Chapter Twenty-Five

Waiting was agonizing. Finally, a nurse opened the door.

"Mr. Müller," she greeted him with a warm smile. "Mary is awake and ready for visitors."

Lydia sprang to her feet beside George.

"Now, before you go in," the nurse continued, "you should know that she's in quite a bit of pain. Rheumatic fever causes a lot of joint pain, so any sudden movements can be incredibly uncomfortable. Take things easy with her."

Lydia nodded quickly and was the first to hurry past the nurse and into Mary's room. Behind her, George thanked the nurse quietly before following his daughter into Mary's hospital room.

The moment he stepped inside, his eyes landed on his beautiful wife. She smiled at him when she saw him, but it seemed forced. He knew when she was putting on a tough face for him.

She didn't look well. Not only did she look weaker and less energetic than normal, but the machines she was hooked up to added another level of discomfort to her appearance.

Had her hair grayed more since George had last seen her? Her skin was pallid as well. Was that a new occurrence?

George stepped up to the bed and took her hand, kissing her on the forehead. "How is my darling wife?"

She hummed thoughtfully but offered him a small smile. "I've been better."

Lydia sniffed and wiped a tear from her eye. "Finally, they let us see you," she said with her mother's toughness.

Mary smiled. "I'm glad you're here." She tilted her head and studied her daughter. "Oh, honey, why are you crying?"

"Crying?" Lydia sniffled again. "I'm not crying."

She sat down on the edge of the bed.

Mary ran her fingers through her daughter's hair. "Oh, my sweet girl. Don't cry. I asked the Father to let me see the new academy buildings open, and in His gracious kindness, He fulfilled my desire. I'm ready, my love. You should be happy for me."

That's when it really hit George. He'd not truly understood the gravity of the situation until that moment.

Yesterday, when he'd been sitting in her office, he'd felt so alone, yet he'd comforted himself with the knowledge that it wouldn't be for long. Mary would recover and would return to her office at Cherry Hills Academy where the two would continue to touch the lives of children for many more years. In his mind, this was out of the blue…unexpected. She had always been such a workhorse and in perfect health. She had always been the one nagging him about his own wellbeing! How could she be giving up like this?

He pulled up a chair to sit beside her, stroking her hair. "It's not set in stone yet, love. Perhaps it isn't the Lord's will."

Mary smiled, seeming to understand his concern, and kissed his hand gently. "Perhaps it isn't. We'll have to wait and see."

George's heart ached in his chest, and all he could do was beg that if it was the Lord's will to leave Mary with him a bit longer, that God would heal her and return her to her work at Cherry Hills. Even still, he understood the situation plainly. Of course, he trusted in the Lord and would never have desired anything against His will, but that by no means meant that his sorrows didn't run deep and leave painful scars.

A misconception that George believed many held about his life was that it was without troubles, since he had so much faith. He knew some people assumed that when he lost someone, he was always just immediately comforted by God and able to maintain his perspective. But that wasn't the case. George was human, and grief struck him the same way it did anyone else. He had great hope, but it took time and prayer to maintain that hope, especially in darkness as great as this.

He lay his head on his wife's hospital bed and did his best to quell the turning of his stomach and the aching of his heart. He inwardly repeated over and over, *Your will be done*, until Mary finally fell asleep.

The next few days seemed to crawl by at an agonizingly slow pace. George and Lydia visited Mary daily, spending as much time with her as the hospital would allow before they knew they had to go home and attend to other areas of their lives. Mary's health hadn't yet returned to her, and she still seemed so weak. In the few hours he had with her while she was awake, he would read scripture to her and talk about his day at Cherry Hills. When she had the strength to ask questions, she would ask about the children to see how they were faring without her. Of course, George had to tell her that they were barely surviving without her constant aid, which elicited a smile that warmed his heart.

Night after night, George slept alone in the bed they once shared. It felt cold. He'd never realized how much heat she'd put off until she was gone. *No,* he had realized. It wasn't *heat,* per se, but warmth. There was a difference.

Heat was a temperature. Warmth was a feeling—a personality, a presence, a spirit. Mary had that warmth about her. As fiery and fierce as she had been, she was also compassionate, kind, and loving. She was a walking contradiction, brimming with ferocity for those she loved and kindness even for those who deserved none. It was that warmth he already missed the most.

It was in moments like these and when he sat beside her hospital bed—and, honestly, any time he thought about her—that he was in the most pain. It was imagining what life had been like with her and recognizing the small pleasures he'd taken for granted that really struck a chord deep inside of him.

He leaned heavily on the Father. In one journal entry, he wrote: "I will walk upright and therefore my Father will withhold nothing that is good for me. If, therefore, the restoration of my dearest Mary is good for me, it will surely be given; otherwise, I have to seek to glorify God by submitting to his will."

He couldn't help but think of the song, *It is Well with My Soul*. He prayed that the Lord would let it be well with his soul, regardless of the outcome.

Chapter Twenty-Six

Doctor Pritchard was good about keeping George apprised as to Mary's condition. He made several suggestions regarding her medical care, including bringing in another professional by the name of Doctor Black to consult on her case.

Doctor Black was renowned when it came to the more uncommon illnesses like rheumatic fever, and Doctor Pritchard thought she was just the woman to bring in on Mary's case. She was scheduled to arrive at the hospital on Saturday morning, and George refused to be late. He barely ate breakfast before he rushed out the door, Lydia close on his heels.

During the drive to the hospital, George sat in the passenger seat in somewhat of a daze. He stared out the windshield almost mindlessly, watching the winter scenery as it passed by outside. The trees were still bare, and the grasses still looked dead and colorless. It would be another couple of months before the weather began to allow for growth and brighter colors.

Lydia remained quiet as well. It seemed she was deep in thought as she drove, perhaps wondering the same thing George was: what would Doctor Black say? George's insides were twisted into knots, and the English muffin he'd barely been able to choke down now felt rotten in his stomach.

He kept trying to convince himself that no matter what happened, it was for the best and for his betterment. That the Lord wouldn't give him a trial he couldn't bear with the Lord's help. He also understood that he and Mary were getting older, and no one was meant to live forever.

It didn't make the idea of losing her any easier.

He tried not to be selfish. He tried to remind himself that Mary was in constant pain and that her health had evidently been failing her for years, but a small part of him was still very selfish…and he didn't want to let her go.

The hospital parking lot was mostly empty, which allowed for George and Lydia to get a spot close to the front. As they got out of the car, Doctor Pritchard called George's cell. George fumbled with his phone for a couple seconds before Lydia took it and answered it for him.

"Good morning, Doctor Pritchard," she said. "This is Lydia."

George couldn't hear what was being said on the other line; all he could hear were Lydia's thoughtful hums and *uh-huh*s.

"Okay, I'll let Dad know. Thanks." She hung up the phone and handed it back to George. "Doctor Pritchard isn't here quite yet, but he said we're welcome to go on in and sit with Mom. Doctor Black is meeting him here at the hospital, so we should have a few minutes with her before either of them gets here."

George breathed a small sigh of relief. As much as he wanted to hear Doctor Black's thoughts, he was also terrified of them. He was more than grateful to have some time alone with his family before their small semblance of peace and hope might be shattered.

As they walked through the hospital, George and Lydia greeted the nurses and candy-stripers who had been helpful and kind to them along the way. Silence fell over them again as they entered the elevator and rode up for four floors before the *ding* vibrated through the quiet air.

Mary's floor was busy on Saturday. Everyone had visitors. George couldn't help but notice that the other patients seemed to be doing better. The young girl who had been in the ICU for the past several days? She was walking around her room and joking with her boyfriend and mother. The man who had been in a car accident? He also looked like he was on the mend.

It was hard not to be slightly jealous of them and their hope, but George banished those thoughts and replaced them with his mantra.

The Lord is good and does good. Nothing but that which is Good, like He is, can proceed from Him.

Lydia turned the corner and opened Mary's door. "Hi, Mom," she greeted cheerily, and it was the lightest her tone had been all morning. It amazed George...how quickly Lydia could change her attitude.

Mary smiled weakly at her baby girl, and even in her frail state, George swore she'd never looked more beautiful.

The nurses had opened the drapes to allow sunlight into the oth-

Fay

erwise dull hospital room. It was unseasonably bright and sunny outside, which didn't match the mood of the day whatsoever. George felt it made Mary look somewhat healthier.

"Good morning, darling," he said as he kissed her forehead. He tried to sound as cheerful as Lydia, though he knew he wasn't nearly as skilled as his daughter at hiding his emotions.

"How is my sweet family?" Mary asked.

"We're good, Mom," Lydia answered. "How are you feeling?"

Mary reached for Lydia's hand, and George couldn't help but notice how weak the effort was. A pang of anguish struck him in the chest.

"I'm happy now," she answered.

"Are they taking good care of you?" George questioned, even though he knew the answer. Everyone at the hospital had been beyond helpful and kind to them, from the doctors to the nurses and orderlies. He just wanted to get Mary talking. Hearing her voice somehow made it less painful.

"Oh, absolutely," replied Mary. "I'm in the best of hands." She glanced over George's shoulder, and he looked behind him to see one of the nurses looking in. The young nurse smiled and waved before moving on to another room.

Mary looked back at George. "Tell me about home."

Lydia immediately took the opportunity and launched into stories about the academy. George quickly joined in, trying to think of the cutest and funniest stories to share with her. They told her of the night before, when one of the boys had pulled a prank on a teacher, and they told her about the clogged toilet that James had to remedy while George was preoccupied with Mary's condition—although they omitted that last bit.

Mary seemed to enjoy hearing the stories. It was refreshing to see her eyes twinkle with amusement and to even hear a quiet laugh every now and again.

About twenty minutes in, George's phone buzzed. He glanced down at the screen. A text from Doctor Pritchard flashed on the lock screen. He was arriving soon. George swallowed, and suddenly, *not* telling Mary about Doctor Black seemed like a very bad idea. But seeing as though they were about to walk in, George decided now was as good a time as any.

"Oh, by the way," he said, trying to sound nonchalant. "Doctor Pritchard is about to be here. He's bringing a colleague with him." He tried to hide his wince.

Mary's countenance fell, and her eyes narrowed on her husband. She gave him *The Look*, the one she probably should have trademarked by now. So George did all he knew to do…he plastered a massive smile on his face and pretended to be oblivious to the displeasure rolling off her in waves.

"Oh?" she questioned. "What for?"

Lydia jumped in to rescue George. "Doctor Black has a lot of experience with cases like yours, Mom. She's brilliant. Doctor Pritchard just wanted a second opinion."

Mary sighed and looked back at George. "I don't want to be poked and prodded anymore. I'm tired. I'm ready to go home."

"I know it's not easy, but please let Doctor Black take a look at you. For us." George had absolutely no problem admitting that he wasn't

Fay

above begging. "If you go home now, you're not going to get any better."

She shook her head, and tears welled in her eyes. "No, George. I want to go *home*," she repeated, her voice cracking.

Immediately, George knew what she meant. He could tell by the look on her face, and tears began to sting his eyes. She was giving up. She was done. George couldn't say a word…he was speechless.

The tears Lydia refused to let fall in the car now rolled over her cheeks. "Mom, no…you don't even know what she'll say. Maybe there's some way she can help you," she insisted.

Mary smiled at her daughter. "Oh, my strong girl," she intoned softly. "I love you so much. So for you I will wait. I'll hear this Doctor Black out. And when she says there is nothing left to be done, I want to go home."

Lydia looked up at George pleadingly, but he knew better than anyone that there was nothing he could say or do. He felt as though his chest was cracking open as he held his wife's hand.

It's not her time, the selfish part of him chanted. *It's not her time!* But he recognized that all of life is but a moment and asked God for grace to make it through this time. The noise in his head began to quiet somewhat.

The Lord is good and does good. Nothing but that which is Good, like He is, can proceed from Him.

He had a feeling he'd need this mantra for a very long time.

Mary squeezed both their hands at the same time. "Promise me that if Doctor Black says there is nothing left to be done, that you'll let me go home."

George summoned his courage and prayed for a voice to speak so that he could finally say, "I promise," before Mary could change her mind.

Mary smiled, seemingly at peace. "Good. Now, tell me more about the children."

Lydia cleared her throat and sat back in her chair, wiping the tears from her eyes. She laughed somewhat uncomfortably before saying, "Umm…right…Oh, did I tell you that little Marissa finally lost her tooth? Yeah, not the prettiest thing. One of the boys actually tied a string to an arrow and—"

Mary squeezed her eyes shut. "Don't tell me."

Lydia laughed. "I know. Horrible."

Chapter Twenty-Seven

Doctor Black was a short Korean woman with almond-shaped eyes and coils of long, dark hair. She looked way too young to be a specialist in her field. George thought there was no way she could be over thirty-five, but she did seem very knowledgeable and held herself the way a sixty-year-old might. George imagined this was what was epitomized as an "old soul."

"Hi, Mary," Doctor Black said as she walked in the room with Doctor Pritchard. "My name is Doctor Black. I'm here to take a look at your case. How are you feeling today?"

Mary flashed her a tight smile. "About as well as I look, Doctor."

Doctor Black smiled sadly. "I understand. I know it's not what you want to hear, but if you'll permit me, I'd like to run a few more tests."

Mary took in a deep breath, and George knew she was ready to argue, which George understood. From the very beginning, Mary's condition had required a myriad of tests and exams, none of which were physically comfortable. It was frustrating that every new round of doctors who were brought in wanted to run their *own* tests to confirm what the other doctors already had.

Lydia scooted closer to her mother's bedside and looked at her pleadingly.

"Very well," replied Mary with a huff. "But I can promise you, there's no point."

"That's quite the bleak spirit, Mary," admonished Doctor Black. "A positive attitude can do wonders. Have a little faith."

"Oh, I have plenty of faith, Doctor Black," Mary answered with one of those smiles she wore when she knew she was about to get on someone's bad side. "I just don't place it in you."

George knew he shouldn't laugh…that didn't stop him, though. He chuckled under his breath, which he immediately tried to cover up under a cough. "Allergies," he muttered around another half chuckle, half cough.

"Winter allergies?" Lydia questioned knowingly.

He shook his head to quiet her and returned his attention to the doctors. "As confident as my wife is, we're happy to run more tests. Anything you think, Doctor Black."

Doctor Black smiled, but her smile didn't reach her eyes. She may have been a bit offended by Mary's remark, but there was nothing George could do about that. "Great. Let's get these tests over with then, shall we?" She waved at the orderlies loitering in the doorway, and they rushed inside.

George and Lydia backed away as they began to prep Mary to

Fay

undergo more tests. When they started to wheel her out of the room, George caught her hand and flashed her a comforting smile.

"We'll be waiting here when you get back."

She nodded. "I love you."

George fought the urge to squeeze her hand. "I love you."

Seeing her this way—knowing that if he *did* squeeze her hand, it would cause her so much pain—created a hollow place in his chest where the realization began to sink in. She was right. It was his Mary's time to go home. And as much faith as he had in the Lord, as much as he wanted to be at peace with it, it made him sick to his stomach.

He released her, and the orderlies rolled her away. Doctor Black then stepped up to him as he watched his wife be wheeled around the corner and out of sight.

"The tests should take us a few hours," explained the doctor. "We'll notify you once they're complete."

George rocked back and forth on his heels, thinking. He nodded abruptly. "We'll just wait here."

"George," Doctor Pritchard stepped in, placing a hand on his shoulder. "You don't want to sit in the waiting room for hours. Get out. It's a nice enough day. There's a park nearby. Why don't you and Lydia go get yourselves some sandwiches from the cafeteria and have a picnic?"

The idea of purchasing hospital food and going on a merry little picnic—the very thing George had done with Mary on their first date—sounded appalling to him, but one look at Lydia told him she didn't want to wait around in a cold, stale waiting room while doctors stuck needles in her mother.

George nodded somberly. "You're right." He smiled at Lydia. "What do you say we run across the street and go to the deli? James has great things to say about their sandwiches."

Lydia swiped at a rebel tear and nodded, jumping to her feet. She cleared her throat of sadness and said, "Yep. Sounds good."

The "nice enough" day turned out to be pretty chilly. To be honest, George hadn't really noticed the cold on his drive to the hospital that morning. Noticing the temperature was beyond his capabilities right now. Still, he and Lydia made the best of it. Instead of sandwiches, they bought soup and hot cocoa and then went across the street to a home goods store where they bought a fluffy, yellow blanket to bundle up in. Yellow was probably George's *least* favorite color, but Lydia convinced him that it was the color of hope, and maybe it would do them some good.

They sat in the park together and sipped on their soup, mostly in silence. The birds chirped quietly, and the few people that were out and about looked like hospital patients trying to get a breath of fresh air beyond the concrete walls. Somehow the park didn't seem much more cheerful than the waiting room.

Lydia picked at her soup somberly. George knew that if he pressed, she'd probably burst into tears and then be *annoyed* that she'd burst into tears, so he left it alone. He also knew that if he opened his mouth, he'd likely admit that he now believed as Mary did—that it was her time to go home—and he couldn't bring himself to take away the hope Lydia clung to so tightly.

When the sun finally set and evening began to roll in, George received a call from the hospital. The results were in.

When they arrived back at the hospital, a receptionist showed them to a private room where they waited for the doctors to give them the news. Lydia clutched George's hand, her foot tapping on the carpeted floor.

Finally, after what seemed like hours, Doctor Black and Doctor Pritchard entered. George and Lydia stood quickly.

"George," Doctor Black greeted them. She smiled, but it wasn't one of those good and cheery smiles. "Lydia."

The two doctors took seats across from them.

George looked at Doctor Black. "I'm ready. Whatever you have to say, please say it."

Doctor Black inclined her head and looked down at her clipboard. "Mary's tests don't look good. Her enlarged heart has severely exacerbated the condition."

"Okay," Lydia began. "What does that mean?"

Doctor Black's gaze met Lydia's, and it was the first time George noticed a glimmer of humanity in those dark, intelligent eyes. "I'm very sorry to say that this is beyond my capabilities."

Lydia's lip quivered. "So…there's nothing you can do?"

Doctor Black sighed as though she wished she could deliver better news. "Normally, pharmaceuticals would be able to remedy this. In your mother's case, however, her organs are too stressed and even damaged. I'm afraid the treatment she would have to undergo would do more harm than good, and it would rob you of what precious, little time she has left with you."

Lydia hiccuped and nodded, trying to hold it together, but she was already losing it. George needed to make sure she was taken care of. He stood quickly and shook Doctor Pritchard's hand, followed by Doctor Black's.

"Thank you very much," he said. "Both of you. You've taken such good care of her, and we appreciate your every effort to help her."

"It was my pleasure," answered Doctor Black.

"George," Doctor Pritchard began. "Would you like to take Mary home, or would you like to stay with her here?"

Lydia sobbed into her sleeves, too much of a mess to get anything out, but it sounded like she was muttering "home."

"We'd like to bring her home," replied George.

Chapter Twenty-Eight

Relocating Mary was a difficult and painful experience. She was suffering so greatly that Doctor Pritchard had to arrange for an ambulance to take her home. George flinched every time Mary did, and he could barely stand to watch the paramedics bring her up to her bed, as painful as it looked. But once she was tucked into her own warm bed, the tension seemed to seep out of her. She melted into the mattress, and she looked far more peaceful.

It was good that Lydia had gone back to her own house to pack a bag, because if she'd been there to witness the pain her mother was in, George wasn't sure she'd be able to handle it. When she did finally arrive at the house, she tossed her bags into her old room and immediately went to sit by her mother's side while George spoke with Doctor Pritchard in the foyer. Doctor Pritchard gave him Mary's medication and the dosages she'd need.

"These should numb her pain substantially," the doctor explained.

"I'm so sorry I couldn't do more."

George nodded. "No, I understand. Thank you, Doctor Pritchard."

"Of course. I'm here if you need anything." He stepped outside and followed the paramedics back to the ambulance.

George closed the door and stood in place for a few moments before gathering himself. The house echoed with silence, and it was a haunting feeling. He looked up, his gaze finding the kitchen, and he remembered all the times he came back from the academy to see her juggling paperwork and phone calls, all while cooking the family a mouthwatering dinner.

Hanging on the walls were pictures of their family throughout the years. As he walked down the hall, admiring each one, he saw their wedding photo. Mary had looked so beautiful in her simple, elegant dress, royal blue flowers woven into the delicate twists of her dark hair.

Beside that photo hung one of Mary and Lydia, when Lydia was no more than a year old. Baby Lydia played on the ground while Mary was trying to hold her up to get her to walk. Mary had looked up and seen the camera at the exact time George took the photo, so her expression had been one of feigned frustration. He remembered that moment and how Mary had burst into laughter as soon as the camera flash went off.

Then came the photos of Lydia's graduation and her college move-in day, when George and Mary helped her get settled into her own apartment.

Looking at these photos, one might think that George was quite

Fay

the photographer, but he knew himself to have a terrible eye for things like this. It was all his girls—it was all Mary.

Somehow she managed to look beautiful in every photo, even when her brow was furrowed or when she wasn't prepared. Each photo radiated with life, joy, and peace.

When he reached the end of the hall and had no more photos to distract himself with, he finally gathered the courage to head up the stairs. With every step, he felt a piece of his heart breaking away and turning to ash.

Mary and Lydia were still talking when George entered the room, though Lydia was consuming most of the conversation.

"Feeling any better?" he interrupted.

Mary's sigh seemed contented. "Much," she murmured. "My bed is far more comfortable than the hospital's."

George chuckled. "I'll bet."

Together, Lydia and George regaled Mary with more stories from the academy and tried to entertain her the best they could, but soon she grew tired and needed her rest. Lydia kissed her on the cheek, and George nearly had to shoo her out of the room to let Mary get some sleep. But for George? Sleep was not on the agenda.

He spent most of the night awake beside his wife, sitting in the adjacent armchair just watching her breathe. He tried to bask in her presence and soak up the last bit of warmth and light she had to offer. He didn't want to miss a single moment.

He drifted off to sleep at some point during the night, and when he woke the next morning, Mary was already deep in conversation with

Lydia. The two were prattling on about academy business, and when it became clear that George was awake, Mary turned to him and said, "I'm ready to go to Cherry Hills now."

George blinked. "I'm sorry, I'm not fully awake yet. What did you say?"

"George, you heard me," Mary insisted. "I'd like to go see the children."

Was she serious? They'd barely gotten her *here*. "That's too far of a trip for you. You're too weak. Why don't I just tell you—"

"I know whether or not I'm strong enough, my love. I assure you, I have enough strength to get me to the academy."

George sighed and looked at Lydia, who seemed just as apprehensive as he was. He had no choice but to agree. What else was he going to do? Deny his wife? That had never gone well for him in the past. Besides, Mary's life revolved around those children. She loved them as if they were her own. He couldn't bear to tell her that she couldn't see them one last time.

"Well," George began, thinking. "I suppose we could call someone to help."

"Call James," Mary suggested. "He can carry me to the car."

George was skeptical, but he glanced at Lydia, who nodded in understanding. "I'll call James," she whispered as she ducked out of the room.

Mary immediately turned and gave George the smuggest smile she could muster. "That man's good for her." She eyed George expectantly.

Fay

"And what exactly is that look for?"

"Well, I expect you to do something about it when I'm gone."

George scoffed. "Darling, you know that I love you with all of my heart, but I'm not about to meddle in my daughter's romantic life."

Mary softened some and nodded. "I just…worry. I'm not sure what will become of her when I'm gone. I don't want Lydia to stop living her own life because she doesn't want you to be alone."

That quieted George. He knew she was right. He was often so caught up in the academy's affairs that he'd forget others had lives as well. Even his own daughter. And he didn't want to steal her life away from her—not when she had so much to live.

"Okay," George replied. "I'll make sure she finds her own path, my dear."

A few moments later, Lydia returned, phone in hand. "James will be here in twenty minutes." She began rifling through Mary's things until she produced a sweater. She draped it over her mother's shoulders after George helped Mary sit up.

Lydia made some breakfast for Mary while they waited, and George took the time to just hold his wife. By the time Mary was finished eating—or, rather, picking at—her oatmeal and fruit, James had arrived. Lydia let him inside, and the two entered Mary's room a few minutes later.

James smiled sadly upon seeing Mary. He stepped up to the bed and kissed her on the forehead. "Glad to see you back in your own surroundings."

She nodded. "Me too. I'll be happier when I can be with the children."

"No problem," James replied. He swept her up into his arms and easily carried her out to the car, where Lydia waited. It wasn't long before Mary was resting comfortably in the back seat, with Lydia supporting her head.

The drive was noisy, which George worried wouldn't be good for Mary, but she seemed to be eating it up. James rambled about the academy's dealings and how the children were faring for nearly the entire drive. As they neared Cherry Hills, however, George called James' attention back to the task at hand.

"James, is there a wheelchair or something we can use to take Mary around?"

"Oh, absolutely," James answered. "I've already spoken to the head nurse, Lizzie, at building two. She should be—Yep, there she is." He pointed at her through the window as they pulled into the lot. He waved at her, and she waved back.

Lizzie, a red-haired, thirty-three-year-old nurse, stood on the porch of the second facility, wheelchair in front of her. Of course, James had everything arranged. He was excellent at things like that.

James helped Mary into the wheelchair while Lydia laid a blanket in her lap. George winced with every movement, silently praying they didn't jostle her too much, but Mary didn't protest at all.

Once settled into her chair, she smiled up at James and said, "Now where are the children?"

"Oh, don't you worry," James answered, wheeling Mary toward the entrance of building three. "We'll take you to them."

Fay

George, Lydia, and Lizzie followed in their wake. They entered the building, which seemed entirely too quiet. When James turned toward the cafeteria, George glanced quizzically at Lizzie, who just smiled and winked. She rushed ahead to open the doors…and George's heart skipped a beat.

The furniture—tables, chairs, trash bins—had all been cleared away, and the doors to the adjoining rooms opened. All of the children who were old enough to understand today's significance were gathered together in the cafeteria waiting for Mary, all holding handmade signs bearing the same message: *We love you, Mrs. M!*

Tears immediately flooded Mary's eyes, and she fanned her face. "Oh, you're making me cry," she sniffled. "You all look so wonderful. Come closer and let me see you!"

George was amazed at how well behaved the children were being. He couldn't believe how slowly and quietly they approached his wife.

James came to stand beside George, watching the scene unfold.

"How did…?" George couldn't manage to finish his sentence.

"I explained the circumstances to them," James replied. "They deserved to know, and I thought they'd be a bit gentler if they understood."

In that moment, George had never been more grateful for James.

Mary reached for each child's hand as they approached her, and they held on as tightly as they dared. George couldn't overhear what any of them were saying, but judging by the look on Mary's face, it was nothing but appreciation for all that Mary had done.

Then came Diana. Diana was barely fourteen years old and had been glued to Mary's side since she'd arrived at the academy six years ago. George could tell she was trying valiantly to hold back the tears as she stepped up to Mary, sniffling and wiping at her eyes.

"Oh," Mary crooned, reaching for her. "My sweet girl. I'm thrilled you're here!"

Diana knelt down on her knees and laid her head in Mary's lap while Mary played with her hair.

"I'm going to miss you so much," she whispered softly.

Mary sighed. "I know. I'll miss you too. But I'll be with our Lord, and I'll always be watching over you."

Diana looked up through red-rimmed eyes. "Promise?"

Mary kissed her forehead. "I promise."

Diana's lip trembled. "Thank you."

"For what?"

"For being my mom."

George had to swallow hard to keep the tears from flowing freely. He was prepared to wheel Mary out then, ending on that high note, when he heard a single voice begin to ring out in the group.

> *"One is kind above all others,*
> *O how He loves!*
> *His is love beyond a brother's;*
> *O how He loves!*
> *Earthly friends may fall and leave thee,*
> *One day kind, the next day grieve thee;*
> *But this Friend will ne'er deceive thee;*

Fay

O how He loves!"

The single child singing was then joined by others, their voices intermingling and rising up with power and love. George could barely believe his ears as he stepped forward, listening to the hymn as the children sang.

"'Tis eternal life to know Him,
O how He loves!
Think, oh think, how much we owe Him,
O how He loves!
With His precious blood He bought us,
In the wilderness He sought us
To His fold He safely brought us,
O how He loves!"

George couldn't look away, and he did his best not to glance at Lydia or Mary, knowing he'd burst into tears at the mere sight of them. Instead, he basked in the beautiful sound of their voices.

A sniffle drew George's attention away from the children, and he finally looked to his left to find that Mary was openly crying. Tears streamed down her cheeks, but they weren't tears of sorrow—they were tears of gratitude. George could no longer contain his own tears, and he found himself breaking down as well.

"Love this Friend: He longs to save thee;

Let the Children Come

O how He loves!
All through life He will not leave thee;
O how He loves!
Think no more of friendships hollow;
Take His easy yoke and follow;
Jesus carries all thy sorrow;
O how He loves!"

Mary reached for George's hand, and he grasped hers. He was overwhelmed by the feeling of awe, as if the Lord's very presence was among them.

"All thy sins shall be forgiven;
O how He loves!
Backward shall thy foes be driven;
O how He loves!
Best of blessings He'll provide thee;
Naught but good shall e'er betide thee;
Safe to glory He will guide thee;
O how He loves!"

When the hymn ended, it was so silent that you could hear a pin drop. Something incredible had taken place. George's heart swelled with joy, warmth, and a happiness so pure and true that he could barely contain it.

Fay

Mary winced as James lay her back in her bed. By the grace of God, George managed not to snap at his assistant. Logically, he knew that James was being extraordinarily gentle and that Mary was just extremely fragile, but it was hard to see, nonetheless.

Lydia tucked her in. "How about a cup of hot tea, Mom?"

Mary nodded. "That'd be lovely," she whispered.

Lydia hurried out of the room.

"Mary," James began. "You know you've always been my favorite Müller," he joked with a smile. "I'm blessed to know you."

Mary's eyes glistened with tears. "Thank you, love. You keep looking after this husband of mine, you hear?"

James nodded. "I hear."

George did his best to smile. "I'll walk you out, James."

He started for the door, but Mary caught him. "George, darling?" She hesitated. "Call my sisters, please."

The words made his heart ache because he knew what that meant. He knew it was time. But he took in a deep breath, prayed for strength and peace, and nodded. "Of course."

George walked James to the door, where his assistant somberly bid him farewell. Then, George made the harrowing call to Berta and Georgina, Mary's two living sisters. They said that they'd get there as soon as they could, and George desperately hoped that "soon" wouldn't be too late.

George returned to Mary's bedroom, where Lydia was letting Mary sip her tea from a spoon. It took every bit of strength George had not to intervene when he saw how difficult it was for her to swallow. He settled into the chair beside them and held Mary's hand.

Over the next thirty minutes, George alternated between reading scripture and reading from one of Mary's favorite novels to get her mind off the pain. Finally, the doorbell rang, and George went downstairs to greet Georgina and Berta.

He opened the door to find Mary's sisters huddled in the cold, tears glistening in their eyes.

Berta was a short woman—much shorter than Mary—and was definitely a bit on the heavy side, but ever since George had known her, Berta had possessed an unearthly confidence. Despite those who ridiculed her when she was younger, she'd turned into a strong, commandeering woman, just like her sister, Mary.

Georgina, on the other hand, was the picture of delicate femininity and civility. Her vivid, green eyes always seemed so gentle and kind. According to Mary, she'd taken after their father in that regard. She was the youngest sister—daddy's little girl—and she carried herself as such.

"Hi, George," Georgina greeted him, stepping inside and giving him a warm hug. She swatted at her tears. "Sorry, we're a bit of a mess right now."

Berta stepped inside as well, closing the door behind her. "How is May-May?"

May-May. Under different circumstances, George might've chuckled. He'd forgotten all about the nickname. Though Mary was still close with her sisters, it was difficult for them to make the drive to Cherry Hills Academy, so he didn't see them often. He'd only heard them call her that nickname once or twice. He'd wondered about the nickname, and Mary told him that Georgina started it. Her youngest sister couldn't pronounce her R's properly when she was a toddler, hence Mary became May, and then May became May-May. It sort of stuck. Eventually everyone—including their parents—called her May-May. Though Mary used to resent it because it made her feel childish, she grew to adore the fact that her sisters had an endearing nickname for her.

Hearing the nickname now was heartbreaking. He knew how much he would suffer from Mary's loss, but he'd selfishly forgotten about her dear sisters who loved her so much.

George hoped that his expression didn't belie his words. "She's doing well. You arrived just in time."

Georgina nodded shakily and reached for Berta's hand, searching for comfort and security. Berta squeezed her hand.

"Let's go see her, then," Berta answered.

George took their thick coats and hung them up while the sisters made their way upstairs.

Mary's room was quiet when George reentered. Lydia sat at the foot of the bed, rearranging her mother's blankets. Georgina and Berta had taken seats along one side of the bed, leaning over their sister and no doubt examining her condition. Though George couldn't see their faces, he knew there were tears in their eyes.

"May-May?" whispered Georgina. "It's Georgina and Berta."

Berta reached out and stroked her sister's brow gently. "We're here, darling."

Mary's eyes fluttered open but only barely. George watched from the doorway to give the women their privacy, but when he saw how much of a struggle each breath was for Mary, he found that he could barely breathe.

She was fine only moments ago, he thought, unable to believe what he was seeing. How had she worsened so quickly?

"Oh, honey," Berta crooned softly. "No, you don't need to say anything. We love you, and we're here."

Georgina looked over her shoulder. "George, come sit with us."

George swallowed and gingerly began to close the distance between them. He sat opposite the sisters at Mary's bedside. Mary turned and gazed at him softly, her eyes losing their vitality by the moment. It was heartbreaking to see the life being drained from such a lively woman, so when she reached for his hand, he grasped it as if he would otherwise drown.

He could tell that she was doing everything she could to cling to life, and he couldn't imagine the pain she was in. Lydia scooted closer and laid her head on her mother's lap while Mary moved her free hand as though she wanted to stroke her grieving daughter's hair—but was too weak. Lydia began to cry softly into the blanket.

He brought Mary's hand to his lips and kissed it. "My beautiful, courageous prayer warrior. You have been the love of my life." George could feel his own voice trembling.

Mary exhaled a contented sigh, and George thought he saw a smile cross her face, so he continued.

"I've loved you since the moment I saw you. I'm not sure I ever told you that, but when you stumbled into that room after chasing your nephew around the house…I fell. I've loved you every minute of every day since." George brushed her hair behind her ear gently. "I'll miss you dearly. But you can go now."

Georgina sniffled, and a tear rolled down her cheek, splashing onto the comforter. "Yes, May-May," she replied. "Just know that we love you so much, and it's alright for you to move on to heaven now."

Lydia sat up then. "Momma, it's Lydia," she began quietly. "I just want you to know that you've been the most wonderful mother I could have ever hoped for. You've taught me what it means to be a strong woman and the value of prayer. I'll always be grateful to you for that. And Dad's right…I'll miss you so much. But I know that this is God's will, and I'm ready to accept it. I love you, Momma."

Mary smiled and turned her face back to George, who was becoming emotional himself. She squeezed his hand with what he imagined must have been all of her might, though it was with barely any strength at all.

"I know," he whispered, his voice thick with emotion. "I love you, too."

It was difficult to watch as her breathing became labored. It made George's heart ache miserably, and he wished he could do something to ease her pain, but all he could do was sit and pray with her.

In her final moments, Mary was surrounded by those most dear to her. George held her hand, Lydia lay her head on her mother's lap, and her sisters sat by her side. George knew she was suffering, but he hoped that their presence helped her.

The moment she breathed her last breath, Lydia broke into sobs, clutching her mother's body.

His beloved wife—his companion who was meant to be with him forever—had left him. It was crushing, but he never once doubted that it was the Lord's will and that God was *good*. Though tears streamed down his face as he grieved his loss, he managed to breathe a prayer of gratitude. He thanked the Lord for His gift in Mary and for bringing her home, where she'd no longer be in pain.

There would always be a part of him missing, but that's what it meant to be a life partner to someone—to be a spouse of forty years. He'd never think of her without missing her, but that didn't mean he would ever resent God for His decision.

Chapter Twenty-Nine

George's throat felt so thick that he wasn't sure he'd be able to get any words out. He could feel that his eyes were puffy, and he imagined that even those in the back pews would be able to see the evidence of his grief.

He pulled his suit jacket on. Its fit had loosened, he realized. Mary would have chastised him. He'd been so focused on the failing health of his wife that he'd completely forgotten to eat. He vaguely remembered how he'd felt in the weeks following the death of his mother when he was a child, and he recalled the same feeling then—a feeling of emptiness in his stomach, one that is impossible to fill.

Mary's death didn't leave him feeling quite so empty. The Lord had kept His promise and comforted George during the night—the time when he missed his wife most terribly. Unfortunately, it seemed the Good Lord had forgotten to remind George to eat. That… or George just wasn't listening hard enough.

He buttoned his coat and turned to look at himself in the mirror. Yep, his eyes were definitely rimmed with a puffy redness. There wasn't any doubt that his congregation would notice, but he didn't mind.

He took in a deep breath and closed his eyes, sending up a silent prayer.

A knock pulled him back to the present moment. He looked over his shoulder and saw Lydia standing in the doorway. For a moment, he almost thought she was Mary, and it took his breath away.

She was even wearing one of Mary's old black dresses. He'd never realized just how alike they looked, and for the first time, he understood that perhaps the Lord had designed Lydia that way for this very reason. To be George's reminder of Mary.

Lydia smiled sadly, holding the door open. "You ready to do this?"

He sighed. "Yes."

Together, they walked out the doors and into the sanctuary.

The aisles were packed with Mary's friends, companions, and even people who had just met her in passing. Mary had been one of those people who'd never met a stranger, and though she had a bit of a spitfire attitude that might've occasionally intimidated people or rubbed them the wrong way, she was still beloved by all who knew her.

About 2,000 Cherry Hills children and orphans had come as well, along with some of the kids who had aged out of the ministry. Because there wasn't room for everyone in the sanctuary, many of them crowded around the television screens in the lobby and even outside. It was standing room only, with people packed in shoulder to shoulder. A fitting tes-

Fay

tament to Mary's life and impact on others.

Seeing all of the mourners who had gathered to celebrate in Mary's life… it was comforting to George. He smiled and shook hands with everyone, thanking people for being there. He saw Sarah Craik, who—with tears in her eyes—hugged him and shared her condolences, along with her belief that Mary was where she was always meant to be.

Across the room, George spotted Lydia again. He liked to keep an eye on her these days. She had taken Mary's death hard, and it took lots of prayer and time alone for her to come to terms with the Lord's will. Lydia assured George that she'd finally made peace with it, however, and it seemed true.

George noticed Lydia smiling with her friends, taking comfort in their presence. It was good to see her liveliness returning. Mary would have hated to see her only child's fiery spirit slowly lose its flame.

He watched as James entered Lydia's group of friends, and one by one the others trickled away to their seats until it was just the two of them standing there. James stepped closer to Lydia and said something with a kind and concerned look on his face. Though George couldn't hear what James said, he imagined it was comforting, because Lydia threw her arms around him and leaned into an embrace.

George smiled. He knew Mary was probably leaning on an elbow in heaven, looking down and thinking, *Told you so.*

Someone lightly touched George's arm, and he turned to see a familiar face. His face lit up, and he gently embraced the woman.

"Susannah," he greeted her warmly. "Thank you for coming."

Susannah Granger. She'd always been one of the Cherry Hills

Academy's greatest financial supporters. She'd known Mary and George for over twenty-five years, and though she wasn't close enough to be considered a family friend, she was certainly a friend of the ministry.

Her smile was sad and filled with regret. "Of course. George, I'm so very sorry for your loss. I can't begin to imagine how difficult this must be for you. Mary was an extraordinary woman."

He nodded. "That she was."

She tucked a strand of graying blonde hair behind her ear. "If you need extra help around the academy during this time, I'm happy to volunteer again."

"That would be wonderful," he admitted. "The children already feel Mary's loss greatly. They'd greatly benefit from having another mother figure present."

She inclined her head politely. "Consider it done."

Someone laid a hand on George's shoulder, startling him. George turned around and froze. Beta was standing in front of him.

"George," Beta said softly, pulling his friend in for a hug.

George barely would've recognized him if it weren't for his voice. They had continued to stay in touch over the phone, but it'd been years since he'd last seen Beta.

Tears stung George's eyes as he squeezed Beta tightly. When he finally released him, George took a deep breath and steadied himself.

"Well, you've changed," George said. "I feel like I've said that to you before."

Beta smiled a sad smile. "I'm so sorry."

"I didn't think you'd be able to make it."

Fay

"It's Mary," he replied softly. "I'm here for you."

Suddenly James was at George's side. He had moved so stealthily that George didn't even hear him coming. George jumped at the quiet man's approach, and then he shook his head, chuckling to himself. "I'm going to put a bell on you one of these days."

The twinkle of mischief in James' eyes was startling…and concerning. "I only feared Mary. Your threats mean nothing," he answered as merrily as he could. "It's time to get started."

George nodded, those words stealing the joy and humor from the situation. "Right, right." He turned back to Beta. "You'll be staying with us—*me*," he corrected himself, clearing his throat uncomfortably. "You'll be staying with me, I assume?"

"If you'll have me," Beta answered.

"Of course. I'll see you in a bit," George said, following James.

He made his way to the podium, and soon the cacophony of voices began to die down. People took their seats one by one, and it quickly became very apparent that there weren't nearly enough seats for everyone present. There were people standing at the back, people standing in doorways to listen, and even people outside the doors.

George immediately started getting choked up at the sight of Mary's influence—how many lives she'd touched.

Oh, don't do this now, George, he chastised himself. He took a deep breath and repeated the mantra he'd recited in his head over and over during Mary's illness. *The Lord is good and does good. Nothing but that which is Good, like He is, can proceed from Him.*

He could do this. With the Lord's help, he could do anything.

He looked down at the notes on the podium in front of him and gathered himself. His gaze returned to the onlookers, the bright lights allowing him to see the glistening of tears in their eyes.

"Thank you all for coming," George began, his voice trembling ever so slightly. "I can't begin to express how wonderful it is to see you all. Mary was such a vibrant light in my life that...well, I selfishly forgot that she was a light in anyone else's. Yet here you all are, lives touched by the same woman." George shook his head in amazement. "I used to ask myself how one person could emit so much energy and life..." His voice trailed off. "She had such a passion for scripture and for the children who flocked to her. I thank God every day for placing her in my life."

George paused and took a moment to collect his thoughts. He could feel his emotions bubbling up again, threatening to drown him, so he repeated his mantra. *The Lord is good and does good. Nothing but that which is Good, like He is, can proceed from Him.*

He smiled. "When we founded Cherry Hills Academy, my wife was my first supporter. She stood by my side regardless of the trials and difficulties, and her faith in the Lord was sometimes even more unwavering than my own. She supported me fully, even when I'd done things that were less than worthy of that support. She lived to see two thousand, seven hundred believers received into communion."

Some of the congregation dabbed at their eyes with handkerchiefs and tissues while others smiled and nodded, and George realized that some of the faces he saw in the sanctuary were the faces of those 2,700 believers. It warmed him to his core and allowed him to continue his eulogy.

"Perhaps all Christians who have heard my story will fully agree that the Lord was good and doing good when He allowed her to stay with me for so long. However, I ask you, my dear friends, to go beyond that. I want you to say it along with me—that the Lord was good and doing good when He allowed Mary Groves Müller, the most wonderful, loving, faithful wife a man could have, to be received by heaven, even though she had to leave at a time when I needed her most." Now the words were flowing easily, as if he had been given a second wind. "Of course, of *course*, I feel a dull, aching void in my heart, and with every day that passes, I miss her more and more, and so do the children. But despite this, my innermost soul still experiences joy because of the joy that I know Mary is feeling. My daughter and I would not ask that she be returned to us, even if it could be done with just a simple snap of our fingers.

"The Lord is good and does good," he stated, and never had the words felt truer. "Nothing but that which is good, like He is, can proceed from Him. And we are satisfied with it."

He then stepped back, thanked everyone for coming, and departed from the podium.

The procession moved from Springfield Community Church to the gravesite, where Mary's body was laid to rest in the ground. Beta stood by George's side the entire time. After, they attended a small wake at the Müller residence which had been organized by James for close family friends only—which, of course, consisted of mostly Cherry Hills Academy faculty and employees.

George made his rounds, shaking hands and thanking people for coming, but there was a sort of numbing exhaustion that was washing over him. All he wanted to do was curl up in a corner and hold something of Mary's. As much as he appreciated James' effort and the comforting words of friends and family, he was ready for everyone to go home. But since he couldn't shut down the wake quite yet, he told Beta he needed a moment and retreated to his room.

Once tucked safely inside of his bedroom, George opened up the window by his dresser. The wind was bitter and unforgiving, slicing right through his jacket. George was not a young or sprietly man by any stretch, but there was something he needed to do.

The roof outside of his window was somewhat slanted, but it was not so steep that it would be overly dangerous for him to climb out… so he did.

He grunted uncomfortably as he tried to fit through the window and find a spot to sit on the roof. He realized that this had been a whole lot easier when he was fifteen and filled with childish rage after the death of his mother. When he finally got comfortable, he exhaled deeply and leaned his head back against the house behind him.

He found peace there for a while, remaining in constant prayer. He laughed to himself. *If fifteen-year-old George could see me now, he'd think I was quite the pious man,* he thought. But that was the thing— he didn't feel like he was striving to be pious or perfectly devout. He was simply leaning into the beautiful relationship he had cultivated with God over the years. He felt like he was talking to a friend. A comforter. A father. The people downstairs provided some consolation, but it was noth-

Fay

ing compared to what He could bring. George just needed a few minutes of quiet, inward prayer.

A few minutes turned into a few hours. He hardly noticed the time passing or that people were driving away on the street below. It wasn't until he heard voices that he snapped out of his meditation.

"I told you he'd be up here," Beta noted.

"Thank God," James panted, leaning through the window. "We couldn't find you anywhere. You had Lydia worried."

George frowned. "Has it really been that long?" He looked up, and—yes, those were definitely the stars. Wow. He shook his head. "I'm sorry. I just…needed some time to think."

Still breathing heavily, James replied, "I totally understand, sir. But please…come inside before your daughter realizes that you're sitting on the roof and that I haven't done anything about it."

George chuckled. "So much for only fearing Mary."

James snorted. "She's Mini Mary."

George couldn't disagree with that.

He climbed inside, joints aching from the chill of the cold. He gave Beta a mock angry look.

"Traitor," he remarked in a weak attempt at lightening the mood.

Beta shrugged and flashed a soft smile. "Just looking out for you."

George followed the two downstairs to find Lydia, who had clearly been upset by his disappearance, though it seemed she was just as emotionally exhausted as he was.

James helped them tidy up the house and then bid them goodnight. Once the house was empty, Lydia, Beta, and George sat in the living room and reminisced about all of the wild times they'd had together growing up. Lydia had heard some of these stories, but Beta hadn't seen her since she was very young, and many of the tales were for more mature ears. Now, these stories were pure comedy. George made sure to throw in a few warnings for Lydia, of course, and she just rolled her eyes.

After a while, George retired to his room and fell into his bed, finally allowing his mind to go blank as his thoughts drifted off. It was the first night of sleep he'd allowed himself to have since Mary's death, and he desperately needed it.

It wasn't a peaceful sleep. He awoke multiple times in the night, seeking Mary's warmth and only finding the cool linen sheets where she used to lay beside him. Tears pricked his eyes, and he scrunched the sheets up in his hands.

Every day for the rest of his life, he would miss her. He would ache for her. There would always be a painful place in his chest where his damaged heart lay. He was missing a vital piece of itself.

More than anything, he wanted to turn over, open his eyes, and smile at his beautiful wife. He wanted to tell her how his day went, share his sorrows and his secrets, and hear her own. He wanted her to chide him when he forgot to eat and shower him with kisses when he finally understood something she was trying to say.

He wanted to not be alone.

But it wasn't meant to be. That ache would remain.

Chapter Thirty

The days seemed dull, and the nights were cold and miserable. The kids seemed to be just as miserable as George, and many sought therapy within the facility to discuss their emotions and feelings of grief. Despite George's faith, he found it increasingly difficult to pray prayers of gratitude. In the past, the passage of time had helped… yet this wound only seemed to fester with time. It grew more painful every day.

Beta stayed for almost a month, and this turned out to be very good for the academy. Beta was able to interact more with the kids he'd formed relationships with in Haiti, and they were ecstatic to see him. They needed that positivity and cheer brought back into their lives after something so tragic.

Beta helped to stave off George's dark depression for a while, but eventually he had to return to Haiti. When he did, he took the last ounce of happiness and joy George had left with him.

Letters poured in from those who knew Mary, speaking words of comfort and hope into George's life. They helped somewhat. He received letters from former students who had lived in the academy before aging out, and every person glowed about Mary, relaying that they'd been devastated to hear of her loss. Most all of them had made it to the funeral.

In one of the letters, a woman raised a question that George had given much prior thought to. What would happen to the Cherry Hills Academy when *he* was gone?

From a legal standpoint, the academy buildings and the land were held by eleven trustees. George's death wouldn't affect the legal standing of the buildings, but who would carry on the work in the same spirit as George had? And of course there was the unspoken question—would the money continue to come in to support the children and the ministry?

Well, that was something George and Mary had discussed and made provisions for years in advance. In all honesty, George hadn't expected to make it this long. Though he did his best to look after his health, he was beginning to experience some health issues.

Years before, Mary and George had prayed together nightly that the Lord would bring someone to them who could carry on the work in their stead. This was around the time that James Wright entered their lives.

George recalled what Mary had said not long after George's second interview with James.

"Do you know what people say about him?" Mary asked.

George shook his head. "What do they say?"

"They say that his beautiful face and radiant smile show the peace and joy that rule his heart," she answered with a twinkle in her eye.

George laughed. "They're that poetic, are they? Or is that particularly flowery prose yours?"

Mary giggled. "Maybe I embellished a little, but it's what they mean."

"And do they say anything else about Mr. Wright?" he inquired with a grin.

"Well, they also say that he is dignified and so gracious that everyone can't help but respect him. And that he is dedicated to his work and is highly intelligent. His lovely voice is nothing to scoff at, either."

George laughed, but she wasn't wrong. "Then it's clear the Lord has sent him to be my successor, is it not?"

Mary smiled. "That's what I was thinking."

As he reflected on this conversation, George felt a bit of joy returning to his heart. He'd been training James without James even knowing what he was being trained for, and this young man had been all but handpicked by Mary. It did truly seem that the Lord had sent James to them, so maybe it was time to tell the man of his intentions.

One morning, while George was in the academy tending to business, he called James into his office. This was nothing out of the ordinary, as the two regularly had conversations in George's office. They mostly discussed issues within the academy, how the children were doing, and what the upcoming months looked like. This morning, though, George had something different in mind.

The door closed behind James as he stepped inside, trusty clipboard in hand. "Alright. Straight to it, then?" asked the assistant.

"Actually…" George began, thinking. "Have a seat, James."

James frowned in confusion, but he didn't argue. He slowly took his seat across from George and set his clipboard down, waiting for George to continue.

George drummed his fingers on the table, a bit lost in thought. He smiled to himself, then nodded in resolve. He was certain he'd chosen the right man. He looked up. "I'm naming you my successor."

James' eyes immediately widened in sheer shock. "I—I'm not sure I heard you correctly."

George was pretty sure he'd heard him just fine, but he repeated himself nonetheless. "I'm naming you my successor."

James immediately shook his head. "I can't be your successor!"

"Why not?"

"Well, because… I'm not like you," he stammered. "You have so much experience and your faith is unwavering. You've never doubted. I… I can't…I can't even begin to do that."

George looked him dead in the eyes. "James Wright, you have more faith and love than you think. You are the absolute perfect man for this job. You were Mary's pick, and I intend to honor that. I've given it much thought and prayer, and I agree with her wholeheartedly."

James seemed to be having a hard time understanding what was happening, yet he still managed to rattle off a list of reasons why he couldn't take the job. "I don't have the skills. Honestly my position as an assistant suits me best. I mean… can you imagine? I wouldn't know the first thing about running this academy. That's why I always come to you to solve the problems! I could never, I mean *never*, run this place the way you do."

George just chuckled. "What are you talking about? James, you singlehandedly tend to ninety percent of the problems that arise in the academy. You *have* been running this place, and you've been running it just as well as I have."

James tried to catch his breath, taking a moment to let everything sink in. George could tell that he'd need time to consider the decision he now had to make, so it came as no surprise when he said so.

"I just…need some time to think," said James. "If it's truly the Lord's will as you believe it is, He'll make it abundantly clear to me as well."

George nodded. "I'm sure He will. Let me know what you decide."

James picked up his clipboard. "Absolutely." He started to head for the door, then hesitated. "Thank you… for your confidence in me."

George smiled. "Just like my faith in the Lord, my confidence in you has never wavered, James Wright."

George knew it wouldn't be long before James returned. Sure enough, his assistant came back a few days later. After prayer and consideration, he had agreed to accept the position, and it was set in stone. Upon George's death, James would take over responsibility of the Cherry Hills Academy and would continue George's ministry so that the children would never go hungry—physically or spiritually.

There wasn't much that James couldn't get accomplished.

After he was named George's successor, he began taking his responsibilities more seriously than he had before—if that were even possible. George felt he hardly had to do anything around the academy. He was ecstatic about James' energy, but he also felt a renewed sense of loneliness in the midst of all of the change. To combat his restlessness, George set to work playing with the children, teaching them what he could, and even helping with their meals.

The greatest gift that George received by James taking over was the gift of time to read and study the scriptures more. George had always spent an incredible amount of time in the Word of God. Knowing God's Word had been the foundation for the unwavering faith he felt. He loved the Bible, and now he loved having extra time to study it.

Many volunteers filtered in and out over the next several months, but none came more frequently than Susannah Granger. In every way she could, she filled the void that Mary had left in Cherry Hills Academy. As far as George could tell, the children adored her. He knew how much they missed Mary. They gravitated towards George, knowing that he felt the same loss, and they would sit with him for hours. Susannah couldn't completely alleviate the pain of loss, but she did her best to distract them.

She was a bit younger than Mary and had all of Mary's liveliness. The children and orphans who were closest to Mary stuck to George's side like glue at first, but after a few months of Susannah's continued presence at Cherry Hills, they began to spend more time with her than George.

Not only was Susannah able to help the children, but she was also able to be there for Lydia. Lydia began to see her as a sort of mother figure after Mary passed. George was thrilled that Susannah was able to provide his daughter peace, though he wished he were strong enough to do

Fay

that himself.

If he were being honest with himself, he would have admitted that he was barely holding it together. He was hanging on by a thin thread. Lydia's staunch support was the only thing keeping him somewhat functional, so he was grateful to Susannah for giving Lydia the comfort he couldn't. There was something special about a woman's touch and motherly love, and he knew this gift was beyond his capabilities.

Lydia had known *of* Susannah before Mary's death, but the two had never really interacted. George credited the fact that they bonded so quickly and so well to the Lord's kindness. This new relationship gave Lydia a reprieve from her sorrow.

And clearly, the Lord wasn't done there.

A few months after naming James his successor, George noticed his personal assistant visiting the house more frequently. It used to be that he hardly ever dropped by unless there was something urgent going on at the academy, but now it was at least a weekly visit.

At first, George didn't think anything of it. James always visited under the guise of discussing some matter with him, so George hardly realized what was really going on. Sure, the excuses were pretty weak, and James had never been the best at bluffing. But it wasn't *totally* out of the ordinary. It wasn't until James began interacting more with Lydia during these visits that George realized what was going on. It made George smile, and he was sorely tempted to snicker at their teenage-like behavior, but he had to admit it was sort of cute. Besides, as the weeks went on, George realized that Lydia's mood appeared to be improving. Whatever little joy and happiness James could provide his daughter, George was willing to accept.

The children were George's pride and joy, and he spent every waking hour with them. He and James would spend hours at Cherry Hills discussing potential issues and their resolutions. He was able to distract himself this way for a while, and it seemed that the gaping hole in his chest—the wound that just wouldn't seem to heal—was slowly beginning to feel less painful.

The nights were still difficult. He still slept restlessly and felt a haze of exhaustion throughout the day. He missed Mary every night and every morning when he woke, but he never forgot to send a prayer of praise to the Lord for easing her pain and bringing her home.

Lydia had since moved back to her apartment, though it was mostly only for appearances. She still stayed in her old room at her family house on nights that George had experienced a particularly trying day. Sometimes she even stayed in her room in the academy when George decided to stay overnight there.

It wasn't beyond George's notice. He knew what his daughter was doing, and though he knew he should honor his word to Mary and ensure that Lydia moved on with her life, he desperately needed the time with her. He needed her distraction. She had a way of capturing his attention through her storytelling as she recalled hilarious moments throughout the day. She made everything funny, and Lord knew that George needed a little humor in his life.

Susannah spent quite a bit of time at the Müller house to be with Lydia. George would be lying if he said he didn't appreciate her being there. She'd help them make meals, and when George needed help with the paperwork that Mary had kept up with over the years, Susannah generously volunteered to lend a hand.

Sometimes, they'd talk late into the night. Susannah would share the pains in her own past while George shared his. They found comfort in each other, which was a small mercy. Though George loved this time with Susannah, he felt somewhat guilty and uncomfortable with the amount of time Susannah was spending at the house. He felt that it was disrespectful to his wife. With this in mind, he eventually asked that Susannah take over Mary's office in the academy so that she could do her work from there instead.

That didn't halt their conversations, though. It only made them more appropriate in George's eyes. Instead of long talks in his living room, it shifted to long talks at the academy.

George struggled to adjust to the loneliness. Lydia was living with him and taking care of him, so he found his loneliness strange and somewhat unwarranted. But it just wasn't the same. Mary had been by his side for forty years, and George had never felt lonely. Not even for a moment. Yet, when he was with Susannah, he didn't feel nearly as lonely. Through her support and belief in his abilities, he found himself feeling refreshed and reinvigorated.

At first, it was a friendship built upon mutual pain and shared time. Because Susannah dedicated so much of her time to the Cherry Hills Academy and to Lydia's edification, she and George were forced to spend quite a bit of time together. But soon it began to morph, and George found himself looking forward to Susannah's visits. When she left, he counted the hours until he'd see her again.

That's when the guilt *really* set in. At this point, it'd been a little over a year since Mary's death. Could his heart truly have moved on so quickly? And if it had, why did he feel sick to his stomach?

He wrestled with these thoughts for so long, begging the Lord to clarify his emotions. Soon, he came to the realization that perhaps Susannah had been placed in his life on purpose.

The thought floored him. There was *no one* else for him but Mary, so he pushed his feelings away and maintained their platonic friendship.

The months seemed to fly by in a blur, and George found that he'd hardly realized the time that had passed. Very little had changed in his own life, but change was prevalent all around him, especially in the life of his daughter.

She and James had started going on lunch dates, and lunch dates had evolved to dinner dates. Soon, it became official. They were a couple.

George found this delightful and amusing. Mary had been right. She was always right. She knew that James would be good for Lydia, and George had, regrettably, scoffed at it. Now he couldn't help but agree.

*They look nice togeth*er, he noted to himself as they left to go on yet another date. And more than that, Lydia seemed truly happy. Susannah had played a huge role in bringing life back into his daughter, but now James was taking over. And George couldn't have asked for a better boyfriend for Lydia. James was thoughtful, respectful, kind, strong, and compassionate. He cared as much for the children as George did, and he never treated Lydia as anything other than his equal.

James *adored* Lydia; anyone could see that. Every time George thought of it, it brought tears to his eyes as he remembered just how much he'd adored Mary when they'd first met. George knew when a man was smitten, and James Wright was smitten.

Lydia, on the other hand, was a bit more difficult to read. She played her cards close to the vest, and it took quite a bit of prying to get her to own up to her growing feelings. In fact, it took a thirty-minute conversation in which George used his patented "Dad eyes," as Lydia called them, to get her to admit how she truly felt about James.

"Fine," she eventually said, a smile cracking across her face, even as she fought it. "Alright. Yes. I love him."

For the first time in a long time, George was truly happy. Everything was how it should be, and it felt right with his soul. He'd prayed long and hard about this relationship, and never once did he feel any reservations about James. The man was a saint.

"Good," George answered. "I'm glad to hear it. I just want you to be happy, Lyds."

"I am," she answered with a contented sigh. "I still miss Mom, you know? I feel kind of guilty being happy."

"Don't," George replied quickly. "Your mother would be thrilled if she were here. I promise. In fact…" he hesitated, not sure if he should continue, but then he smiled and said, "your mother actually predicted this."

Lydia's eyes widened, and she sat forward in her chair. "What? She did?" Her cheeks reddened. "How could she have seen this coming? I certainly didn't. I'd never really thought of him as anything more than… well, *James*."

George laughed. "I don't know. Your mother had a way about her.

But I tell you that so you'll know that she really would approve. She'd be happy."

Lydia smiled softly, and George was once again astounded at how much she looked like her mother. "Thanks, Dad."

It was nice getting to focus on others' lives and the joy they had rather than dwelling on his own loss. Knowing that James would very likely be his future son-in-law, George began spending more intentional time with him—as if he hadn't spent hundreds of hours with him already.

James never mentioned anything to George about his budding relationship. He kept things strictly business when they spoke, despite George's prodding. It wasn't until about eighteen months after Lydia and James officially began dating that James finally came to George to discuss the matter. By that point, George knew full well what James was there to ask.

"Will you make her happy?" George asked.

James stammered. "It's all I want to do."

George nodded with a smile. He remembered that excitement. "Then of course you have my permission, James. I already think of you as family. It'll be nice to make it official."

James reached across the desk to shake George's hand. "Thank you, sir."

George chuckled and accepted his hand. "Better get used to calling me George."

James laughed, and George had a deep sense of knowing that this was right. He attributed it to the Lord's voice. What George *hadn't* expected was Lydia's less-than-enthusiastic response.

Fay

He'd been washing the dishes, quietly humming a cheerful song to himself, imagining that James was down on one knee popping the question. He missed that giddiness, so he borrowed some of the joy he knew Lydia must have been experiencing. Of course, that assumption went down the drain when Lydia marched through the door without a word and went to work on her laptop.

Confused, George dried his hands on a kitchen towel and walked into the living room.

"Umm," he stammered, not sure what to say. He was pretty sure today was the day.

Then he heard a sniffle. That definitely wasn't normal.

"Lyds, what's wrong?" he asked, stepping into the living room.

"Nothing," she answered quickly.

He tried to think of a way to let on that he knew without *actually* revealing that he'd known, but it was a lost cause. He sat beside her on the couch.

"Did… something happen between you and James?"

She turned and looked at him with red-rimmed eyes. "I know you know. He said he got your permission first."

George blinked. Wasn't she supposed to be thrilled? That's how he was picturing all of this going down. He figured he'd have to put in earplugs to sleep at all with the girly, lovestruck music she was bound to be playing all night. Not that Lydia was that type of woman; it just seemed more appropriate than the response he received.

"I…" George was perplexed. "I'm sorry, but I'm confused. Isn't this a good thing?"

She stoically returned her attention to her laptop. "It would've been...if it had happened at a different time."

"Different time?" George still had no idea what was going on. "What's wrong with now?"

"You need me here," Lydia finally said. "If I spend the rest of my life with James, who will spend the rest of their life with you?" She shook her head. "I can't marry him."

A wave of guilt immediately washed over George. Had he really seemed so pathetic recently that his daughter felt she couldn't live her own life? He suddenly remembered what Mary had insisted he promise her. It had seemed somewhat ridiculous at the time, but as always, Mary was right. She'd feared that Lydia would be unable to spread her wings, and here she was, turning down the man she loved because she was afraid of what would happen to her father.

"Oh, Lyds," George sighed. "You aren't abandoning me. I promise you that. It's *wonderful* that you've found James, and you owe it to yourself to pursue that. If you truly love him, then marry him."

She looked at him. "I do everything for you around here. I take care of the laundry, I fix your meals, I even remind you when you need to stop working and go to bed. I'm hardly even at my apartment anymore."

He chuckled. "I'm a full-grown man. I'm sorry if I haven't acted like it as of late. You know it's been difficult for me, but I need to take better care of myself, and I know how to do it." George took her hands in his and squeezed them. "Do you want to marry James Wright?"

She took a deep breath. "More than anything."

The words warmed his heart. "Okay. Then don't let me stop you.

And don't worry; it's not like we'll never see each other again. You both work at Cherry Hills, so we'll be seeing a lot of each other every day. You can nag me all you like then, and I'll get a break in the evenings."

She grinned widely and jumped up, kissing George's cheek. "Love you. I have to go," she said quickly, the words tumbling out. "I need to go find James."

George laughed. "You do that."

Then Lydia was right back out the front door, and George realized that yet again his life had irrevocably changed. But even if he didn't particularly *love* change, he was beyond thrilled for the change in Lydia's and James' lives. They were good for each other, and Mary had seen it long before George did. James would make her happy, and together they would only strengthen the academy. George's wish had come true. Not only was James going to be his successor—and a worthy one at that—but Lydia was going to be at his side.

The first thing George wanted to do was tell Susannah…and then he remembered that same guilt he felt every time he thought of her. Resigning himself to only consider her a friend wasn't enough. Even a mere phone call to share celebratory news felt like a betrayal to Mary's memory. So he dispelled the desire to call her and settled for washing the dishes.

"Lord," he prayed. "Please tell my darling wife the news we're receiving down here." He smiled fondly as he returned to the sink and scrubbed at a plate. "Tell her of the joy we're experiencing." Okay, this particular plate was really not coming clean. "And please ask her how in the *world* she managed to do so many dishes while keeping up with everything else I threw at her."

Let the Children Come

He decided to just let the dishwasher give the plate its best go, and he stepped away from the sink.

Chapter Thirty-One

Days passed, then weeks. At the academy, James and Lydia were acting like two lovebirds, always perched on the same branch. They drank up each other's presence, a bright smile gracing their faces whenever they caught sight of one another. George watched with fatherly curiosity as he worked. It was both heartwarming and heartbreaking to George.

He missed that feeling so much. He missed getting to see Mary's smile and hear her laugh. He missed that companionship.

Beside him, someone tugged at his shirt. He was startled out of his thoughts and turned to see Diana—now almost sixteen—standing beside him with a set of keys in her hand. She jingled them softly. George recognized those keys.

Awhile back, one of the academy benefactors had provided a small, reliable sedan for the kids to learn to drive with. Diana was obviously over George's excuses and was ready to go for a drive.

She cleared her throat expectantly.

George chuckled. "Something you need, Diana?"

"Yep," she answered. "We're gonna have a chat. While I drive."

George was a bit taken aback. He arched a brow. "Is that so?"

"Yes, sir," she replied swiftly. "Let's go."

George followed Diana out to the car. The petite girl slid into the driver seat and whipped her deep auburn hair back into a bun at the nape of her neck before strapping in and starting the engine.

"Okay, now what you'll want to do first is—"

"I know," she interjected, shifting the car into gear. She backed out of the driveway at an alarming speed. Well, it wasn't *that* fast, but considering George was pretty sure she'd never driven a car before, it was terrifying.

"Whoa," he gasped, gripping the seat. "Slow down a bit, Diana. Are you trying to give an old man a heart attack?"

Diana glanced sidelong at him. "I barely coasted down the driveway."

"Oh. Well…be careful." George strapped himself in.

Diana turned down one of the rural, country roads and rolled her window down, enjoying the warm breeze that entered. George could smell the faint perfume of buttercups the children had planted along this road. Mary had helped get them growing years ago, and the flowers kept popping back up every spring.

As Diana turned down another road, George thought to remind her of the speed limit and then discovered that she *was* driving the speed limit. She was actually a very good driver. She stayed perfectly within the lines, didn't have a white-knuckled grip on the steering wheel, and seemed confident overall.

She'd *definitely* been practicing.

He eyed her suspiciously. "Who have you been driving with?" He knew that if she named one of the other children, he was going to lose his mind. He'd warned them for so long that student drivers couldn't teach other student drivers. There needed to be a real adult in the car.

He'd been so expecting to hear another kid's name that when Diana finally answered, it took a second for the name to register with him.

"Susannah."

George blinked. Susannah had been giving driving lessons? Had this been to everyone or just Diana? George hadn't noticed. "Oh. That's nice of her," he replied.

Diana nodded. "Mm-hmm. She's been great."

The *whir* of the tires beneath the car filled the silent air for a few moments.

"You know, since she's been teaching me how to drive, we've had a lot of time to talk," Diana continued.

"Have you now?" That was good. She'd been a great help to Lydia as well, and Diana had been so close to Mary. It was good that Susannah was extending her reach.

"Mm-hmm," she said again. "She's not like Mrs. Müller. She's softer spoken and can't deal with too many negative emotions. But everything she does, she does for the benefit of others. In that way, she's very much like Mrs. Müller."

George had to agree. "I suppose she is."

Diana kept her gaze on the road. "I just thought you should

know that none of us would think any different of you if you loved her back."

That floored George. *What did she just say?* He stammered. "What?"

"Come on," Diana drawled. "Several of us have seen how comfortable you two are with each other. You were so... broken after Mrs. Müller's death. It hurt all of us to see, so when you started healing, we noticed that too. And Susannah's played a huge role in that."

George couldn't speak. He stared at the setting sun, refusing to look away.

"You know I wouldn't say any of this if I didn't believe it," Diana then said softly. "Mrs. Müller was like a mother to me, and I think I was closer to her than anyone else in the academy, past or present." At George's quizzical look, she insisted, "She told me so."

"I don't mean to speak for Mrs. Müller," continued Diana, "but I think she wouldn't mind if you and Susannah were to find happiness in each other. Loneliness isn't a good look on you, Pastor George."

George shook his head. "I couldn't. It's not about *loneliness*. I miss her. I miss Mary. Susannah can never replace her."

"That's the problem," Diana replied swiftly. "You keep thinking that if you and Susannah love each other, she'd have to 'replace' Mrs. Müller, but she doesn't have to. She can't. Mrs. Müller is what you needed for all those years...but the Lord called her home. Maybe now He's sent someone else to help you along your path."

Those words rattled George.

"I'm sorry if it seems like we're overstepping."

"*We?*" asked George.

Diana shrugged. "A few of us have been thinking this for a while, and I was the one elected to tell you. Don't be mad?"

George found himself chuckling. "How could I be mad? It's kind of you all to look after my wellbeing."

"It's only fair after you've dedicated your life to looking after ours," said Diana, a small smile on her mouth as she looked at George.

George could feel a spark of warmth in his heart, lighting him up from the inside out. He still wasn't sure how he needed to proceed, but Diana had definitely given him another perspective.

"Eyes on the road," he quickly said, mostly joking.

Diana quickly returned her eyes to the road. "I know, I know."

When the two returned to the Academy, Diana hugged George tightly.

"Thank you," he told her.

She released him and smiled proudly. "I spent a lot of time with Mrs. Müller. I *know* she doesn't want you to be alone, especially with it affecting your health so much." She pulled at his baggy shirt again. "You look awful, by the way."

"Thanks," George replied sarcastically.

"No problem," chirped the young girl. "Keep us updated on the gossip. It gets boring around here sometimes." She waved as she ran inside.

On the drive home, George kept turning Diana's words over in his head. He felt *so* guilty even just considering the idea of pursuing a relationship with Susannah, but what if Diana was right?

When he arrived at his house, he spotted himself in the reflection of the car window. For the first time, he noticed how sallow his cheeks had gotten, and how the life had leaked from his eyes. That wasn't how he was meant to look. He had to start taking better care of himself for the sake of the children under his care.

How selfish it was of him to be so caught up in his own grief that he neglected the kids he'd promised to love. He hated that reflection, so he quickly turned away and headed inside.

Lydia was in the kitchen cooking when he came in. She peeked her head around the corner.

"Hey, Dad," she called.

He breathed out slowly. It was good to see her, and he could use the time with her. Life had felt so hectic, and with James attached at her hip, he hardly got a chance to have any real conversations with Lydia anymore.

"Hey, Lyds," he replied with a smile. "Are you here for the evening?"

James then stepped out of the kitchen, wiping his hands on a towel. "I am as well, if that's all right with you." He motioned to Lydia. "I just agreed to help make dinner."

"And I invited him to stay for dinner," Lydia followed quickly.

"Oh," George replied, his heart sinking ever-so-slightly. He'd longed for some quality time with his daughter, and seeing Lydia and James goofing off together so happily was not a great remedy for his guilty conscience.

"Sure," he said after a long pause, deciding that it was silly for him to deny them that happiness. "Of course. James, I barely saw you today. I hope you weren't too under water with your to-do list."

James smiled as he set the table. "Thankfully I'm pretty used to the work by now."

George helped Lydia carry the Italian-style pasta to the table, and together the three sat down for their evening meal. After a quick prayer, they dug in.

As they ate, George noticed how the conversation always made its way back to James and Lydia's wedding, and how it wouldn't be long before they were terminating Lydia's lease and buying a house together.

George remembered that excitement and did what he could to contribute to their plans, though it seemed they were more excited to just talk about it and express their joy than to actually *plan* anything.

After dinner, James and Lydia watched a movie with George before James headed home. While George washed the dishes, he wondered whether or not he should mention his conversation with Diana to Lydia. He decided against it, afraid that Lydia would feel it was a betrayal to her mother's memory.

They were two months out from the second anniversary of Mary's death, but it didn't seem long enough. He wasn't sure it would *ever* seem long enough. Mary was still so much a part of him. He couldn't imagine *trading* her for anyone else, and that was what this felt like.

"Want a cup of tea before bed?" asked Lydia as she came into the kitchen, freshly showered.

George shook his head. "Will I see you at the Academy tomorrow?"

"I have some errands to run in the morning, but I'll be at Cherry Hills in the afternoon." She tied her wet hair up in a messy bun. "Okay, I'm headed to bed. Goodnight."

"Wait," he called after her. "You're staying here?"

"I thought I would," she answered. "Is that all right?"

George loved that Lydia liked to spend time with him, but he immediately remembered Mary's words. Lydia didn't need to take care of him anymore. He could take care of himself.

"Lyds, go home," he insisted.

"This *is* my home," she argued.

George smiled. "It'll always be your home, but don't stick around because of me. Sometimes I like the peace and quiet." It was a total lie, but one that needed to be said.

Lydia raised a brow. "Are you sure?"

George nodded. "Yes. Go home. Get some rest. I'll see you around Cherry Hills."

She sighed but relented. "Okay." She rose up on her toes to kiss George on the cheek. "Don't hesitate to call me if you need anything."

Lydia packed up her overnight bag and headed back to her apartment. The moment she was gone, the house felt all too quiet. He could hear the ticking of the minute hand on the clock, and the *tap tap tap* of the branches on the windows.

He made his way into the kitchen and turned on the stove. The blue fire illuminated the kettle. He fixed himself a cup of tea and headed upstairs to his bedroom, knowing full well he wouldn't get any sleep that night.

Fay

To say that he wrestled with himself would be putting it lightly. His thoughts were a tumultuous storm. He prayed that the Lord might melt away his guilt and grief if it was His will that he pursue Susannah.

It didn't happen overnight. He considered it for days, then weeks. The more he saw Susannah around the Academy, the more he became aware of his own loneliness, and the void she seemed to be filling in his life.

George wasn't meant to be alone. He desperately needed a companion, and though he'd told Lydia that he'd be fine without her, he now realized just how false that was. Mary had done so much for him. How could he possibly imagine that he could do it all himself?

The eyes of the children were on him, as well. Since his discussion with Diana, he noticed that many of the kids would watch his interactions with Susannah, small though they may be. The childish giggles filled the Academy every time Susannah and George even *passed* each other in the hall.

Though the onlookers somewhat annoyed George at times, he couldn't bring himself to be angry with them. After all, they only wanted what was best for him. And he had to admit…it was sort of cute. Susannah had to notice, but if she understood what was happening, she never said anything.

James and Lydia came over nearly every evening. It was under the guise of planning for their upcoming wedding, but George suspected Lydia was concerned for his wellbeing. It was nice, though, because Susannah typically came over as well. Lydia liked to involve her in the wedding planning, and Susannah was thrilled to oblige.

"And the flowers?" Susannah questioned, then gasped as inspiration bloomed in her mind. "What about calla lilies?"

"Actually, I was thinking red. Poppies," replied Lydia. "Any objections?"

"Hmm," James mused. "Aren't some people allergic to poppies?"

Lydia narrowed her eyes at her soon-to-be husband. "Those people can wait outside. Poppies are magical."

Susannah laughed. "I think what Lydia means is that we'll make sure that no one attending is allergic to poppies."

George's head was spinning. He'd been through all of this before with Mary, and like mother, like daughter, Lydia's version of wedding planning was simple, direct, and quick.

As the conversation continued, George found himself looking at Susannah more and more, both for approval and to just look at her. She was such a gentle, calming presence. And for a moment, in his mind's eye, he caught a glimpse of her in a wedding dress.

That's when he knew. He'd been praying for so long, but he was almost afraid to know the answer. Now it was right in front of him.

Susannah was *meant* to be a part of their family.

The moment he realized it, everything in him relaxed. Then came the scarier question, What if she didn't feel the same way?

He was nervous. *Nervous.* He couldn't believe it. How long had it been since he'd actually felt these butterflies?

"Are you sure about this?" he asked self-consciously as he stood on the porch of building three.

The wraparound veranda was beautifully decorated with every color of calla lily imaginable. He'd gone off a hunch that since Susannah suggested this kind of flower for Lydia's bouquet, vibrant lilies were her favorite.

"Absolutely," answered Diana as she hopped off a ladder. She looked up to admire her work. The fairy lights she'd hung glowed softly in the fading light. He imagined that from a distance, it truly did look like he was standing in a fantasy world.

"This is a little…much, don't you think?" he asked again.

Cody, one of the other children lending a hand, scooped up the ladder. "Trust me, Pastor George," he said in a tone that was all confidence. "Women *love* this sort of stuff."

"Ahh," George answered. Seeing as though Cody was fourteen, surely he'd know.

Diana just smirked. "Don't overthink it. She's going to love it." She checked her watch. "Okay, she should be here any minute." Diana clapped her hands loudly, commanding the attention of all the other orphans. "Everyone scram. Let's give them their privacy."

George got the impression that they'd probably be hunkered in the bushes watching and listening, but he could live with that.

Diana gave him a thumbs up and hurried off with everyone else, leaving George to stand awkwardly on the porch.

This is ridiculous, he thought. *I'm too old to be making grand gestures like this.* Besides that, he'd seen nothing to indicate that Susannah was any sort of romantic. He was totally going off of Diana's recommendation here, and maybe Diana had no clue what she was doing!

That was it. He had to call it off. He'd be better off just getting a cup of coffee with her. She'd—

Headlights illuminated the gravel drive. George immediately looked up as Susannah's car parked in front of building three. No turning back now.

Susannah stepped out, a wide smile on her face when she saw George. "So, I take it there *isn't* an emergency in building three?"

He shook his head, suddenly at a loss for words. "No. I—umm. Well, there was. You see—" Wow. He really had gotten no better at this.

She stepped up to the porch, and her fingertips ghosted across the calla lilies.

"These are so beautiful," she whispered. Her eyes glittered as she stared up at the lights. "Who hung these?"

"Some of the children," George immediately answered. "They helped me, I mean."

"I see," she answered.

She walked along the porch, admiring every lily, and George was relieved to see how much she seemed to enjoy the display.

"How long did this take you?" she marveled.

"Hours," he answered without thinking. "But we had fun doing it."

Susannah finally turned to look at him. "What is all of this for, George?"

He had to do it. Now was the time.

He reached out and took Susannah's hand in his. He slowly knelt

Fay

down on one knee.

"Susannah Granger," he began softly, shaking his head. "I know this must seem so bizarre and sudden to you, but you've been on my heart for weeks. *Months*," he amended. "You've been such a solace to me after the passing of my wife, and your presence has healed wounds in Lydia that I never could've hoped would mend on their own.

"Your kindhearted nature toward the children in our care and your dedication to the work the Lord has placed on your heart has helped me more than you'll ever know." He hesitated for a moment, then said, "And I want to ask if you'd do me the honor of marrying me."

From the look on Susannah's face, she never saw this coming. For a long moment, she didn't speak, and it terrified George.

"I…" she breathed quietly. "George, I had no idea…" She shook her head. "I've prayed about this for months. I felt a tugging on my heart every time I was near you, but I was so afraid to tell you so. You and Mary were… you were epic. I had no idea that you felt the same way." She then nodded emphatically. "Yes, George. I will absolutely marry you."

A wide grin broke across George's face. He wanted to jump up and hug her—but suddenly realized that he couldn't get up. His knee felt locked into position. Embarrassment flooded him as he chided himself.

Idiot, he thought. *You're not some spritely young man whose knees work properly!*

His smile turned sheepish. "I'm thrilled. Beyond thrilled. And now I'm incredibly humbled, because I need a hand getting up."

Susannah burst into laughter and reached for his hand, but before she could even begin to pull him up, a swarm of children surrounded them, all chortling.

"Pretty embarrassing, Pastor George," remarked Cody.

George chuckled and accepted their help to stand, then immediately embraced Susannah.

"Thank you," he whispered.

"For what?" she asked.

"For being in my life."

Susannah pulled away and placed a hand on George's cheek. "Thank *you*, George Müller, for being in mine."

George felt his heart swell. It was the first time he'd been so genuinely filled with joy and anticipation that he was rendered speechless.

"I can't wait to tell Lydia," he gushed. "She's going to be so happy!"

Susannah cringed. "Wait, George. Why don't we keep this to ourselves? At least until after her wedding," she suggested. "Her big day is coming up! I wouldn't want anything to overshadow that."

Yet again, Susannah managed to amaze him.

"You're right, yes," he replied with a nod. "Okay," he addressed the children around him. "Do you think you all can keep this a secret for now? And can you please gather up all the calla lilies and get them into Miss Susannah's car?"

A cacophony of squeals was released into the air before the children readily obeyed.

Chapter Thirty-Two

James and Lydia's wedding came faster than George could comprehend. Within three months, the wedding was upon them. Everything was immaculately decorated at the Springfield Community Church, and George swore it had never looked more beautiful. Per Lydia's request, vibrant red poppies adorned the chapel.

George wasn't ashamed to admit that his eyes filled with tears when he saw Lydia. Her dress was simple and elegant and not overstated at all, but she glowed in it nonetheless.

"Oh, honey," said George as he took in the sight. "I wish your mother could have been here to see you. You are absolutely stunning. I'm so proud of you."

Lydia sniffled. "Dad, stop, you'll make me cry, and I'm going to ruin my makeup." But she hugged him anyway, ignoring the wrinkles she was no doubt creating in her satin dress. She held on tight and George did the same. This would be the very last day that his daughter would be *his*. From now on, she and James would be a team. She'd call James when she needed comfort or a shoulder to cry on. She'd call him to kill the bug in her room and be the handyman. But George would always be her dad, and he knew that.

When he walked her down the aisle, he thanked God for every moment Lydia had been in his life. James stood near the altar, waiting with anticipation for Lydia. George knew just from the look on James' face that he would adore Lydia for as long as he lived, and that was all George needed to know. Lydia would be taken care of, the academy would thrive, and the Lord's work would continue.

George and Susannah shared their intentions to get married soon after Lydia and James' wedding. Lydia was ecstatic and pressed the two to have a real wedding—even a small one—but George and Susannah decided that the money was best spent elsewhere. They opted to invite family and just a few very close friends and hold the ceremony at the small chapel adjacent to Springfield Community Church. It was a beautiful and simple ceremony, and they held a small reception afterwards to celebrate.

That evening, Lydia prepared a wedding dinner for everyone. It was the happiest day George had experienced in two years. He reveled in the laughter and held Susannah close, thanking God for his new companion. He readied himself for the new stage of life that was beginning.

Chapter Thirty-Three

Susannah immediately proved herself to be an invaluable companion, and George loved her and greatly appreciated her contributions around the academy. Susannah's presence made Mary's loss easier to bear, and his new wife gave him a sense of companionship that he'd dearly missed.

She was wonderful with the children, as she'd now spent nearly two years with them consistently, and the children loved her as much as they had loved Mary.

George had his hands full with her. She had all of Mary's spirit and every bit of her grace and kindness, which made her a force to be reckoned with. They had their rough spots, of course. She felt that George overworked himself, and George felt that Susannah nagged too much. They argued far more than he and Mary had, though eventually the arguments faded, and they learned to love and be loved in harmony.

The first two years following their marriage weren't pure bliss, but they were as close as George had been in a while. With Lydia now living with James, George was relieved to have Susannah by his side. They ate every meal together, laughed together, read the scriptures together, and prayed together.

With James and Lydia now so effectively tending to the needs of the academy, George was given more free time than he'd ever remembered having. Desiring to be intentional with his new season, he began to pray and ask the Lord for guidance regarding the next few years of his life. And just as George knew He would, the Lord answered. It was time to carry the Word about faith far beyond Springfield.

The Cherry Hills Academy blog had skyrocketed in popularity, and information about the ministry had become extremely accessible worldwide. Because most people had heard of the miraculous happenings at Cherry Hills at one point or another, George had received frequent invitations to speak at churches and events. After years of refusing because he was too busy at the academy itself, George finally felt it was time to accept some of these requests.

Together, he and Susannah began to travel all over the country before venturing out into other areas of the world, including England, Scotland, and Ireland. Many people came to hear George speak, and George was consistently humbled by the scope of what God was doing through his ministry. Though he relished in the opportunity to minister in smaller cities, he was also given platforms on larger scales. He was *renowned,* and he couldn't believe it. He hadn't realized until now just how well known he'd become. It was astounding to him. He didn't feel worthy of all the attention the news gave him, but he was happy to be a vessel to enact God's will. The Lord's hand continued to guide his path, and he followed enthusiastically.

"I missed you so much," cried Lydia when she first saw Susannah and George walking out of the airport. She nearly leapt on George but held herself back. "Right. 'Old bones,'" she mocked.

George chuckled. "Glad to see you still hold me in the highest regard."

James stepped out of the car. "George," he greeted him fondly. "Here, Susannah, let me get that for you." He picked up their luggage and loaded it into the back of the car.

Though Lydia had clearly intended to take them straight home, George convinced her to take them to the academy first, where George was met with a gaggle of squealing children. George scarcely managed a breath between all of his greetings and the children pulling at him from all sides. He embraced the staff, who were equally as excited to see him, before James finally managed to get him to the peace and quiet of George's former office.

James sank back in his chair with a sigh of relief. "I think it's safe to assume they're thrilled with your return."

George smiled. "I find it humbling." He looked around the small office. James had changed quite a few things since moving in, but George thought the changes were wonderful. "Are you feeling more comfortable now?"

"Yes and no," he answered. "You've left some big shoes to fill. I'm no longer freaking out when we don't receive donations like we used to. The Lord has seen fit to honor our prayers, even in your absence. Though I still have moments—lots of them—of doubt, it's nowhere near as bad as before. God takes care of His children when we put our total, unconditional faith in Him."

"See?" George said. "I told you."

"I suppose you did," he replied. "What you *didn't* tell me was exactly how much work and headache went into running this place."

George laughed. "It is *a lot* of work, but the joy it brings balances it all out. Besides, it seems that you and Lydia have done a wonderful job here. You don't give yourself enough credit."

James sighed. "Well, now that you're back, I suppose I'll be taking more of a back seat for a while."

George scoffed. "Of course not, James. You've both worked so well together. Besides, Susannah and I will likely be off again on another tour soon. I've spoken to other pastors who are interested in our visit."

"That's wonderful," James replied. "Well, if you'd like, I can show you how I've been running things here. That way, if I'm doing something wrong, you can point it out yourself."

George chuckled. "Sure. Let's take a look."

They walked through the academy buildings, and as James showed George how things had been progressing with the children, George was beyond pleased with the hands in which he'd entrusted Cherry Hills.

Though Beta had retired from his work in Haiti, he had continued to run The Samuel Program from his home in California. While George was home, Beta even came and visited for a while to catch up with his old friend. The two picked up right where they'd left off. Beta was always proud to see the work George had done and the children flourishing under his care.

Beta and James had remained in close contact with each other while George was gone. Beta would let James know when new orphans were approved for immigration and when James might expect more applications at Cherry Hills Academy. It kept both of them busy, and George thought that there was nothing better for Beta's spirit than to continue working through his retirement.

As expected, George and Susannah left again on another tour that lasted one year, during which time George spoke at over 300 engagements. During the tour, he met hundreds who had known of him and his ministry, and he encountered even more children and orphans who had aged out of his program and gone on to create full lives for themselves. Everyone was thrilled to see him, and each face brought back memories dear to his heart. These now grown adults were true gifts from God, and George felt blessed to be able to see them again.

Every time George and Susannah returned to Cherry Hills, they only stayed for a little while before heading out again. Honestly, George felt as though he was of little use to Lydia and James, who seemed to have such a rhythm going at the academy. Susannah kept him in check when jealousy began sneaking in, and then they'd both have a laugh about the fact that he'd been *jealous*. The children at Cherry Hills Academy were his children just as much as Lydia was, and he had a bit of a difficult time fully turning over the reins, but he knew it was best.

In September of George's seventy-third year, he and Susannah headed out again to begin their next missionary tour. Since the previous tours had taken a lot of energy out of George, they opted to stay a bit closer to home.

They traveled across the country and spoke in churches where they were invited, but they also had to turn down many invitations due to lack of bandwidth. George's messages varied widely, but he always emphasized the same truth of the Word: unconditional faith in Jesus Christ produces miracles through prayer.

There were times when George came across situations that blatantly went against the Word of God, and he fearlessly spoke out about it. He felt empowered and led by the Lord to say what needed to be said, even when it wasn't the most "politically correct" message.

George and Susannah experienced miracle upon miracle during their missionary tours as well, which they attributed only to the Lord and His mercy. No matter where they went, it seemed that God had placed a hedge of protection surrounding them, and people flocked to hear the words they had to say.

Over the next few years, George and Susannah continued their tours. They even journeyed to more dangerous areas of the world where their message wasn't quite as tolerated as in the United States and Western Europe. Still, they always made it back safely to Cherry Hills, where their

Fay

ministry continued.

James was the perfect son-in-law, and everything he did seemed blessed by the Lord as well, though he was prone to worry. George encouraged him to let his fears and worries go and to trust wholly in the Lord. James sounded as though he were trying exceedingly hard to do so, but George knew it would take time and practice for him to settle into a rhythm of peace. Faith has a way of growing when practiced.

Of course, it wasn't long before George and Susannah left again. After much prayer and study in the Word, they felt called to travel to India. During that time, George fell ill due to heatstroke and was sent to the countryside in Kolkata to recover. It wasn't long before he was able to continue his work, but when he was well again, he received a harrowing call from James.

"George, I've been trying to reach you for almost a week now," James said, out of breath and frantic.

George, confused, immediately looked at Susannah. "We haven't had any messages." Then again, they'd been far out of service, and they hadn't exactly paid for all the upgrades offered by carriers. "What's happened, James?"

"It's Lydia," he breathed quietly.

Every muscle in George's body locked up. "What's wrong? What's wrong with my daughter?" he practically exclaimed, and Susannah clutched her chest.

James was practically sobbing. "She was starting to get so weak… too weak. And she was in so much pain…"

"James, focus. What is wrong with Lydia?"

"She has cancer."

"What?" George couldn't believe what he was hearing. His heart was pounding, and blood was roaring in his ears. His precious daughter was not well. Meanwhile, he was on the other side of the world. How could he have left her like this?

"James," he shouted. "Talk to me!"

James seemed to be trying to gather himself, and it took all of George's strength not to get frustrated with him. "They say it's terminal."

Terminal. That word made it feel like Pastor Craik all over again, but this time it hit so much closer to home. His heart ached, and his entire body seemed to fail him. He practically lost his balance and had to hold himself up against the railing of the porch.

Susannah tried to come alongside him and hold him, but he could hardly feel it.

"They say that all they can do is…" James couldn't seem to finish. Then he swallowed roughly and said, "They can make her comfortable. That's it."

George sank to his knees, and the phone fell from his hands. He immediately bowed his head in prayer and began frantically asking the Lord to look after his baby girl, his only child.

Susannah picked up his phone, and George could vaguely hear her asking for more details, but he couldn't focus.

By the time the phone call was finished, Susannah had tears in her eyes. George couldn't bring himself to ask what had been said. Susannah lovingly helped him off the floor and guided him to the couch, where she practically cradled her husband in her arms.

Fay

"Everything's going to be alright," she assured him, though there was a note of uncertainty in her voice. "If the Lord means to allow Lydia to return home, then you know her soul will *rejoice*."

George nodded. "I know," he choked out. "But a father should not have to outlive his children."

As he said the words, sobs began to overtake his body. He couldn't imagine life without Lydia. Even when Mary died, Lydia had been his rock, his strength. She was the blessing that the Lord had always seen fit to give him, and for the smallest moment, George was terrified.

George knew that Susannah was right. If the Lord chose to let this cancer take Lydia, she would be dining with Jesus in paradise. But George was still human, and he was more than afraid. The idea of losing her wasn't just horrible… it was paralyzing.

"I have to be with her," George whispered, heart breaking. "I can't be here anymore, Susannah."

"I know," she answered quickly. "We will be with her. I'll organize everything." She kissed him gently on the forehead. "Stay here." She stood, scooped the phone up from the table, and hurried into another room.

By some miracle, Susannah arranged a flight for the next morning. She insisted that George get some sleep, but his night consisted of pacing the floor, praying fervently, and sobbing uncontrollably. He didn't understand the Lord's will, but then again, he never had. He just had to rest in the knowledge that the Lord truly did have everything under control. Of course, "rest" felt out of the question entirely.

The next day flew by in a haze. George and Susannah loaded up a rental car, and Susannah drove them to the airport. George stared out the window, watching the beautiful Indian countryside pass them by.

It's impossible to describe the sinking feeling one gets when one hears news this grave, but George would have said it was something along the lines of a sledgehammer occasionally drilling a poisoned spike into his chest. The sensation pulsated and left him feeling weak and alone, even with his wife sitting next to him. It was a truly hopeless feeling, and try though he might to allow the Lord's Spirit to comfort him, sadness had a firm grip on him.

George was almost catatonic as they made their way through the airport. Susannah had to speak for him on multiple occasions as they moved through security and the different terminals. By the time they finally boarded the plane, George had sent up countless prayers to the Lord, all requesting the same thing:

Please, Lord, let me see Lydia before she passes. Please, Lord, let me see Lydia before she passes.

Chapter Thirty-Four

America's customs had some improving to do, George thought as they made their way through the endless line. He couldn't help but be annoyed. He'd barely snapped out of his haze when they touched the ground in Springfield, and they still had to deal with the frustrations of the United States customs system.

Susannah rubbed his arm soothingly. "We'll be there soon," she continued to assure him.

George was beyond all thought, manners, and sympathy when he made it to the customs booth.

"Good afternoon," the woman behind the desk said monotonously. "Passports, please."

George slapped the passports on the desk quickly and tapped his foot nervously, waiting for her to clear them. The woman looked at him suspiciously out of the side of her eye, and Susannah apologized for his behavior.

After a couple moments of reviewing their passports, the woman looked up. "What was your business in India?"

Susannah spoke up before George had the opportunity. "We're missionaries. My husband was speaking in different churches."

"I see you've been all over," noted the woman. "How long have you been gone?"

While Susannah continued answering the woman's ridiculous questions, George's mind was on his daughter. He pulled out his phone to call James, and the woman behind the counter immediately zeroed in on him.

"Whoa, whoa, whoa," she exclaimed. "Sir, you have to get off your phone right now."

George stared at his phone, then back at the woman. "What?"

"No phones in this area." She jabbed a bony finger towards a sign that stated explicitly that. He knew that, but still tried to make the call.

George was just about to lose his cool. He was about to say something along the lines of, *Listen here. My daughter just got diagnosed with terminal cancer, and I'm being forced to wait in an outrageously long line while her life may very well be draining away. Now I'm going to call my son-in-law to find out where she is. Okay? Okay.* Fortunately for everyone involved, the Lord's voice spoke to George and softened his heart.

Taking a deep breath, he gentled his tone and said, "I'm sorry. You're right." He put his phone away. "I'm afraid we're in rather a large rush. My only daughter was diagnosed with terminal cancer, and she may not have long left. I'm trying to see her before…" He choked on the last words.

Fay

The customs woman looked absolutely grieved for him. She nodded softly and slid the passports back to Susannah. "I understand. You have my thoughts and prayers. Welcome back to the United States."

George tried to catch his breath and smiled as best he could at the woman. "Thank you."

Susannah linked arms with George, and they hurried to baggage claim. After securing their luggage, George phoned James while Susannah hailed a cab.

"Where is she?" George questioned immediately.

James seemed to breathe a sigh of relief. "She's at home," he answered.

Home, George thought. That sounded like Lydia. It also sounded as though she knew what was to come and had resigned herself to that fate. The thought broke his heart a little more.

"We'll be there soon," George answered, then hung up the phone.

Susannah flagged down a cab, and they hopped in.

The cab driver was kind and tried to keep up conversation with Susannah, who, for the sake of pleasantries, responded well. George, on the other hand, was beyond zoned out. He took in the familiar sights of his city, his home. He had pictured his return very differently.

When they'd returned from their tours in the past, they were met with excited children and smiling faces—Lydia's among them. Like her mother before her, she had always been so vibrant and filled with life. George couldn't remember a time when she wasn't dancing or leaping or running or doing *something* active.

When they arrived at James and Lydia's house, they unloaded

their bags quickly. George had been so eager to rush inside just ten minutes prior, but when Susannah made a move for the door, George stopped her.

"Wait," he breathed, staring at the forest green door. "I need a second."

Susannah came up alongside him and wrapped her arms around him. "My darling," she whispered softly. "It's time to go in and see her."

Tears in his eyes, George quietly asked, "What if she's already gone?"

Susannah gently stroked his face. "Then we'll face it together, but I don't believe she is. I can feel it." She squeezed his hand. "Do you really want to spend what could be your daughter's last moments standing on her porch?"

George shook his head. "Okay. Let's go inside."

Together they entered the house, and Lydia's presence was everywhere. It'd been so long since they'd visited James and Lydia's home that George had practically forgotten how much influence his daughter had on the place. Every piece of décor seemed to fit her personality perfectly—intelligent and chic, but oh so colorful.

Footsteps came quickly down the stairs, and James rounded the corner. When he saw them, he seemed to sag with relief.

"Thank the Lord," he said. "She's upstairs."

George rushed past him and took the stairs two at a time, which was quite a feat at his age. He pushed through the door into the master bedroom and took in the sight of his darling daughter.

Lydia was propped up in bed, which probably made her look

healthier than she really was. The curtains had been opened to allow the sun's fading light through the wavy window panes, and the brilliant light made Lydia's skin look like it had some color.

She smiled when she saw her father, though George thought he caught a wince. "Daddy, you came home!"

George stepped up to her bedside and knelt, kissing her hand. "Of course I came home," he answered. "You're my baby girl."

She sniffled and wiped at a tear. George was doing his best to fight off his own tears to avoid distressing her further.

"How was your trip?"

"Never mind that," replied George. "How are you feeling?"

"I'm alright, really," she insisted. "Doctor Williams has taken excellent care of me and given me medications that make me very comfortable."

Comfortable, George thought. There was that word he'd begun to hate. All the doctors could do was make Lydia *comfortable*. His heart began to ache painfully again, so he squeezed his daughter's hand tighter.

Lydia, keen as ever, sensed his worry and gripped his hand back. "Oh, Dad, don't be sad. I'm okay with this. I've accepted it. Just…" She took in a deep breath, and George could tell it was hard for her to breathe, which only made his misery worse. "Please look after James for me?"

Right… James. George suddenly felt awful for not greeting him better. He remembered his devastation when he lost his Mary, and that was after they'd had so many wonderful years and memories together. He couldn't imagine losing her at Lydia's age. The thought crippled him.

"Don't worry about James, honey," he urged. "We'll be there for him. And he'll be there for us."

She smiled. "Thank you." She eased back into the soft pillows of her bed. "That makes me feel so much better."

George didn't know what to do, so he just sat beside her on the bed and began to pray with her.

A couple minutes later, James and Susannah joined them, and they spent the rest of the evening talking about George and Susannah's adventures across the globe. George did his best to keep the topics lighthearted, but he couldn't help his worry.

When it became too late for Lydia to stay awake, Susannah sat beside her while James and George stepped into the hallway to talk.

"I'm almost afraid to ask…" George gathered his courage. "Stage four?"

James nodded, and it was clear from his every movement that he was already grieving the loss to come.

"How long?"

"One, maybe two weeks."

Those words were crushing. "How…how is this possible? How did we not catch it sooner?" He didn't understand. She was so progressed… yet they'd never noticed anything.

James looked just as stunned as George. "I don't know."

"You were with her every day," George said, his voice slightly accusatory. "You didn't see her in pain?"

"She'd hurt her hip a while ago," James answered defensively. "She was playing with the kids and she hurt it… I assumed it was just that!"

George raked a hand through his gray hair, hands trembling. He knew James couldn't have done anything about it. "I understand," he answered, willing his voice to be gentle.

He had to remind himself that these weeks were a gift. He'd prayed that the Lord would give him enough time to get home, and He'd done that. Anything more was just an added blessing.

"I wanted to fight more," James said weakly. "The doctors said there was nothing to do, but I wanted to try more…"

"What did Lydia want?"

James looked up, a deep sorrow in his eyes. "She wanted to fight too. She's such a fighter…" He took a moment to gather himself. "But after the third round of tests came back and yet *another* doctor gave her only a few weeks left, she said she didn't want to be in a hospital. She wanted to be home."

George nodded. He understood the panic and helplessness James was feeling, because he'd been feeling the same thing when Mary had made the decision to leave the hospital. It wasn't giving up. It was acceptance.

"All right. We'll set up a substitute at the academy so that you don't have to split your time there."

"Okay," James answered numbly.

"Then we'll spend every minute we can with her," said George. "I'll make sure that you have plenty of privacy with her as well. I'm sure you have lots of things to say." He remembered how much he had felt needed to be said when Mary was leaving him, and he could only imagine that James felt the same.

"I just…" James began. "I'm having a hard time…"

"I understand," George said, placing a hand on his shoulder.

Tears began to well in James' eyes. He cleared his throat and straightened up. "I want you to know that it's been bliss. Every second of every day… bliss. I wouldn't have traded a second of it, not even knowing what was going to come."

"Then you tell her that," George encouraged, gripping James' shoulder tighter. "Make sure she knows."

He nodded. "Okay."

George stepped back into Lydia's room and kissed his daughter on the forehead before beckoning Susannah out. Behind them, James went in and sat by Lydia's bedside, holding her hand. George was once again grateful for James in Lydia's life. He'd been more than a help to George, and he was the perfect husband for George's daughter.

"James has the spare bedroom made up for us," Susannah said once they were alone in the hallway. "We'll stay here until it's time to leave."

"That sounds good."

Susannah and George made their way to the spare bedroom and tried to sleep. After tossing and turning in his bed for quite some time, George broke down in tears. He tried to quiet himself to keep from waking Susannah, but she hadn't been sleeping, either. She wrapped her arms around him, and he held her back tightly.

Thoughts and worries bombarded his mind, and his heart was heavy with grief. How could this be happening? To *Lydia*, his faithful, God-loving daughter? She was so young and had so much to live for. If

James were right and their marriage had been bliss, then why was she being taken? It seemed like a crime to steal her away, but he wholly trusted in the Lord. Despite the pain he was in, despite all of his human wonderings, he knew that the Lord's will was right and perfect.

With that in mind, he did his best to get some sleep. He wanted to be the best father he could be to his daughter for as long as she had left.

Over the next two weeks, the family did exactly as George said they would. They loved on Lydia and spent every waking moment with her. They played games together, shared meals in Lydia's bedroom, and talked of James' plans for the future.

It was hard for George to listen to some of their conversations. Anyone watching could tell that James was being eaten up inside, yet he insisted that he would be alright and that life would go on. Lydia begged him to find another wife, but James could hardly consider such a thing. It pained George to know that their happiness together was coming to an end.

Susannah was a saint and a nurturer. She took splendid care of Lydia, tending to her every need. The two only grew closer, which George scarcely thought was possible. They spent one-on-one time together while James and George discussed other arrangements, including gathering some of the orphans to the house to say goodbye to Lydia. When they were finally able to pull it off, Lydia was beside herself with joy, though it was difficult for her to express it. The children and orphans sang songs, just as they had when Mary passed, and they held Lydia's hand and prayed with her. George didn't have the strength to hold back tears this time. As Lydia began to hug each child with the small bit of energy she could muster, he had to excuse himself so he could be alone with his tears and not affect the joy in the room.

As the days came and went, so did Lydia's strength. He could see her vitality waning more and more each day. Soon, she looked like she was close to death, and Susannah was having to do everything for her. Lydia didn't have the strength to sit up… or even smile.

James spent hours on end in her room with her. Try though she might, Susannah couldn't get him to leave her side for food or rest. George appreciated that quality in his son-in-law, but he worried for him all the same. This was going to take a toll on James. George knew. He'd gone through this very thing not long ago.

The doctors had been right. About two weeks after George and Susannah arrived home, George knew that Lydia didn't have much time left. As they had every day for the days prior, the family gathered around her bedside. She was barely able to keep her eyes open, but she smiled softly at her loved ones.

George sat beside his daughter and kissed her hand gently. "My sweet, darling Lydia," he whispered. "I've always been so proud to call you my daughter, and you've been the greatest joy and blessing of my life." His voice shook. "Give your mother a kiss for me."

Lydia looked like she understood, and tears welled in her own eyes. When Susannah came and said her goodbyes, George had a hard time holding back the tears. He couldn't hear what she was saying, but whatever it was, he knew Lydia heard her.

Finally, James came to sit by his wife's bedside. George wanted to leave them alone, but couldn't bring himself to do it. He needed to be there. He couldn't bear the idea of leaving his daughter in her final moments.

"Lydia, my love," James whispered so quietly that George almost couldn't hear. "I've loved you for so long, and you never knew it. I think I loved you before I even knew it." He laughed at this thought, though it was a short, pitiful sound. "You are so much stronger than I am. I praise God that he entrusted me with your heart and wellbeing. I'm so sorry that I couldn't help you through this…"

Lydia's tears spilled down her cheeks, and George's heart broke knowing that she was a fiery mind trapped inside an ailing body. She probably had so much left to say… and he hoped that she'd been able to say most of it before she'd gotten to this point.

"I'll love you forever," James continued. "My life will never be the same, but I want you to know that you've given me the happiest days of my life. I'll forever remember that and hold them dear to my heart."

Susannah gripped George's arm and buried her face in his shoulder, quietly sobbing into the sleeve of his shirt.

James stroked Lydia's cheek. "I didn't deserve you. Lord knows I didn't. But I'm grateful for you all the same. I love you, my beautiful Lydia."

Lydia seemed to breathe softer then, closing her eyes as tears streamed down the sides of her face. She looked like she was trying to reach for him, and James clutched her hand tightly. She took in a deep breath and settled into the pillows behind her.

Over the next few minutes, her breathing became more and more shallow, and the time between her breaths lengthened. Every second was agony for James, George, and Susannah, who could do nothing but watch their beloved Lydia fade away.

When she breathed her last breath, James dissolved into agonizing tears. Though George tried to comfort his son-in-law, he knew there was little that was going to help apart from the Lord's peace.

Susannah and George gave James his privacy and retreated downstairs, where George let his grief flow freely. He knew for certain that Lydia was with Jesus, yet his heart was heavy. He could barely breathe. Over the next few hours, Susannah had to rock him gently so that he might have some comfort.

Chapter Thirty-Five

There is no pain like that of the loss of a child. George was certain. Though he wanted to conduct Lydia's funeral, he knew he would choke on every other word and opted against it. James gave a beautiful speech, but he barely got his words out before breaking down.

Like with Mary's funeral, all of Cherry Hills' children and orphans came to Lydia's funeral. The family received countless letters and emails from the many people who had known her, all expressing deep grief.

One of the more comforting things was how the donations flooded in to help pay for Lydia's funeral. With every message and every donation, George felt his heart mending a little more. Lydia's effect on people was evident, and the joy she had brought to so many warmed George's heart and soul.

After a while, George threw himself into his work. He and Susannah again began touring and spreading the Gospel, but after almost two years, their preaching tours came to a close. It was time for George to come home, and it was time to confront his own grief.

Since then, James had found his peace with Lydia's death. His good work at the academy had continued, solidifying George's belief that he'd chosen the right man to continue in his footsteps. He and James continued to spend plenty of time together, going over the academy's donations, expenses, and needs. When a problem arose, they continued to seek out the Lord in prayer rather than to rely on man's strength. Because of this, the Cherry Hills Academy continued to flourish.

In seventeen years, George and Susannah had traveled approximately 200,000 miles. George was eighty-seven years old when he retired from traveling, though he didn't feel it at all. Susannah had been an excellent traveling companion. She'd greatly assisted him in the circulation of tens of thousands of tracts and Bibles in many different languages, and her passion and work ethic were an inspiration to all who met her.

It wasn't long after their retirement, however, that Susannah's health began to fade. It didn't happen all at once, but George could steadily see the lack of energy in her body. He had experienced this enough times now to know what it meant. Eventually, his wife declined to the point where she was no longer able to venture out of the house.

James was a blessing. He set up a video feed for Susannah so that she could still interact with the children. Since returning from their tours, Susannah had begun a study group with forty-six children in the Academy. It was geared towards the mature believers amongst the children and orphans, and it was meant to strengthen them spiritually. The study was her pride and joy, and George was grateful that James could allow her to continue it even into her last days.

Susannah's life was fruitful up until her last breath. The last words George heard from her were a prayer. She asked that the Lord would continue to shower his blessings on George and the academy, and though George found it strange that she didn't include herself in that prayer, it made sense the next morning when he woke up… and Susannah didn't.

Since the day his mother died, death had seemed to surround him. George was painfully aware of this. To anyone looking in from the outside, it might have seemed like George was living a cursed life. After the death of his mother, brother, father, Henry, Mary, Lydia, and now Susannah, death appeared to loom over him like a constant shadow… yet George never felt that way.

In spite of all the world's influences and attempts to sway George from his life of faith and obedience to the Lord and His Word, George felt that he'd lived a *blessed* life. His life had been full of miraculous events, remarkable opportunities, and rich relationships. He refused to lose faith.

George believed that death was only the beginning and that this world was not his home, nor was it the home of those he'd lost. His had been called *home*, and he'd soon be with them again. What he was feeling wasn't joy per se, but he knew that the Lord was merciful and good.

Let the Children Come

George would continue his ministry for several years to come, preaching radically and giving generously. Under James' care and supervision, the academy continued to thrive.

Though George spent hours and hours with the children of the Cherry Hills Academy, he managed to continue his messages at Springfield Community Church, where the new pastor enthusiastically offered that George should become a frequent guest speaker.

George spent the morning on March 9 at the academy helping James. After Susannah's death, George began spending more time at the academy than he did at home. He even moved the majority of his belongings—which were few—to his room there.

James seemed to appreciate this, and he'd latched on to George. Though James wouldn't admit it, his faith had grown astronomically. George noticed that whenever there was an issue, James was calm and collected. He was no longer the worrier he had been when George was running the place, James would simply ask that George pray with him, and then he would set about fixing the problem.

James relied on the Lord in everything, and it gave George peace to know that the children and orphans would continue to have beautiful lives for years to come.

In the afternoon, George made his way to the office that had become Susannah's after Mary's death. He sat down in the chair behind the desk and exhaled softly, taking in the mostly empty room.

After Susannah stopped using it, the room was hardly touched.

Fay

Occasionally someone needed a document or two from the filing cabinet, but caretakers and staff mostly remained outside the room out of respect. Susannah and Mary had been such massive parts of Cherry Hills Academy that it felt dishonoring to dismantle their office.

The one thing that hadn't changed was that calendar on the wall—the one that had a different scripture for each day. As the years passed, Susannah had changed the calendar—just as Mary had—but she always purchased the same brand so that she could continue to read the verse of the day. Before leaving the office and heading over to the church to speak, he flipped the calendar to the next day, March 10, and the verse warmed George's heart:

> *"His master said to him, 'Well done, good and faithful servant. You have been faithful over a little; I will set you over much. Enter into the joy of your master.'"*
>
> *—Matthew 25:21*

George memorized it as he had many other verses.

That evening, on March 9 of George's ninety-third year, after leaving the office, George delivered a message to a prayer meeting at church that was both cautionary and encouraging for his church body. In many ways, the sermon summed up the passion and faith that George had carried throughout his adult life. It was on Revelation 3:14-22 and the church of Laodicea—the lukewarm church. He *urged* his congregation to never be lacking in zeal, as Paul said in Romans, and to passionately go about the work the Lord had laid out before them.

"'Therefore, be zealous,' says the Lord," George quoted. "'Be *repentant*. Behold, I stand at the door and knock. If anyone hears My voice and opens the door, I will come in to him and dine with him, and he with Me.'" George closed his Bible, returning his gaze to the listeners in the audience. "The Lord desires this relationship with us," he stated. "He wants us to be *zealous* for Him and His Word. To 'grope for him in the darkness,'" he continued, his voice strong and powerful.

George paused as he considered his next words carefully. Exhaustion was beginning to take over, so he made his way past the pulpit and sat down on the steps leading up to it. When one of the men in the front pews began to stand to help him, George simply lifted a hand to assure him he was alright.

George knew his time here was short... and he was ready. He didn't want to leave his church, but his soul ached to return to the Lord and to dwell with Him forever.

Smiling, he said, "I've had many of you come to me and tell me what miracles you've seen through my work with the academy. I want to encourage you that this is not a phenomenon or something I've had *anything* to do with. This is purely the work of the Lord, and He wants to do the same in your life if you'll allow Him."

Several people nodded in agreement.

"I spent too many days listening to voices that were not the Lord's," George said with a sad shake of his head. "I won't waste another day believing what God *didn't* say."

Fay

An applause filled the room, and when it quieted, George finished his sermon. "I say all of this to you today so that when I am gone, you aren't discouraged. I want you to be set aflame by the Lord so that no one on this planet can extinguish your light. The Lord calls us not to be lukewarm or to go about his work halfheartedly. He calls us to be passionate, fearless, and above all else, *faithful*. After all, we are the 'bride of Christ,' are we not? He wants us to be faithful spouses. May this encourage you to be just that."

After the sermon, many came to George with questions, and George was honored to answer them. He gladly shared what knowledge the Lord had given him. Being able to speak to his congregation had deeply nourished his spirit.

He went to bed that night thinking of the verse for tomorrow on the calendar:

> *His master said to him, "Well done, good and faithful servant. You have been faithful over a little; I will set you over much. Enter into the joy of your master."*

On Thursday, March 10 at about 7:00 in the morning, Diana, who had aged out and since become a volunteer at the academy, brought a cup of tea to George's room. There was no answer when she knocked. When she opened the door, George Müller lay on the floor beside the bed. He had probably risen to take some nourishment, had felt faint, and fell to the floor. The coroner's report said he had died of heart failure an hour or two before he had been found by Diana.

It didn't take long for the news of George Müller's death to travel. Thousands of cards, emails, phone calls, and text messages came into the Cherry Hills Academy from all over the world. Dignitaries communicated condolences. Christians, Jews, Muslims, and even atheists wept as they pondered the loss of a true "man of God." Flags were flown at half-mast around the country.

Over a thousand children gathered outside the church. They cried, recognizing that they had lost a father for the second time in their lives. The tears that ran down their young cheeks were far more compelling than any words. Springfield had never before witnessed such a spectacle.

James Wright gave an address, reminding everyone who had gathered that death comes to all, but those who are trusting in Jesus Christ for their hope of eternal salvation with God the Father, there is no sting of death. The sermon was from Hebrews 13:7-8 – "Remember those who led you, who spoke the word of God to you; and considering the result of their conduct, imitate their faith. Jesus Christ is the same yesterday and today and forever."

Ed Groves, the nephew of Mary and George, sang the closing song:

"'Tis so sweet to trust in Jesus,
Just to take Him at His Word;

Just to rest upon His promise,
Just to know, 'Thus says the Lord!'
Refrain:
Jesus, Jesus, how I trust Him!
How I've proved Him o'er and o'er
Jesus, Jesus, precious Jesus!
O for grace to trust Him more!"

Tens of thousands of people reverently stood along the route of the funeral procession to the cemetery that followed.

There were many things that could have been said of George Müller during his long life. He was a caregiver to many and a generous beneficiary to the missionaries he had the privilege and honor of helping. He was a compassionate husband and understanding father. He knew when to fight… and when to take the medicine. Through trials, blessings, and miraculous provision, George kept his eyes on Jesus. But most importantly—more important than any of his accomplishments—George was a man of unwavering, undying, and unconditional faith. He was an ordinary man who put his full trust and faith in God, and God used him in extraordinary ways.

Epilogue

Yes, George Müller was a real man who lived from 1805 to 1898. He was born and raised in Prussia. He was a hellion during his youth, and the untimely death of his mother exacerbated the issue. Something mentioned in the novel but not in detail was his trip with his friend, Beta, through the European continent: a trip paid for by George's father. Beta would later convert to Christianity and his transformation would be instrumental in leading George to the truth of the gospel.

George's conversion was quick and transformative after he heard the truth of God's word. He'd already been studying to be a minister at the University of Halle in Germany, but at that time, the term "minister" was used loosely. Back then, this meant a cushy government job, which George's father was thrilled about. A ministry degree was more akin to getting a modern-day political science or government administration degree.

Fay

Incidentally, this was the same university that August Francké, pastor, theologian, and philanthropist, had taught Greek and theology for thirty-six years. Francké brought passion for Christ to the university, but that passion had long since died out when George began attending."

But when George decided to go into the Christian pastorate and not the government, his father did really disown him, and sadly they never did have the close father/son relationship he longed for, even though George did reconcile and share the truth of the gospel with his father. Shortly after that, his father died without George ever knowing for certain if his father had come to trust in Jesus Christ.

After completing his education, George wanted to become a missionary, but was turned down. He began preaching by memorizing other preachers' sermons, but found they were not effective. Consequently, he spent a tremendous amount of time studying and praying and became quite a powerful and knowledgeable teacher.

Early in George's pastoral ministry, he was paid with "pew rents." This practice is not something currently used in our society, but it was commonplace in the 19 and early 20 century, even in America. Renting the pews meant exactly what it sounded like: people had to pay to hear the word of God preached every week. The closer to the pulpit, the higher the rent. Being closer to the front meant that more people could see the importance of the person paying the rent and be aware of their wealth. George objected to it because it did not cause him to trust God for his provision, and he thought it violated the scripture against giving the rich a prominent place in worship. So, he convinced the church to put a box at the back of the auditorium and anyone could give what they were led by God—a donation box.

Henry Craik, another one of our characters from the novel, was truly George's best friend throughout his ministry, as well as his co-pastor. Henry was a brilliant linguist and his books on the Hebrew language were studied in seminaries for years. They pastored a church in Bristol, England for many years. It was there in Bristol that George and Henry started the Ashley Down Orphanage.

In writing this book there was the question of where all the orphans came from since we do not have such the crisis that existed in George's day. Charles Dickens, of *Oliver Twist* and *A Christmas Carole*, was a writer during George's time, so if you can picture it, that was the society George was living in. Dickens was also a contemporary of George and wrote glowingly about the sincerity and genuineness of Müller's faith, and the orphanage after visiting it.

Though orphans are still a prominent issue, they're not as commonly found in the US. So, I tried to bring some of them here. But there is a problem here, and that is homeless mothers, fathers, and children. They sort of fall beneath the cracks of society, yet show tremendous strength in adversity.

About a year before passing away, George Müller gave a sort of "review" of his life in which he touched upon the several departments of the work, saying:

"God has led me to the founding of many schools. In England, Scotland, India, Straits of Malacca, British Guiana, Essequibo, Belize; in Spain, in France, in Italy, and other parts of the world, there are these schools, 117 in number, and in them there have been educated a hundred and twenty-two thousand young people; out from among whom, more than twenty thousand have been converted (the masters have so reported); but in heaven I expect to meet many more than forty or fifty thousand. In regard to the Holy Scriptures: 279,000 Bibles, in various languages, and 1,440,000 New Testaments, have been circulated, to His glory: God abundantly blessed this part of the work, particularly in Spain, in Italy, and in Ireland. As to missionary operations, through the goodness of God, sums amounting to £258,000 [close to US$40,000,000] have been sent out to Missions, alone. In the circulation of tracts, which was particularly laid on my heart, God has granted me to circulate 109,000,000 of books, pamphlets, and tracts. More than twenty thousand persons have been brought to the Lord Jesus through the instrumentality of the four hundred or five hundred missionaries for whom the Lord sent means. Out of the 9750 orphans that I have been enabled to receive, between four and five thousand have been brought to the knowledge of the Lord; and we have at the present time about 1600, in the Orphan Houses, who are believers."

In addition to all of the above, George and his second wife, Susanna, spent seventeen years traveling around the globe preaching and telling the story of faith to crowds of thousands at a time. They traveled over 200,000 miles. He met with dignitaries from around the world, including the Queen of England and the President of the United States. He was also instrumental in starting the Plymouth Brethren denomination. Incidentally, one of the missionaries he supported was Hudson Taylor, who started the China Inland Mission. He was also a friend and contemporary of Charles Spurgeon.

He died of a heart failure very much like I describe in the book. The whole world mourned his death. His funeral was attended by thousands.

George never saw the orphanages or ministries as his—they were God's. He bristled when people referred to them as "Müller's Orphanage." Another interesting quirk about George Müller is that he didn't like his picture taken. He didn't want people to idolize him—God was to get all the glory.

I wrote this book hoping to find the next "George Müller." This century is ready for him or her. Will you be that one? I would love to hear your story of faith, what is God doing in your life of faith? Write me at tom@tomfayauthor.com.

My next project is a Bible study and study guide that digs deeper into the life of faith as taught and lived by George Müller. If you would like to be added to an email list, go to my website at www.tomfayauthor.com/study-guide. I will notify you when it is ready for publication.

Acknowledgements

There are so many people I must thank for their help in this project. First, thank you Lon Ackelson and Bella Zammit. I have started over, writing this book a number of times. But many others gave me great insight into the direction of the project, and their input has been invaluable. Thank you Brock, David, Jamie, Kourtney, Margaret, Catrina, Pamela, Sarah, William, Nicole, Lisa, Chris, Jessica, Lindsey, Sarah, Scott, and Art.

However, I must thank most of all Rose Reid—Rose, I couldn't have done it without you. Thank you for all your help. I look forward to more collaboration. I also want to thank Susanna Fleming who worked countless hours and countless projects to make the book successful. Susanna, I am so encouraged as to what God has for you in your life of faith.

But most of all, I must thank my wife, Anna, who encouraged me to keep going, checked the work, and gave invaluable insight into the project, and never gave up. I couldn't have written it without her. Thank you, Anna!

It was Anna that suggested the name of the book. It comes from the Gospel of Luke chapter 18:

[15] "People were also bringing babies to Jesus for him to place his hands on them. When the disciples saw this, they rebuked them.[16] But Jesus called the children to him and said, "**Let the little children come** to me, and do not hinder them, for the kingdom of God belongs to such as

these. ¹⁷ Truly I tell you, anyone who will not receive the kingdom of God like a little child will never enter it."

About the Author

After graduating from the Grand Rapids School of Bible and Music with honors in theology, Tom began to feel a calling on his life to move into the ministry. He moved to sunny San Diego, California, where he entered the pastorate and founded the Southern California Bible College. He then entered into the business world, making and losing and making fortunes as an entrepreneur in everything from real estate to telecommunications.

In 2016, he graduated from Fuller Seminary with a Masters of Arts in Global Leadership. Though he found ministry work to be incredibly fulfilling, he loved storytelling and sharing his experiences with others, which is what led him to become an author.

Now a student at Duke University as he works towards his Doctor of Ministry degree, Tom aspires to lead an authentic, challenge-filled life. When he isn't writing, studying, or spending time with his wife, family, and friends, he enjoys sailing, traveling, and hiking.

To learn more about Tom, visit him online at: www.tomfayauthor.com.

Made in United States
Orlando, FL
19 April 2022